The Namesake

Truth is Freedom

adam e bradbury

The Namesake

©2017 Adam E Bradbury

All Rights Reserved

This is a work of fiction. Any resemblance of the characters or situations to actual persons, living or dead, businesses, companies, events, or religions is entirely coincidental.

Cover art based on copyright free images from pixabay.com

ISBN: 1973970325
ISBN-13: 978-1973970323

DEDICATION

Heather – love of my life – you have been so understanding. The world of Amynthia has leaked out of the page and into your life more than once and you have been so very generous in not insisting I reach for the mop and bucket. Thank you for giving me the space, for taking so much care and time in reading my drafts, and for giving me your honest (and brutal) opinions.

Thank you. This is for you.

ACKNOWLEDGMENTS

I owe a great deal to my friend Alan Barrington Deane, the first person to read my manuscript. Alan, your encouragement and honesty were pivotal in turning a first draft into a novel. I must also thank Krystina Kellingley, my creative-writing 'go to person'. Krystina, thank you so much for all your help and support.

The skills of a professional copy editor are an essential component in getting a story into print. I am extremely grateful to Bridget Cook for giving me so much of her time. Bridget, your meticulous approach and carefully considered comments have helped me raise my game and produce a novel that I am really proud of. Thank you.

A special thanks to the author, Scarlett Tillie Bell, for her help in my characterisation of Laban. Thanks is also due to my beta-readers Toby and Liz and to everyone who took the time to read, listen to, and provide feedback as my manuscript went from draft to draft during the re-write. I owe you big time.

Mostly though I must thank Pops who called me 'Dude' and made me laugh, and Ma who kissed my bruises and taught me to be a trier. I love and miss you both.

PROLOGUE

The girl had no name. None of them did.

She closed her eyes and drew air deep into her lungs, tasting the scent of the flowers that grew outside the glassless window of her cell. She had worked hard. It had been hot, it was always hot in the fields, but now the cool velvet sky of the night was here and she was grateful for it.

She held her breath and listened for her cousins, but the doors and corridors separating her from them left her isolated, cut off. All she could hear was the sound of her own heart beating.

Its rhythm unsettled her. She had been told that she would die when it stopped beating, and that one day it certainly would. She would go to heaven of course. She would serve her family with loving diligence, and the nine orders of angels would surely grant her passage to the holy garden. No, she was not afraid of her own death. Nevertheless, the rhythmic sound in her ears made her nervous. What would it be like the moment that it stopped? What would the journey to heaven be like?

She needed to pray; to join with her cousins and praise the Living Saints.

She picked her clean smock from the back of the door, slipping it over her head and threading her arms through the shoulder straps in one motion. She pulled open the door to her cell, her shoes were waiting on the threshold where she had left them, where she always left them. She slipped them on and headed down the stone-floored corridor to the refectory.

The door was open and the chatter and noise of her cousins was all around. The two rows of tables that ran the length of the hall were laid for the evening meal. Women and girls, each dressed in a white smock, tied at the waist with a light blue cord like her own, were finding seats, talking and laughing.

As the girl entered the hall a group of women began to sing The Praise, and the faithful fell silent and took their seats. The voices warmed themselves on the dark wooden panelling of the walls and climbed into the rafters, floating back down to the devoted as if from heaven itself.

> 'We praise the Three Living Saints.
> We thank them for their gifts and their care.
> For their love and the fare
> That sustains our bodies and nurtures our souls.'

The choir sang with one voice.

In the years to come the girl would think back to the simple way in which the Trevelian namesakes, her cousins, would sing their verse; each voice taking the same notes as the others. It would not be until the bloodshed and violence came that she would hear voices sing in harmony for the first time. When she looked back across the years she would often think how strange it was that the killing had given their world such beautiful music.

But these were memories that lived in the future, not thoughts that lived in the present. This night the girl took her seat as she always had. Sitting with her cousins, wrapped in the music of praise, she knew nothing of lies, or of war, or of the harmony that could be found in music.

She did not know what her journey to heaven would be like. She did not know when her heart would stop beating. She did not even know that she had no name.

*"Of our present and our past,
Of our future state.
Of our beginning and our end,
One thing will persist,
Our property in the namesakes."*

The Telling; final stanza

CHAPTER ONE

Mason hated the dry season. He should have thought to bring some water, but he had left as soon as the news reached him.

He squinted into the sun, studying the horizon as the transport manoeuvred itself around the potholes and ruts in the road. In the distance a thin column of smoke pointed from the sky to his destination. He drew air in through his nose and exhaled through his mouth, whispering her name with the last of it.

'Jess.'

His body rocked from side to side and he tightened his grip on the handrail. There was nothing he could do until he got there. Today the familiar track leading like the spoke of a wheel out to the farmlands seemed to stretch on forever. The vehicle bumped and crawled along, unhurried and unconcerned, a ribbon of dust rising into the still air behind it like the tail of some great rodent.

Another fifteen minutes and the transport was alongside the vast steel-framed structures of the nursery tunnels, its wheels crunching over broken glass and debris.

As it came to a halt Mason flipped the switch above his head and spoke into the air.

'Sir.'

The intercom crackled with static for a moment before a voice, made tin-thin by the speaker, bounced into the cab.

'Mason.'

'Sir, it's as you feared. Looks like a bomb of some kind. The last ten or more metres of number two glasshouse are completely missing.'

'Is she OK?' the voice in the speaker spoke straight away, eager to know.

'I can't see her. I'm going to take a look now.'

'Let me know as soon as you find her, Mason.'

'Sir,' the word meant "yes".

He pushed the switch to a second position and spoke to the cold machinery sitting in the cargo hold.

'Bring out three medi-tubes and follow me into the glasshouse.'

The screen above his head showed a ramp descending from the back of the transport.

He did not wait to see the black cube respond to his command, kicking up a skirt of dust as it slid from the end of the ramp. Instead he squeezed his bulk from the cramped cabin as quickly as he could and pulled on the lever that made the access hatch slide back.

He squinted into the daylight and looked down at the debris littering the normally well-ordered area. The air, heavy with the unmistakable smell left by munitions, pushed him back through the years. He walked down the three steps from the transport and picked his way through the glass-strewn pathway to the nursery tunnel.

It took him a moment to spot her. She was crouching behind the collapsed wall of a soil-conditioning pit. She had her back to him and was kneeling. Beside her he could see the prone body of one of the Trevelian namesakes. Pale and still; another shadow resonating with his past. He took a breath and walked over to her, placing his great hand on her shoulder.

'You OK?' his voice soft.

Jess did not look up but touched her hand to Mason's, dropping her cheek to its back. He could feel her tears on his skin. He crouched down next to her.

'She looks so peaceful,' she said, 'neither of them show much sign of injury, some cuts, some blood around the ears, but other than that...they're just dead.'

'I've seen it before...' Mason's voice was gentle, careful not to inject emotion where it would not be useful. 'The injuries can be due to the pressure wave. A quick death at least.'

He looked around and spotted a second body lying a few metres away.

'Your father said that three of the girls were killed.'

Jess pushed a stray strand of hair back behind her ear and stood up.

'No. Two. I thought the other one was dead when I got here and called it in. But she was still alive, the others have taken her back to the welfare unit and are looking after her.'

He nodded but made no reply.

'We need to get them out of here,' said Jess after a few moments.

'I've got some medi-tubes.'

He looked around for the flat-sided stone that had followed him from the transport. It was taller than Mason with just enough clearance to fit through the opening. It stood there, silent and grey, three black tubes each large enough to hold an adult, floating in front of its bulk.

'Give me one of those,' he said

The device approached and gently lowered one of the medi-tubes to the ground at the dead girl's feet.

'Put one over there and then give us a little room.'

He nodded towards the other body and the device obeyed, carefully lowering a second canister to the ground by the other dead girl and moving five or six metres back into the tunnel.

Mason watched in silence as Jess opened the nearest tube by touching her thumb to its top. It split into two down its length, each side folding up and back to reveal a flat bed on which a patient could be placed.

'Give me a hand would you please,' she said.

Mason was easily capable of moving the body on his own, but he waited as Jess crouched and slid her hands under the dead girl's armpits.

'I can feel her sweat on my fingers,' she said.

Mason looped his hands under the dead girl's knees and waited for Jess to look up at him. 'Ready?' he said.

She nodded and they lifted the petite body, her dead weight forcing Jess to hold her breath as they shuffled over to the tube. They slid her onto the bed and the sides closed around her like a clam around a pearl. There was a slight vibration as her body was scanned and then a red line illuminated along its length where the two halves of the lid met. It signified that there was no sign of life within.

'All this technology,' said Jess, 'today it's just a body bag.'

Without exchanging any more words, they moved to the second girl, loaded her into the other tube and retraced their steps back through the wreckage of the tunnel to the transporter. The only noise came from the stone as it retrieved the two medi-tubes.

***

'Let's get the bodies on board and then go and check on the others,' said Jess, leading Mason out of the tunnel and toward the transport.

'Do you know what happened?' he asked.

'Like I told Popos, there was an explosion.'

Mason nodded, 'OK,' he said, giving her the space to unload what was in her head.

'I was in the workshop. The girls had been out working for a couple of hours and I went back there to take a seed inventory. I didn't hear it; it was the fire alarm relay that got my attention. It took me a few minutes to get out here and by the time I arrived the girls had got themselves organised and were at the muster point.' She took a breath. 'They did a great job sorting themselves out.'

'OK,' he said again.

'When I got here it was more or less as you saw. Three of them had been turning the soil in the front pit. I thought they were all…' she shook her head, 'I should've checked more thoroughly before I called in. It's my responsibility. If the others hadn't been there I'd have lost her too!'

Mason touched Jess's arm.

'It's OK,' he said, 'you did everything right.'

Jess nodded and gave him a smile.

'…they took her back and I stayed out here, waited for you.'

Mason nodded.

'Go and talk to your father,' he tilted his head to the transport, 'I'll get things organised.'

She nodded and fought her neck-length auburn hair back into a tight ponytail, both hands fully employed, and headed up into the cab of the transport.

Mason walked to the rear of the vehicle where the large black cube still sat in the dust. Six more of the stones had unpacked themselves from their crate, their grey featureless bodies standing in a circle around it, waiting for him.

'Control,' Mason spoke into the air and one of the stones moved from the circle and came to a stop in front of him.

'I want a sweep of the surrounding one thousand metres centred on this point for any signs of undetonated explosive devices.'

A small 'copter pulled itself from the side of the command unit, unfolded its four wings and flew like a huge insect into the sky high above Mason's head.

The command unit spoke almost immediately in an authoritative voice that was neither female nor male, 'No explosive devices are detectable within the surrounding one thousand metres Sir.'

'Determine the centre of the explosion and carry out a forensic scan from a fifty-metre radius back to the point of the blast,' said Mason.

The 'copter scooted to a point above the missing end of the nursery tunnel and the remaining stones began to move to points on a circle centred on its position.

'Once you've completed the scan, transmit the data to my personal code, then I want you to repair the damage. Clarification?'

'None Sir, your wishes are clear.'

'Don't begin the repairs until Mistress and I have left the area.'

With that Mason turned from the command unit and waited for the bodies to be loaded into the transport.

***

Nicholas Alexander Michael Trevelian, Patriarch of the Family Trevelian, stood alone in his office. He could feel anger wrap itself around the inside of his skull. He wanted to be out there. He wanted to be with his daughter. He wanted Jess in his arms.

He looked out toward the irrigation canal whose crescent defined the boundary to his private gardens. On a typical day, he would walk its curve in the fresh early-morning air. He would watch the light dance across its water making black tongues of shadow appear and vanish across its skin, losing himself in the scent of the flowers that he loved to nurture. Here, in the decadent lushness of his garden, he would find his centre before the heat of the sun and the responsibilities of a Patriarch climbed onto his shoulders for the day. But today he had not done these things. Instead he had imagined the carnage; imagined what his wonderful Jess must have been faced with.

His right hand ran down the full length of one strand of his beard, his fingers slowing over each of the ribbons knotted into the plait. As he touched them the muscles of his shoulders and neck relaxed.

The speaker buzzed and then a voice.

'Popos. Popos it's Jess.'

'Jess, are you OK?'

'I'm fine. Mason's here now and I'm fine.'

Nicholas allowed himself to breathe. His hand dropped from his beard and moved slowly across his chest.

'Get yourself back here as soon as you can, Jess. I want you here. I want you safe.'

'Don't worry. I am safe. Mason's here. We'll be back before dusk.'

'Come see me as soon as you get in. A father needs his daughter.'

He paused. He could feel that Jess had something more to say.

'One of the girls survived, father, I got it wrong, two were dead and one survived.'

'Right. How is she?'

'She was in a bad way, but they took her back to the welfare unit. We're going to go back there first and make sure she's OK before we return.'

'Come see me,' he said.

'Don't worry.'

The static from the speaker faded to silence.

Nicholas's eye was caught by a small brown bird, half the size of his fist, as it hopped across the lawn in front of his office. He had always been impressed by the way nature would spot and exploit an opportunity. How it would adapt to its environment. Four short decades ago this entire region had been desert; infertile barren dust, incapable of supporting anything but the lightest touch of life. Now it was a bountiful garden that fed the city, and nature had moved in and made it her home. He watched the bird for a few moments, glad that she had seen fit to make her home in his handiwork.

Could it all have been for nothing?

He watched the bird for a few moments more before losing sight of it behind an immaculately presented hedge. He relaxed a little. Jess was safe and Nicholas Alexander Michael Trevelian was in control once more.

***

'Connect me to the office of the Head of Civil Security.' Nicholas spoke into the air and the static spilling from the comms unit gave way to a series of rhythmic clicks.

'Nicholas,' the voice was formal but friendly, 'what can I do for you?'

Normally Nicholas would have enjoyed being addressed by one name. It would have reminded him of happier, less complicated days. But today the use of his first given name by someone of similar high rank was simply appropriate. He turned from the open window of his office and faced the comms unit.

'Citizen Owen, there's been an attack on the Trevelian holdings.'

There was a pause.

'I see, and the nature of this attack?'

'A bomb.'

Silence, and then in his typically clipped tone as if striking each consonant on an anvil the Citizen said, 'I find that difficult to accept Patriarch.'

'I've yet to receive a forensic report, but it was a bomb. Out in one of the production sectors. There'll be an impact on our crop delivery.'

Again, silence as the Citizen considered and calculated.

'Surely it is more likely that some accident has resulted in an explosion, a fuel cell left in the sun, a spark in a chemical store.'

'It was a bomb, Citizen.'

'I find it difficult to accept that anyone would be able to hatch such a plot without my office being aware of it.'

There was a pause as Nicholas sucked in his lower lip and leaned in toward the comms unit.

'My thoughts exactly, Citizen,' his voice low and quiet.

A silence hung in the airwaves between them. There it was, Nicholas's accusation. After a long pause, Citizen Owen spoke. His words chosen carefully and delivered slowly.

'Patriarch. You will appreciate that intelligence is a fragile creature. It must be nurtured and cared for. One cannot expose it to the world until it is ready, or act every time a concern is raised. The rights of the citizenry must be protected.'

'So you do have some information then Citizen.'

Silence.

Nicholas could sense the knots tighten in the Citizen's stomach.

'What was the nature of your intelligence, Citizen?'

There was no reply.

'Citizen Owen,' Nicholas's voice was raised, 'tell me what you know and tell me now. I have two dead souls out there and I need to be making some decisions.'

'Forgive me, Nicholas Alexander Michael. I appreciate that you need to know all you can,' the voice returned to the formal clipped tones and language of its office, 'but the nature of my intelligence is such that I cannot share it. Even with you. In any case the information is not credible.'

'The fact that an attack has been made on my estate this morning would suggest otherwise would it not?' Nicholas raised his eyes to the ceiling.

'I shall of course keep you appraised of my enquiries,' the Citizen offered.

Now it was Nicholas's turn to be silent.

'Patriarch, are you still there?'

'Keep me informed,' said Nicholas. 'I shall make available to you anything that we find from our own investigations. In the meantime, I request that Trilogy be convened to consider this matter.'

There was barely a heartbeat's pause before the Citizen replied.

'But Sir, to convene Trilogy, surely a hasty move. Might I respectfully suggest….'

Nicholas's tone became abrupt and directive, 'Citizen Owen, I wish you, to see to it, that Trilogy is convened, and that this matter is discussed,' and with that he ended the transmission without waiting for a response.

He stepped away from the comms unit. There it was again: the anger he knew would never be his friend. He looked back out over the gardens, his tall athletic body showing nothing of the age that it had earned.

'Bloody fool,' he said under his breath.

He sucked in his lip again and considered the Citizen's response. He had expected him to be a little more forthcoming. Unless? If someone of rank were implicated?

He shook his head. But then….it would only take one feeble-minded fool to act on his words.

Nicholas knew too well that fools were capable of anything. Particularly fools who believed that "right" was on their side.

***

The inside of the hut was dark and humid and Jess paused for a moment to allow her eyes to adjust. She could sense the faces of the girls and women, the Trevelian namesakes, watching her; their shadows clinging to its walls, waiting to see what she might do next. She walked to the table in the centre of the room where the injured girl had been placed.

An older woman was seated next to the table. She did not look up but held the unconscious girl's hand as she spoke, her voice gentle, soothing.

'Mistress is back now, and Mason-of-Trevelian is with her. We will all be back at Halls before you know it.'

Jess looked at the bloodstains on the tablecloth under the girl. 'How's she doing?'

'She sleeps, Mistress, the azrapone holds her.'

Jess touched the girl's cheek with the back of her hand and looked at the thin metallic band that ran from temple to temple across her forehead. She was drawn to the slow hypnotic rhythm of the light that sat at its centre, glowing brightly and then fading slowly to nothing. As a little girl, its blueness had made Jess imagine that it was the eye of some mythological beast.

'Good. I'm glad we had one to hand,' she said.

She looked at the girl, held somewhere between sleep and death. She was about the same age as Jess, perhaps a year or two younger, maybe eighteen or nineteen. Her face should have shared the thin pale symmetry of all the Trevelian namesakes: deep brown eyes framed by long dark hair. But her face was distorted and disfigured down one side where the skin had swollen around a deep cut.

'That looks painful,' said Jess.

The woman pulled the girl's hand to her lips and kissed it.

'Her flesh was badly torn but we've cleaned the wound. There'll be no infection.'

'Can she be moved?' Mason had approached the table and spoke to the older woman. She nodded.

'We can bring a medi-tube,' Jess added.

'No, we can move her, Mistress.' The woman looked up and addressed the namesakes standing around the walls: 'Six of you take her out to the transport and get her strapped in across the front seats'.

Some of the younger women moved toward the table. The first four to arrive each knotted a corner of the bloodied tablecloth. Two more positioned themselves on either side of the girl and then with an unspoken signal they lifted the corners and sides of the fabric to form a stretcher and carried the girl outside. Others moved tables and chairs from their path to allow the girl and her bearers to pass.

'Please make use of the Family's medical suite if you have need of it,' said Jess.

The older woman looked her in the eye and touched her hand to Jess's arm.

'Thank you, Mistress, I had intended to ask the medical suite to carry out a scan.'

Jess blushed at having suggested the woman would have done anything other than what was best for one of the girls.

'I'll leave it to you then,' she said.

Jess followed the namesakes outside and watched as they loaded themselves into their transport. The machine came to life as the older woman spoke into the console in the cabin and took her seat. It reversed from its location executing a slow three-point turn and trundled off through the gate toward the residential Halls.

'You OK?' asked Mason

Jess turned to face him. The pleasant afternoon sun felt warm on her back as they looked at each other. The beautiful blue sky and sweet smell of water in the air held no hint of the ending of two innocent lives. She nodded.

'Thanks.'

She looked around the courtyard, the hub from which she managed the Family's lands for her father. The machinery, the seed store, the gullies running around the perimeter which would channel water to the underground tanks when the rains came. Orderly, organised, familiar.

'Why would someone want to attack us? All we do is make the food.'

She looked up into his face. His eyes were looking at her but she could tell he was seeing something else. She changed the subject.

'Thanks for coming out so quickly,' she said.

He smiled, back with her, back in the moment.

'Jess, I'll always be there for you, you know that.'

CHAPTER TWO

She was awake, but she couldn't open her eyes. No, she thought, that's not quite it. She was sure that she could open her eyes if she so chose, but something in her heart said, no, keep your eyes closed, rest. So she kept them closed.

She was aware of voices around her. The voices of some of her cousins, aware of them but unable to make sense of what they were saying.

Then she was floating, floating above the ground, outside in the sunshine. She could feel the sun's warmth on her skin. Then it was cold again and she felt the gentle rocking motion of her cradle and she slept.

When finally, she did open her eyes, it was night-time. She could tell by the taste and smell of the air that the sun must have set some hours before. She was in her cell. She could not understand why the light was on so long after dark. It should be out and she should be asleep. She tried to get up from her bed but was unable to move her arms or her legs. She tried to cry out but could not make a sound. She caught sight of a movement in the corner of her eye, there was another person in her cell. She fought for breath and felt a sudden fear grab at her heart and make it sink into her feet.

'Be still little one,' it was the voice of one of her cousins. 'You're quite safe. You're in your cell, rest'.

She could see her now, standing over her. The light in the ceiling produced bright bands of golds and silvers around her blurred head. For a moment, she thought that she must be in the presence of a saint, then she knew it could not be as she had recognised the voice.

'The azrapone has been helping you to sleep and is now releasing you from its arms. It's night but we're all still awake and I'll stay with you as long as you need me.'

Her blurred face leaned in and the girl felt the azrapone slip gently from her temples. She felt a kiss on her forehead, slow and loving, and then the life came back to her body. She pushed herself into a sitting position and carefully put her feet down onto the floor. She felt a little dizzy but managed to stand. Her cousin, sitting on the chair next to the bed, reached out and squeezed the girl's hand.

She could feel her cousin's eyes on her as she made her way to the wash room, splashed water onto her face and drank from cupped hands. It made her feel a little better to taste the water and feel its coolness run down her throat and into her belly. Her face felt hot and she couldn't fully open her left eye. She put her fingers up to her face and neck and blindly explored the cuts that covered one side of both. Her fingers recoiled as they touched her swollen skin.

'What happened?' she asked.

'What do you remember?'

She paused and looked down, noticing that her arms and hands were also covered in bruises and cuts. She held them out in front of herself and turned them around and over, taking in each injury. Remembering.

'We were turning the soil. It was good soil but it needed turning, so three of us decided to work on it for an hour or so. Another week and it'll be ready to take a crop....'

Her voice trailed as she remembered.

'I said I'd go and fetch some forks from the tool shop... then there was shouting. It was me, I was shouting...the others were just lying there...on the ground, just lying there. I couldn't make them hear me. Then I could taste blood in my mouth and then.... I don't remember.'

She looked around at her cousin whose eyes met hers. There was always an understanding between cousins, and in that look the girl came to know what had happened.

'They're gone, aren't they? Dead I mean? They're both dead.'

'Yes.'

She turned back to the sink and held it with both hands. She felt as if she would vomit.

After a moment, her cousin spoke, 'There was some kind of accident. They were killed, you were hurt. Mistress has brought them back to us and they're being prepared for the final witnessing. They'll be put in the ground at dawn.'

The girl straightened her body. She winced, suddenly aware of the stiffness in her left shoulder and hip.

'I'd like to help with the preparations,' she said.

'There's no need, others have the tasks in hand.'

'I should like to assist. I need to.'

She walked back into the room.

'I must dress.' She walked over to the hook on the back of the door and reached up for her smock, the movement forcing a sharp intake of breath.

'You must rest. Your injuries. If you don't rest they'll take longer to heal.'

'My injuries aren't serious.'

'But you must rest little one. You were nearly....'

'I need to see them and say goodbye.'

There was a short silence.

'If you're sure.' The woman stood, her kind eyes filled with concern. 'You'll need to be properly dressed for the witnessing. Wait here and I'll fetch some vestments.'

The woman turned back to the girl as she reached the door and said, 'Mistress may want to speak with you. If it's too painful, look for me and I'll intercede.'

The girl nodded at her cousin as she left. She sat on her bed, stretched her neck and shoulders and waited for her clothes.

***

Jess stood in the shadows facing the small wooden door next to the fireplace. The scent of roses and lavender spilled out through the little doorway, carried on the back of the flickering yellows and golds of the candlelight. The chapel was situated in a room that ran across the back of the refectory so that it was as long as the hall was wide. Through the doorway, Jess could see shadows moving across the large stone flags of the floor.

Two hooded figures wheeling a large brass bowl moved through the doorway toward her. As they passed she could see that the water it contained was dirty: a cloudy red-brown that sparked here and there as its eddies caught the reflections of candlelight. She realised it had been used to wash the dead girls, and the thought made the breath catch in the back of her throat. She moved to one side to let them through.

'Mistress.' One of her namesakes, a woman perhaps in her early forties seated just inside the doorway, rose and bowed as Jess entered the chapel. 'There was no need for you to attend.'

Jess smiled and touched the woman's shoulder.

'Of course I will attend. And the Patriarch will be here before the dawn'.

The woman gave a gentle smile, her mouth the only part of her face visible from beneath her hood.

Jess looked across the chapel to the two tables at its centre. The benches that normally filled the space had been moved back to the walls to make way for the laying out of the bodies. She looked at the dead, their naked skin touched by the candlelight. So pale and still, so much less than life.

She looked up at the banner hanging at the far end of the chapel. Its large gold letters floating on their blue background proclaiming that "Our Faith Sets Us Free". She watched the namesakes as they worked together in hooded silence, attending to their dead cousins in preparation for the final witnessing. It struck her that this was indeed a community united in faith.

Her eyes were drawn to the stained-glass windows that held the faces of the Three Living Saints. Normally she would feel some sense of serenity or comfort as the sunlight brought them to life, but tonight the faces seemed flat and lifeless and offered her no solace. She felt cold and alone and realised that this was the first time she had been in the chapel after dark.

A figure, its head, like the others, covered by a hood and tilted to the floor, entered the chapel. Jess watched as it carried two pristine bundles of white cloth, each neatly folded and tied with a scarlet ribbon like some perfectly wrapped gift. It placed a bundle next to one of the dead, stood perfectly still for a moment and reached out a hand. Its arm, scarred and bruised, was the only thing that suggested the special connection it shared with the newly dead.

Jess watched the figure, motionless, outside of time. She approached and placed her arm around its shoulder. The hooded figure did not react, they both looked down at the dead girl on the table in front of them.

After an age, Jess spoke, 'I expected you to be resting.'

'Mistress.' The girl turned to Jess and gave a subtle nod of her head. 'I wanted to attend them. We were working together when it happened.'

'I know. I'm sorry. May I help you in your task?'

The girl handed Jess the second neat parcel and they walked over to the other table. Jess placed the package at the feet of the second dead girl and untied the ribbon. The girl touched her hand to the dead girl's shoulder and looked into her face.

Jess was suddenly aware of three namesakes standing behind her. She turned and acknowledged them but they seemed to hesitate.

'I'm intruding,' she turned back to the girl, 'I just wanted...' her face felt hot, she was in the way.

'Thank you, Mistress,' said the girl with a slow nod.

Jess smiled and moved away from the body, returning to the space under the stained-glass windows.

The girl and one of her cousins unfolded the cloth and laid it out along the table next to the dead girl so that equal lengths dropped onto the floor at either end.

The girl reached across the pale skin of the corpse and placed her hands on its hip and shoulder. She stopped for a moment, the flesh was icy cold. She felt a knot tighten in her belly, the body's lack of life suddenly tangible and real. She rolled the body onto its side, cradling it to her own chest as if giving comfort to a child. Her cousin arranged the cloth under the body and she rolled the cold flesh back to the table. Gathering up the lower end of the shroud, she pulled it up so that it covered the dead girl to the shoulders. Her cousin gathered up the other end and formed it into a pillow under the dead girl's head.

The girl looked at her dead cousin for a moment. It was as if she were asleep, framed in the newly washed white linen of a soft and comforting bed, not a corpse but a sleeping girl. She slid her arms under the pillow, tilting the sleeper's head up. The other woman took the scarlet ribbon that had been used to tie the shroud and passed it under the pillow. She then tied it across the dead girl's eyes, holding them closed.

When their work was complete the girl turned to her cousin and they embraced. She could feel the warmth of her cousin's body and was grateful for it. It chased away the coldness of death.

A single chime from the small service bell standing in a frame at the end of the chapel moved through the air, its light crisp tone prompting those present to form a line and file out of the chapel. Only two women were left, each seated on wooden chairs positioned next to each other and between the two tables holding the shrouded bodies. They would keep a vigil for the remainder of the night; chattering to each other and to the dead girls about anything and nothing, until the dawn came and it would be time to give them back to the earth.

***

Nicholas Alexander Michael Trevelian entered the refectory an hour later. The sound of the many conversations taking place around him made him stop just inside the door. The tables, normally arranged in lines running the length of the hall, had been moved to form three sides of a square and his eyes were drawn to the two white candles standing in tall brass candlesticks at its centre. Their flames were barely visible in the brightly lit hall, but he felt compelled to take a moment and acknowledge their presence.

There was no reaction from the namesakes to the arrival of the Trevelian Family Patriarch, only Jess acknowledged him, slipping from the bench where she had shared a meal and rising to her toes as she kissed his cheek.

'Popos.'

'How are the preparations?'

'They're both ready,' she nodded and gave a tight-lipped smile.

'And the community?'

'In good spirits. I'm surprised, I thought in the circumstances, with the way the two of them met their ends... I had expected the celebration to be muted. But as you can see...'

Nicholas took in the room. The women were smiling and talking, some were laughing. This was a celebration of two lives well-lived and the passage of two pure souls to a better place. To paradise.

'You feeling any better?'

Jess gave a nod, 'A little. I know you're right, it wasn't my fault. But...,' She looked around and shrugged, "the journey well-made" as they say.'

Nicholas extended his arm to Jess's shoulder, gently stroking it with his thumb.

'You'll be OK. So will they,' he said.

He was suddenly aware of the smell of roses and lavender, scents that he would always associate with this place. The last time he had been here was for the festival of the harvest at the end of the previous season. The memory would normally have brought him a smile.

'Their faith has brought them together,' he said.

Jess nodded, not taking her eyes from his face.

'I envy them,' he said, 'what we might see as an utterly abhorrent act, the taking of two young and good lives, to them makes perfect sense. Their faith allows them to come together, to celebrate those lives. I envy them.'

'Their faith really does set them free doesn't it,' said Jess.

He looked around at his namesakes. He smiled down at her and reached a great arm around her shoulder, pulling her close in to his side.

***

The girl did not eat much of the food that had been prepared for the feast of the witnessing. Instead she had taken a place on one of the benches and lost herself in the light of the candles. She was held in their movement, staring at them, unaware of the passage of time until the sound of the chapel bell ran through her, making her jump.

The conversations in the room began to dry and the girl watched as some of her cousins began extinguishing the lights that ran around the walls. As they went out the atmosphere in the hall moved from one of celebration to one of serene silence. Soon the only light in the room came from the two candles, and the only sound was the faint and intermittent splutter of their hot wax.

The girl stared into the flames. She watched as the souls of her two dead cousins made them dance and flicker.

Jess and her father stood side by side where they had been talking. They had turned to face the candlelight, beyond which they could see the dim outline of the chapel door. This time, just before dawn, was The Reverence, the final witnessing. Lit only by the candles, the souls of the newly dead, this was a time for a silent and private contemplation of those that had moved on. Jess and her father stood in silence, unable to fully share these moments with their namesakes.

In the chapel, the two women who had been holding vigil were now standing in the darkness at the feet of the two dead girls, their heads bowed. As the first light of the dawn entered the chapel through the stained-glass faces of the Living Saints, the shadows cast by the trees in the graveyard on the other side of the window made their images appear to move as they looked down on the dead. A few minutes later, when the sunlight had become strong enough to reach the far wall of the holy place, the two women began to sing. Their words told of the ending of mortal life and the passage of the eternal to paradise.

The women left their charges and entered the refectory. Their voices were joined by those of the others and their words floated up into the rafters, allowing the building to add its own soft echoes of remembrance. The girl opened her mouth and heart and joined her voice to those of her cousins. Tears welled behind her eyelid, bursting through the swollen flesh and running down the scar that broke the symmetry of her face.

Two women began working their way around the hall removing the shutters from the windows. As each was taken down the soft dawn sun entering the room made the light from each of the candles less and less significant until their flames were barely visible.

When the final shutter had been removed, the singing stopped and those gathered waited for the last of the reverberations to leave them in silence. Then, in the gentle light of the dawn, the two bodies emerged from the chapel into the stillness of the hall. Each was carried by six women holding onto their shrouds, helping them float in serene sleep. The namesakes formed a line behind the shrouded bodies.

The girl walked over to the nearest of the two candles, drawn toward its light. The metal candlestick felt cold and was thick enough to fill her hand. She wrapped both hands around it and lifted it gently from the floor. She carried the candle over to the others, followed by one of her cousins who took the other.

The girl waited at the front of the procession for the chapel bell to ring twice more, once for each soul. She could feel the sound move through her and waited for it to die away completely before leading the procession out through the stone arch of the doorway. She breathed in the beginnings of the morning and led the way around the building. The candlestick was heavy and her arms ached holding it out in front of her. The only sound was the delicate gravel-crunch of the procession's feet on the narrow pathway behind her.

The smell of the damp soil from the two shallow grave-pits cut into the flesh of the earth filled her head. She removed her candle from its holder and knelt with it at the end of one of the graves. A stream of wax ran down one side and over the back of her hand. She let it solidify on her skin, its heat a soothing distraction. She watched as the two bodies were laid next to the openings. Again, she thought the girls looked more asleep than dead, cocooned, resting. She watched as her cousins untied the scarlet ribbon from each face and pulled back the cloth, exposing the bodies to the sunlight. She was so close she could smell the lavender from the water in which they had been washed.

Two of the women entered each pit, and the bare-flesh bodies were carefully handed to them. Each was placed onto the soil with the greatest care.

The girl felt a shadow on her shoulder and looked up. One of her cousins had placed a waist-high frame next to her. She slotted the candle into the cradle in its base and stood. The frame held a small silver bowl of water over the candle. She was handed a purse made from a single piece of fabric drawn into a bag and held closed with a copper-coloured ring around its neck. She slipped off the ring and tipped the contents into the bowl, drawing a circle of red dust on the surface of the water. The dust fizzed and frothed as it came to life and expanded.

One of the women spoke.

'Such as you are now, so will we soon become. Your souls go to be weighed. We ask the nine orders of Angels and the Three Living Saints to look upon you in the shadows of this world, and grant you passage to the holy garden.'

The woman looked across at the girl and gave a nod. She picked up the bowl and tipped it across the body which lay in the pit in front of her. The liquid continued to expand as it drew itself across the pale skin, the fungi that had been woken by the warm water releasing enzymes that hungrily ate the flesh away as she watched.

With that the women began to cover the two visibly decomposing bodies with earth. They worked in silence as the dawn sun rose a little into the sky. Their last task was to leave a small sapling on the top of each otherwise unmarked grave.

'A History of Amynthia'. Prof. E. Fuller

From this great distance we can see so very little of the details of Amynthian society; how they occupied themselves, what they did for work or for pleasure. They seem to have left no clue that will help us discover their private lives. What we are able to deduce relates to their structures of governance, and central to this was Trilogy.

To the general population of Amynthia, Trilogy may have been an irrelevance; a throwback to a time of feudal governance, to a time before the war: its pomp and ceremony considered either to be an embarrassment to modernity or a theatrical expression of nostalgia. It was something to be relished, celebrated, enjoyed perhaps, but mostly something to be ignored. But to those who could remember the last years of The Great Conflict, Trilogy surely had never ceased to be the cornerstone of society. Those who could remember the motivation behind its formation must have appreciated that its structure and function had been designed to prevent their world spiralling out of control as it had before. It enshrined both the role of religious faith in law-making and the limits within which it could act. It provided the outlet and the muzzle for the forces that had all but brought humanity to extinction.

The Trilogy, it seems, comprised elements whose duty it was to care for three aspects of society: the will of the people, their physical health and their spiritual wellbeing.

The custodianship of the people's spiritual health was entrusted to the three so-called Living Saints. They formed the lowest order of Trilogy and held the city's moral compass. They were lifelong appointments drawn from the ranks of The Seminary, the religious college in which girls and boys from the more refined, or perhaps simply the wealthier strata of society would be enrolled at the age of seven. A Seminarian could only rise to the rank of Living Saint on the death of an incumbent, so the majority of Seminarians must have followed some other path. A graduate of the Seminary was not permitted to stand for an elected office, so typically a career as a technocrat or senior administrator seems likely. Their spare time would be spent debating religious text, and arguing abstruse points of doctrine with one another no doubt.

We do not know the names of those given the task of caring for the population's physical health, but we do know that this duty was manifest in the production of the food on which Amynthia relied and that this duty was shared between three families. Their collective voice carried more weight at Trilogy than that of the Living Saints. In matters of debate, the physical health of Amynthia would take precedence over its spirituality.

The most senior element of Trilogy was The Authority: an individual appointed for a fixed term of one year to ensure the rights of the citizenry were protected. The Authority was not allowed to propose any of the business of Trilogy or take part in any debate, but would ensure that the Rules of Council were properly applied and provide a casting vote should the three Families and the three Living Saints fail to reach an agreement over some issue. The Authority, it seems, also had an absolute right of veto over any decision made at Trilogy. The will of the people was held above all else. It was sacrosanct. The Authority was appointed by lottery from the membership of Council, the elected parliament of Amynthia, and was supported by a team of clerks who were versed and expert in constitutional law and could provide 'argument' or advice should a casting vote be requested.

On the whole, Amynthian society was ambivalent toward the Trilogy, except for their attitude to the Families. With their perceived hold on the food supply, and their reliance on the slave-class of namesakes, the Families drew only criticism.

Reproduced from 'A History of Amynthia' with the kind permission of the estate of Prof. E. Fuller.

CHAPTER THREE

The inside of the capsule was lined with an opulent red leather skin. It ran in a continuous length up the walls and across the curve of the ceiling, broken only by the portholes which drew a dotted line along either side of the craft. The red skin and darker carpet would suck up any sounds made by the occupants, lending a feeling of intimacy to spoken words. But Nicholas, Jess and Mason sat in silence.

Jess looked at her father. He was wrapped in his thoughts, his eyes unfocussed, directed at his hands held prayer-like on the table between them. His jaw was clenched and she could see the muscles in his cheeks pulse. In the two weeks since the accident she had watched as his shoulders took on the full weight of Patriarch. She wanted to say something, to offer some support. But what advice could she offer to this great leader?

He looked up at her and winked. She smiled back and turned to look through the porthole. In the distance the mountain range that separated the farms from the city looked on, its distance making it stand still as the craft sped through the dry air just above the ground.

The capsule slowed as it approached the mountain which sat like the hub of a wheel at the centre of the great city of Amynthia. The craft's mirrored outer surface reflected the streets and buildings around it, twisting them to destruction at each of its tapered ends.

It slowed still further and entered a tunnel which took them into the mountain's heart and then up through a shaft to its peak. Here the Chambers of Trilogy commanded a position designed to be both awe-inspiring and inaccessible to the vast city spilling out across the plateau from which the mountain grew.

***

Mason-of-Trevelian left Nicholas and Jess in the capsule and made his way through the ornate wood-clad entry corridor to the Family's rooms. He had arranged for their quarters to be opened, aired and dressed but etiquette required that he physically check the rooms prior to their arrival.

His large body moved quickly from room to room, his eyes sweeping the corners and shadows for anything out of place. He could taste a slight stagnancy sitting under the scent of the newly delivered flowers, but all appeared to be in order. He finished his search in the exquisitely decorated syndicate room, its walls covered with pastoral scenes of wild animals and crops, punctuated by geometric designs in gold leaf.

'Sir,' he spoke into the air and his master's voice responded almost immediately.

'Mason.'

'The apartments are ready for you.'

'Thank you.'

Mason lifted his head to the Trevelian Family crest which looked down into the room from the centre of the high vaulted ceiling. Could it all have been for nothing? All the years of work, all the sacrifices? He knew Nicholas was worried. He crossed to the window making up most of one side of the room and stared down at the city, his city, stretching away under the picture-framed blue of the sky.

A few minutes later Jess and her father entered the room. They had both changed into the simple blue gowns which Mason had laid out for them in the entrance hall, each bearing the white shell-like emblem of the Family Trevelian on the chest and back.

'A long journey well-made is ended.' Jess smiled at Mason as he recited the formal age-old saying, his arms held wide.

'Mason, would you please signal our arrival to The Hub and confirm the arrangements for tomorrow's meeting,' said Nicholas.

Mason dropped his hands and held them behind his back.

'Already done Sir, Hub has confirmed that the other parties have all arrived, apart from The Authority who is due before dusk.'

'Thank you, Mason.'

Jess could see her father's shoulders drop a little as he relaxed. She knew that he had been anxious since calling for the meeting of Trilogy. He turned and smiled at her.

'It's never been the battle, always the waiting that gets to me,' he said, reading her thoughts.

'Come Popos, let's have something to eat.'

'No. I want us to go over a few things again before we relax. We must be sure to state our argument properly at Trilogy.'

Nicholas moved to one end of the chest-high crescent shaped table that swept around the centre of the room.

'Let's start with a recap of what we learnt out at the tunnel please.'

'Give us the aerial view from the scans taken from the scene.' Mason spoke into the air as he walked over to the table. The space ringed by the horseshoe started to glow and an image of the blast area appeared before them.

'Show us the point of the blasts.' Two red circles appeared on the image at Mason's command, each repeatedly shrinking to a point and reappearing to mark positions on either side of what remained of the tunnel structure.

'So, we know that there were in fact two devices, and that they were located outside the glasshouse on either side of the soil production pits,' Nicholas spoke rhetorically; he, Mason and Jess had discussed and dissected the evidence endlessly since the attack.

'And we know that both devices were triggered by a crude timer, but that they contained a relatively sophisticated explosive similar to that used by our civil defence militia.'

'Not similar Sir,' interrupted Mason, 'identical. The explosive was certainly military in origin, the chemical signature is unmistakable. And it was pure and unadulterated. The method of delivery however, as you note, was amateurish, crude.'

'And we also know that someone from outside the Family Trevelian planted the devices.'

'That's correct,' said Mason, 'no Trevelian family member, no staff-of-Trevelian, and no namesake had any contact with either device. The traces of cell-line that we found at the scene originate from elsewhere Sir.'

'And when challenged we can evidence this statement, including the meticulous elimination of all staff-of-Trevelian?' asked Nicholas.

'All your staff, present and past, were included in the review. I can produce a very detailed and well evidenced account for the record if so required by Trilogy.'

'So. Who then?' Nicholas stepped back from the horseshoe and turned to look out through the window.

'Someone with access to munitions, or with the rank to gain access,' said Mason.

'It was Adam Charles Percival,' said Nicholas, cutting off Mason's words.

Both Jess and Mason were silent.

'I haven't said anything up 'till now because I didn't want you upset,' he was speaking to Jess, 'I know the two of you were close as children.'

Jess's eyes were wide, her head shook.

'But I don't want it to come as a surprise to you tomorrow during Trilogy.'

'No. No, Popos, there's no way. Adam could not have done this. Not taken a life, no way.'

'I'm sorry, Jess,' he turned to face her, 'Adam was behind this. I'm sure of it.'

'No,' her voice softer, her eyes looking at the floor, 'I, I don't believe it. I don't believe he could.'

'Tomorrow we'll find out,' said Nicholas.

***

'We're already considered an irrelevance by much of the population. If Trevelian seeks to use this as an excuse to increase the powers of the Families still further he will have a fight on his …'

Demeter's gaze hit the young man directly between the eyes. She was the most senior of the Three Living Saints and had a reputation for taking naïve young men off at the knees. He swallowed hard, his voice a whisper now; taut with adrenaline.

'But he means to argue that a state of martial law be granted,' he continued. 'He means to strengthen his Family's standing and curtail our influence.'

Demeter's voice was measured, calm.

'And you know this.'

'I'm sure of it.'

'You. You are sure of it.' She stroked a crease from her sleeve. 'Before we go making an issue let us first determine if we have one.' She smiled at him, her expensively blackened teeth showing through her thin lips. She faced forward and continued with her lecture.

'Seminary is the foundation of our society's morality, and we three Saints represent the Seminary here at Trilogy. We are the force which guides Amynthia's moral compass. There's no leverage a Family can bring to curtail that purpose or dilute its potency. The Trevelian Patriarch has given his opening statements, nothing more. We'll wait and see where he takes his argument and then we'll respond to it.' Demeter put her hands into her lap, her thumbs touching, fingers slowly moving apart and together almost imperceptibly. 'And it is inappropriate and unseemly for the Living Saint of War to rant like a pubescent youth.'

The young man sat back in his seat, his scowl drawn into his high collar.

Demeter looked around at the ornate symbols and figures carved into the wood-clad walls lining the room's circumference. She had always admired the craftsmanship exhibited here; the way the artisans had incorporated the woodgrain into their designs and anticipated the way light and shadow would fall on their work. The inside of the Chamber of Trilogy was truly a thing of beauty.

As protocol dictated the Three Living Saints had remained in the Chamber during the recess. They were the lowest order of the Trilogy and were required to be seated in the circle before the other members returned. They waited. She waited.

After a few minutes, the wide entrance door swung open and the Patriarchs of Trevelian and Percival, and the Matriarch of de-Monte entered the room followed by a small entourage. Demeter watched as the three Family-heads walked up to the raised platform on which she and the other Living Saints were seated. Shoulder to shoulder they took their places at the lecterns facing her. Here was the physical manifestation of their status: their heads higher than those of her and her fellow saints. Not for the first time she felt this indignity as a barb in her side. She smiled.

The large bell hanging from a stand by the wall rang out three times. As its last chime raced around the curved wall, leaking out into the adjoining corridors, The Authority, the highest-ranking member of the Trilogy, entered the chamber. Clad in the blue and white cloak of her office, she climbed the steps rising from the opening in the floor of the platform. She took her place in the chair from where she would look down on the other members. The tableau symbolised the hierarchy of Trilogy and captured the history that had brought it into existence.

'We reconvene debate.' The Authority made the announcement that signalled the end of the recess she had called an hour before.

'Nicholas Alexander Michael Trevelian, you have presented evidence from which I think you mean us to conclude that the devices used to destroy your property contained military grade explosive.'

'Yes, Authority.' Nicholas looked up at her as he replied.

'And you have stated that the cell-lines present on the residue were not of your Family.'

'Or of my staff, Authority.'

'You leave us to make the obvious inference that someone with sufficient rank and privilege to gain access to military supplies was involved.'

Nicholas gave a nod.

There was silence for a moment.

'And so, your finger points...?'

'No, Authority, I don't accuse. I only state the facts to Trilogy and suggest that we be allowed to check the cell-line material we recovered at the site of the attack against others.'

'And by others you mean… who exactly?'

Nicholas took a breath before he replied. 'I ask for permission to have the fragments of cell-line recovered from the site of the explosion compared to those of a member of the Percival Family.'

The atmosphere within the chamber intensified.

'You suspect the attack was perpetrated by a member of the Percival Family?' It was Demeter, speaking now as the Living Saint of Famine, who voiced the thoughts of her two colleagues from Seminary.

'The Families are one,' said The Authority, 'you each share the burden of producing food for the city. What motive can there be for one Family to attack another?'

Nicholas glanced to his side at Charles Edwin George Percival as he spoke.

'I believe that Adam Charles Percival, first son of the Percival line, was behind the attack.'

Charles did not turn to look at Nicholas, but stared directly across the room at the Living Saints. His face marble-white.

Nicholas continued, 'Adam has for a long time opposed the use of namesakes. He's spoken publicly more than once about the prohibition of their use. I believe that he's been moved to violence by his own misguided rhetoric, and that the attack was intended to gain publicity. I believe it to be an attempt to stimulate calls for the abolition of the namesakes.'

Charles did not move but continued to stare straight ahead. His face began to colour. It was Demeter who broke the silence.

'The Right to speak is a fundamental freedom afforded to all our citizens. The first-son of Percival has done no more than exercise this right. There's a great chasm between speech and violence. I take it you have some evidence which allows you to bridge this gap?'

'It's exactly this evidence that I seek,' said Nicholas.

'You've no right to ask for such a thing based on a whim!' The two Living Saints seated on either side of Demeter stamped their feet in agreement as the Living Saint of Famine continued, 'It's not for a Family, not even a Patriarch, to cast doubt on the behaviour of any citizen. Seminary provides the moral compass to which a citizen must align and it is for its representatives at Trilogy, myself and my honourable colleagues,' she tilted her head to indicate them, 'to highlight or call for any such action. It is not your place…'

'Do not preach morality to me Saint.' Nicholas's voice was solid with emotion. 'Everyone in this room understands the true nature of The Seminary's morality. You have no right to claim the moral high-ground.'

'I will not allow you to speak of The Seminary in that way!' The Living Saint of War got to his feet as he shouted. 'Your antagonism toward us is well documented, what we see here is your use of this situation as an excuse to harass us.'

'I'm not interested in walking on eggshells around your nonsensical sensitivities. You, like me, are a servant of society, and you, like me, must live under the yoke of the law.'

All three of the Living Saints were now on their feet, two of them screaming their objections across the chamber with sharp-fingered emphasis.

Charles Edwin George Percival leant forward and touched Nicholas's arm. The yelling from the other side of the platform died away.

'My friend Nicholas does not mean to cast aspersions or cause offence. His tactic is, I'm sure, rooted in the purest of motivations.' Charles looked directly at Nicholas now: 'I don't believe that my son could be moved to violence. His very thesis is one of benevolence toward our communities of namesakes. He couldn't take life from them.'

Nicholas put his hands on the bench in front of him and dropped his gaze. The saints retook their seats. Charles continued.

'If there is offence in this matter dear friends, it is mine to claim. My son has made no secret of his opposition to our way of life; of our holding property in the namesakes. His position is that using them as we do, to undertake the necessary drudgery of food production, is anachronistic. He points out that over the years our reliance on them has diminished to a point where we now only need them for certain aspects of the production of food. For work we have not yet managed to fully automate; work which still needs the sensibilities and sensitivities of human mind and touch. My son's argument is simply that this too must change, as surely it will in time. He says that our property in namesakes, their enslavement, is no longer justifiable and must be ended. He does not advocate violence, only change. Yes, he wants it to stop. He makes no secret of this. But he is an intellectual, his thesis is one of kindness not one of violence.'

'Fine words from the head of a Family,' it was the Living Saint of War who spoke. 'You're at the very heart of the system which your son seeks to overturn.' Demeter shot the young man a glance and he fell silent.

Charles turned, ignoring this comment, and spoke directly to Nicholas: 'For some reason you suspect my son of perpetrating this terrible attack on your holdings. Surely you can see that he could no more cause the death of a namesake than he could keep quiet about the injustice he feels in their treatment.'

Nicholas shook his head.

'Why do you accuse my son, Nicholas?'

'Because he's a hot-head. Because he has the rank to obtain munitions. Because he's a self-centred young fool who believes that an end justifies the means. I say that by this act he seeks to find the public eye so that he can spread his rhetoric to the wider community.'

'You have no evidence that Adam has done any of this,' said Charles.

'Adam has been very vocal about what you described as his 'thesis', Charles, and you and he, in fact we all, must recognise that this is no good. No good at all.' Nicholas turned to address the room, 'Adam has been giving public talks, to any that will listen, stirring up support and creating ill feeling for months now, and during this time there have been numerous minor acts of vandalism against my holdings, acts culminating in this last violent act.'

'There, exactly.' Charles had once again stepped forward to speak. 'Adam is an orator, he speaks, is this the criticism? How can this be a crime? Forty years ago, our society enshrined The Right to speak one's mind, no matter how it might be perceived or to whom it might cause offence. The Right is held by many, including your humble servant, to be our finest and noblest achievement. My son simply exercises this right in order to shape the course of our society. And do we not say, "that the future belongs to those that would change today."'

'I do not attack or challenge The Right of free speech,' said Nicholas, his voice taut, 'but you know full well that should free speech result in a crime, those responsible must be held to account.'

'So, what then is your argument, Nicholas? You want my son to submit to a cell-line test, so you must think him responsible for planting the bomb himself, or do you accuse him of incitement? In which case, what is the point of subjecting him to a test?'

'Submit Adam to a cell-line test and, if as you say, he is innocent of planting the bombs himself, then I shall accuse him of incitement. Anything, so long as he's brought to heel and his dangerous ideas are taken out of circulation.'

The Living Saint of War erupted. 'So you do stifle free speech. There is the true motivation. Now we see it.'

Nicholas threw up his arms and Charles stood in red-faced silence, visibly angered by Nicholas's last comment. It was Rebecca Catherine Valerie de-Monte who stepped forward and into the silence. So rare was it for the de-Monte Matriarch to speak at Trilogy that every eye in the room turned to look at her.

'Honoured members of Trilogy,' she addressed the Living Saints directly, 'take your seats and find peace. Nicholas does not challenge The Right, but he's lost two young lives, something that would put any man into a provocative frame of mind. Not all those here are old enough to remember the last years of the war, but no one can be more committed to The Right to Speak than those of us who lived through it, including Nicholas. I need not remind you of his role in those dark hours before our society was reborn.'

The temperature in the room had cooled. The monsters that lived in the stories of The Conflict could be found in the nightmares of all Amynthia's citizens. Rebecca continued.

'Trilogy should not be concerned with guilt or with innocence, only with truth. If Adam were to submit willingly to a cell-line test this would do nothing more than establish that truth.'

The eyes in the chamber came to rest on Charles. He exhaled deeply and rubbed his forehead with the fingers of his left hand.

'I can't ask Adam to do that.'

Rebecca tilted her head to one side.

'Why not?'

Charles straightened and turned, looking directly at her.

'Because he's gone. He disappeared about a week or so ago.'

'Shortly after the attack,' said Nicholas.

'Yes. It doesn't mean he had anything to do with it,' Charles added quickly, 'he's often taking himself off somewhere. It doesn't mean anything, it's not significant...' Charles's voice trailed and his eyes dropped to the lectern in front of him.

Again, it was Rebecca who broke the silence, her words soft but clear.

'Nicholas, it was you who convened debate. I assume your intention was to ask Trilogy to vote on a motion. I suggest that we have given sufficient air to the subject and that you should now offer a motion on which we can vote.'

'Thank you, Rebecca, and please, forgive me for my hot and ill-considered words.' Nicholas's apology was offered to all. 'My intention was to ask that Adam's cell-line be compared with what we found at the site. But since his whereabouts is unknown, such a sanction, if granted, would not help us, as no sample could be obtained from him.' He paused and considered for a moment. 'However, another option is available to us. I propose, that in light of the significance of the attack on my holdings, Trilogy vote on the following motion: That in the absence of his son, Charles Edwin George Percival provides a sample of his own cell-line for comparison with the residues recovered from the site of the explosions.'

Charles's face reddened but he said nothing.

There was silence as those present waited for The Authority to give her endorsement to the motion. She stood and spoke clearly so that her words would be captured by the spherical flower-like head of the recording device next to her.

'Votes will be cast as follows,' she said, '"Yes" will be cast to signify that Charles Edwin George Percival,

Patriarch of the Family Percival, does provide cell-line samples this day for comparison with the residues recovered from the site of the explosions at the holdings of the Family Trevelian. "No" will be cast to signify that none shall be provided. I give authority to Trilogy on behalf of the elected Council in the matter of this vote.'

She allowed a moment to pass as protocol demanded and seeing no objection from those present she called on each member of Trilogy in turn to cast their vote.

'The Living Saint of War...'

'No'

'The Living Saint of Plague...'

'No'

'The Living Saint of Famine...'

'Yes'

'Rebecca Catherine Valerie de-Monte, Matriarch of the Family de-Monte...'

'Yes'

'Nicholas Alexander Michael Trevelian, Patriarch of the Family Trevelian...'

'Yes'

'Charles Edwin George Percival, Patriarch of the Family Percival...'

Charles looked ahead and into the eyes of the Living Saint of War. 'Yes,' he said.

'Then let it be recorded that votes were cast in this question four to "yes" and two to "no" and that no casting vote was required. Nicholas, would you please supply the samples retrieved from your estate to the clerk of Trilogy.'

Nicholas turned to look over his shoulder at Mason who had been sitting with Jess in the shadows below and behind him throughout the proceedings. Mason got up from his seat and held out the small ornate wooden box containing the capsules of cell-lines he had retrieved from the nursery tunnel. He handed it to the clerk who had appeared from behind The Authority's raised chair and all eyes watched as she carried it out of the room.

'All members of Trilogy are to remain within Chamber while the comparison is undertaken,' said The Authority.

The Living Saints stood as The Authority nodded her acknowledgement to them and to the Family heads and left the Chamber the way she had entered it, via the stone steps that led down through the central platform. As she descended the bell was rung seven times to signify the conclusion of Trilogy.

The Living Saints made their way from the platform and removed the chains of office that each of them wore about their necks, handing them to their staff in the lower benches. Each heavy gold chain held a large medallion at its centre bearing an emblem that signified the owners so-called 'deed': War, Famine or Plague. The staff took the precious emblems away to the side of the chamber in a cloud of violent whispers leaving Demeter and the other two Saints in silence.

Nicholas, Charles and Rebecca had likewise removed the tabards which displayed their respective family crests and retired to the lower benches to wait.

'Thank you, Rebecca, for your intervention. I forgot myself,' said Nicholas.

'Nicholas, Trilogy is a place for politics not anger, but yours was understandable. And Charles, you acquiesced and agreed to be tested?'

'No, Rebecca, I did not acquiesce. By agreeing to be tested I made a formal statement of my son's innocence. Once this nonsense is concluded I'll be asking for a formal statement of apology from the Trevelian Patriarch and insisting on an appropriate level of compensation.'

A silence sat on their shoulders, daring any to speak; it was Jess who broke through it, leaning forward and touching her father's shoulder.

'Father, Mason and I will return to our rooms, would you like us to bring you anything?'

Nicholas turned and smiled at her, understanding her attempt to diffuse the situation.

'Thank you, Jess, no. I won't be long. I'll join you as soon as the results are announced.'

CHAPTER FOUR

The girl lay paralysed as her mind, sitting in the space between sleep and wakefulness, refused to assert itself, refused to banish the nightmare. She lay in the dark, motionless, feeling the presence of the intruder looming over her in what should have been the safety of her cell. She tried to move her legs, tried to lift her body, tried to shout for help, but her mind ruled otherwise. It held her in her bed, powerless. With only a blanket for protection there was no escape from The Menace whose foul breath she could now feel on her face.

It made no difference that her eyes would not open or that her room was black with night, she could see every detail of the pale and scarred face that hovered an inch away. It was so close to her own that she could tell that it was cold, cold like the skin of her dead cousins the day she had touched them and said goodbye to them in the chapel. Cold pallid skin. Translucent. Veins visible across its cheeks, spreading out like irrigation channels. Pale pale eyes. Eyes so strange, not brown like her own or those of her cousins, but blue, a pale pale blue.

She knew it was a nightmare, just a dream, that no one was in the room with her. She knew that she was alone. She knew all this was in her mind. But she knew that The Menace meant to harm her, meant to bring her to dreadful harm. She knew she must escape. She knew she must get away.

Her limbs would not move; she was pinned to the bed. She summoned all her will and managed to cry out, a small and almost silent cry, but a sound nonetheless; if she could force herself to make a sound, however small, she could force herself to wake up and then she would be safe. Again, she cried out. The Menace opened its mouth and grinned. She understood it to mean that it was hopeless for her. There would be no escape. Even if she could wake herself from this malaise The Menace would return as surely as sleep itself. It would be waiting here for her.

Crooked broken teeth were visible behind its thin white lips. The girl inhaled as hard as she could, breathing in the stench of rancid decomposition, and then, with all her might she let out another cry, not of fear but of battle. Again, she took a breath and yelled. The Menace backed away, trying to find a shadow that was untouched by the light coming from the girl's mouth with each scream. A third cry, for blood, for vengeance, filled with anger and challenge. 'Come and fight me,' the cry said, 'come and fight me if you dare'.

The sound and the light poured from the girl's mouth into the room.

The shadows were all gone now. There was no spot, no place, no corner left in which The Menace could find a darkness to hide itself. It ran from wall to wall, trying to find an escape from the torture of the girl's screams, its frantic motion making the tattered black robes that covered its bones form tormented knots around its body. Swirling and turning, faster and faster the robes formed bindings around the creature's head and neck. Locking its limbs to its body. Bindings that held it tighter and tighter to itself, crushing it. Every movement it made caused the robes to grip and crush and shrink, pulling The Menace into a tight knot. Each scream that the girl made was louder and brighter and as she hurled it into the cell The Menace was pulled further and further into the wall opposite her bed. Pulled and constricted and trussed-up, until finally it had gone.

***

Later, as the sunlight brought her cell slowly from darkness to light, the girl woke. She got up from her bed and made her way to the washroom. The memory of her nightmare had left only a faint feeling of unease. It was not until she had finished washing and caught sight of herself in the polished metal wall behind the sink, that she remembered. The reflection in the wall was vague and indistinct, but the girl could see the line of the scar running down her face. It took the same course, from corner of eye to lip, that she had seen on the face of the ghoul during the hours of darkness. She touched her fingers to the scar, feeling the roughness of the tissue, and remembered how The Menace had threatened and taunted her.

The ache growing at the back of her head reminded her that it was time for the first meal. She collected her smock from the door, threw it on and headed to the refectory.

Taking her usual place on one of the wooden tables, she immediately reached for the jug of hot caldi in front of her. The tendrils of vapour waved at her from above its rim. She closed her eyes and breathed in its sweet earthy aroma. She filled a cup and brought it to her lips, pulling the smell up through her nose, letting it fill her head. She drank, and as the liquid traced its warm path down to her stomach she relaxed. She drained the cup and exhaled deeply.

She liked to sit in this particular place, though she could see that it was no more or less special than any other. She liked the colours in the wood of the panelling opposite her. Perhaps it was just that it was familiar she thought. She refilled the cup and took another sip, feeling the calmness grow inside her as the benevolent care of the Family Trevelian, her Family, wrapped itself around her in the routine of another day.

'Good morning cousin.' It was one of the younger girls that jumped into the seat to her left. Her hair was cut into a short bob signifying that she was below the first coming-of-age. But the girl thought that she was not far off, perhaps twelve or thirteen.

'How are you this morning? Did you sleep well? What do you think we'll be working on today?' The new arrival reached for the caldi jug, asking questions and chatting away with seemingly no expectation of an answer. Indeed, no answer was possible as she did not appear to need to stop to take breath. She only fell silent when the morning praise began.

The girl smiled at the youngster and closed her eyes, tilting her head to the rafters, allowing the music of praise to trickle down across her forehead. She had always loved the choir, the generous gift of space and peace which its music offered to those who knew how to receive it. Her mind resonated with the physical sensation that each note triggered. She was entirely held in the music, there was no room for anything else.

Once the praise had been sung, the cousin serving food to her table returned with a plate of bread and a bowl of thick hot paste made from cereals grown by the community and harvested only days before. She put them in front of the girl and her young neighbour. The younger girl reached for her spoon as soon as it was placed in front of her. She smiled as she ladled the contents of the bowl into her mouth and moved the thick porridge around its inside. She licked her spoon as she looked up and smiled.

'What's wrong with your face?'

The girl reached up and touched her hand to the scar on her cheek.

'Nothing. I was in an accident that's all.'

The youngster turned her attention to the distorted reflection in the back of her own spoon.

'I wish I had a scar,' she said, 'I think it looks good.'

The girl smiled back, 'I had a bad dream last night. I'd almost forgotten it.'

'Was it scary? What was it like?'

'No, well, it was scary at first. Something was trying to get me and I couldn't get away. A man I think. Trying to get me. And I couldn't run away. Not at first. I was just sort of stuck there unable to move.'

The younger girl was transfixed by the story, licking the back of her clean-as-new spoon.

'He had a strange see-through skin and stared at me with these pale blue eyes. I could feel his breath on my face. But then I shouted at him…'

'Come now cousin,' an older woman had taken a seat opposite the two of them as she had been talking, 'it's not kind to frighten our younger cousins with ghost stories. There's no danger lurking in the night here my sweetling,' she addressed the younger girl, 'only the kinship of cousins.'

'Forgive me, you're quite right,' she smiled at the younger girl who smiled back from behind her cutlery. 'It was just a dream.'

The three concentrated on their breakfasts for the next few minutes until the young girl had all but cleared both her plates.

'I used to dream of a man with blue eyes,' she said, one last morsel of bread waving in the air, 'he was kind though, he never frightened me. In the dream, he used to sing to me. I can't remember the song,' she thought for a moment, 'it was nice though. I liked it.'

The bell in the chapel rang, signalling the start of the working day, and the girl drained her cup. Her body relaxed in response to the liquid's taste and warmth.

She made her way outside and joined one of the queues waiting for a transport. Once inside she closed her eyes and relaxed in her seat as the vehicle plodded its way out to one of the fields, the motion rocking her in her cradle. She realised that she had not fully shaken off her night terrors. Those eyes, the stench of decay. But the chatter and closeness of the cousins around her helped her to relax, their voices gave her comfort. She was with them, part of them, they were part of her. She dozed and when the light came streaming in through the side of the transport as its door swung up and open, she woke with a start, surprised to find their journey over.

She walked out into the sunshine with the others, took two or three steps from the transport and it hit her. This was Primrose Section. This was the place where it had happened, where she saw them die. This was the first time she had been back. A cold panic grabbed at her and she screamed.

She was aware of her cousins all around her. They were speaking. They were speaking at her. She could not see their faces or understand what they were saying. Her feet were frozen to the floor. Her panic was replaced by an odd feeling of calmness, as if a great weight had landed on her and crushed the panic out. How strange, she thought to herself, for my feet to be frozen on such a hot and sunny day. Then all she could see were swirling colours and all she could feel was nothing at all.

CHAPTER FIVE

Rebecca Catherine Valerie de-Monte, head of the Family de-Monte, sat on the wooden bench behind and below her place in the circle of Trilogy. Her hands resting in her lap, palms uppermost one on top of the other, her chin slightly raised and her eyes partly closed, she sat perfectly still. There was not even a hint of her body taking in and exhaling breath. Calm and aware of her surroundings she waited for The Authority to return with the results of the cell-line comparison.

Charles Edwin George Percival, head of the Family Percival, traced a path that hugged a small section of the circumference of the room. His body moved from light to shade to light, turned and returned again and again. As his body walked his breathless lips moved, trying to catch up with his racing mind as it moved between anger and outrage.

On the end of the same wooden bench on which Rebecca found her meditation, Nicholas Alexander Michael Trevelian, head of the Family Trevelian, sat. The fingers of his left hand slowly explored the ornate design skilfully and beautifully carved into the bench's side. He could feel the wings of the de-Monte crest, each feather rendered in meticulous detail, and to either side he could feel the edges of the crests of the Percival family and his own. As he sat there, part of a room whose every fraction held layer upon layer of symbolism, he wondered if anyone outside of Trilogy understood or even gave a thought to this depiction of the three families; the four vertical pillars that divided the design into three panels, one for each family. Did they simply accept that they represented earth, water, air and sun, the elements required for the production of crops, or did they see them as he did, as the bars of a cage: a symbol of the servitude that applied to him and his family every bit as much as that imposed on his namesakes. He wondered also if the relative position of the de-Monte crest was ever noted by wider society. The great powerful wings wrapping the Trevelian and the Percival coats of arms. He wondered if anyone outside of Trilogy even noticed the symbolism: that the de-Monte Family was in some way different from the Percivals and the Trevelians.

He looked across to the other side of the Chamber where the Living Saints of Plague and of War were listening intently, heads bowed, as Demeter, the Living Saint of Famine explained some intricate point to them.

'What do you suppose has got her so animated?'

Rebecca opened her eyes and followed Nicholas's stare.

'I'd say some tedious technicality of protocol was being explained. You know what our friends from the Seminary are like. I sometimes feel that the irrelevant details are all they care about. Never have I come across one of their number that could see the big picture.' She paused, allowing her eyes to scrutinise them for a moment. 'I'm worried about Charles.'

They looked at each other.

'He loves Adam. Adam's not as strong as your Jess, and Charles indulges him. Your words were hard for him to hear. Especially hard to hear at Trilogy.'

'It's regrettable,' replied Nicholas, 'but I couldn't stand by. Things have gone too far. I know you understand that.'

Silence.

Rebecca closed her eyes and returned to her thoughts, leaving Nicholas alone with his. His fingers went back to their work of tracing a path across the carved bench-end as he waited for the Chamber's bell to signal the announcement of the cell-line comparison.

***

Mason stood by the large window that looked down on the city from the syndicate room of the Trevelian apartments. His thick-set muscular body looked like it could trample and smash the buildings and structures of the vast urban conurbation below. All it would take would be the smallest movement of a vast foot or hand.

He was alone with his thoughts. Jess had retired to her private room and his master was still in Chamber. He felt for the two small indents below his left wrist and pressed them, first one at a time and then both together, allowing him to slide the prosthetic hand from his stump. He blew on the truncated limb. Strange, he thought, the sensation that his fingers were hot and itchy, like they had been in a glove on a hot day, when of course he had no fingers to feel anything. The connection plate that was set into the bone at the end of his forearm glowed, first blue, then red, then blue again, winking back and forth like some domestic appliance that needed attention. He dropped his left arm back to his side and placed the hand on the floor next to him thinking, not for the first time, that it looked like some strange five-legged creature. He thought it almost funny that he should have survived countless bloody battles without a scratch only to lose a body part constructing the city that stretched out before him.

He touched his right hand to the window. He could see the rooftops of the high-rise residential blocks caught in the last rays of the sun. Here and there flags showing allegiance to God or gods, or to one of the Living Saints, swam in the warm late-summer breeze. Lights had begun to illuminate the streets that swirled and curved their way between the blocks. He could not see them, but somehow, he could feel the myriad lives playing out in those streets and rooms below him. Lives so different from his own and his master's as to make him suspect they belonged to a different species.

'Mason, please fetch Jess, I'm on my way and I need to talk to you both.'

'Sir,' Mason spoke into the empty room in response to his master's voice.

There were no communication nodes in the private rooms so he would have to physically find Jess. He headed toward her room, leaving the city and the sun-set to their own devices.

When he and Jess returned, they found Nicholas standing in the same position occupied by Mason a few minutes earlier. He had his back to the view and was looking across to the central horseshoe-shaped table at an image of a building that Jess did not immediately recognise. Mason crossed the room to take in some of the details.

'Popos, have the results of the analysis been announced?'

Nicholas's attention took a moment to shift from the image to his daughter. 'Yes. Yes, the results have been announced.'

Jess approached him as he spoke. She could see the concern in his eyes. Concern for her. She reached out and touched his arm.

'It's as you thought, isn't it?'

Nicholas nodded. 'There was a positive correlation with the Percival cell-line.'

Jess stared at her father, 'But…'

'It means that either Charles or Adam handled the explosives. That can only mean Adam.'

Jess put her hand to her mouth. She turned and looked out of the window, 'I can't believe it. I've known him all my life.'

'I'm sorry Jess. There's no doubt, Adam definitely handled the explosives.'

Jess wrapped her arms around herself and Nicholas pulled her into his body. She tilted her head to the side to rest it on his chest. They looked out across the city together, their backs to the room and to Mason.

'I know it's not what you wanted to hear,' his voice soft, 'but The Authority has accepted the correlation and already acted.'

'Acted?'

She turned to face her father. He noticed the way the light from the window lit the right side of her face, banishing the shadows that would have been cast by the light of the display image. He knew that by the end of this conversation Jess would no longer be his little girl. Their relationship was about to change.

'I know you're ready, Jess.'

She frowned and shook her head, not understanding his meaning. He placed his hands on her shoulders and looked down into her eyes.

'I remember holding you the day you were born. You were so tiny.' Jess felt the warmth in his smile as he spoke. 'I finally knew what it had all been for. Everything that we had been through in the war. All the work to build a new world. You being born allowed me to see that it had been worth it. If a beautiful life like yours could thrive in the world we were creating, then there was some justification for it, for all of it. You were my hope. You always will be.'

He pulled her forward and kissed her forehead. These next seconds would change the space between them forever. It would be the last of their simple father-daughter life together. Where now there was closeness and intimacy, there would be distance and formality. He took a breath.

'Council have decreed that Adam be arrested and held on charges of terrorism and treason. Charles has been confined to his Chateau and his holdings have been temporarily put under the control of the Family Trevelian.'

Jess stared up at her father, not yet seeing where he was leading her.

'Council are nervous that if I personally take control of the Percival estate, it could jeopardise both the Percival and the Trevelian quotas for the season.'

'That's nonsense Popos, and you know it. I can keep things running while you're away, you know I can.'

'I have no doubt in your abilities Jess. I've more faith in them than you do.' He smiled. 'But Council have been clear that I'm to retain control at home. They feel that will at least guarantee the Trevelian quota. Which is why I want you to take control of the Percival holdings for me.'

Jess's face froze.

'The Authority has made sanction on behalf of Council, Jess. You've long since had the right to hold a second given name. I can't tell you how much it meant to me when you decided to earn that name rather than simply claim it as your birth right when you turned twenty.'

Jess stepped back slightly, she knew now what was about to happen. It was too fast. She needed to think, to process this. She wanted to be in control but it was happening so fast, happening right now.

'Popos... I...'

'You're more than ready Jess. I want you to move to the Percival Chateau and oversee their production quotas. I want you in charge there.'

Jess looked up into her father's eyes and found the trust and confidence that had always been his gift to her. She felt his strength flowing in her veins, pushing back her self-doubt. If Popos said so, then she was up to the task.

'You must become Mistress-of-Trevelian to control the Percival estate.... It's time you took your second given name my daughter.'

He drew her into his body and held her in his arms for the last time.

'Jess *Nichola* Trevelian,' he whispered, 'Mistress-of-Trevelian.'

Jess felt the warmth of her father's arms around her and pushed her face into his chest. She felt her tears come and when she stepped back she saw that her father's eyes were also wet. She blew out a breath and smiled at him. The moment that had just passed between them had been the moment their shared world changed. Childish ways and language were behind her now, behind them both. She would no longer be able to call her father Popos. She was now of rank. Her old life gone. A new life begun.

***

Mason had no task to perform. Once he had entered their destination into the console, the capsule took care of itself. He could hear the voices of his master and the new Mistress-of-Trevelian, Jess Nichola (he liked the sound those names made next to each other), but he could not make out their words; the plush carpet and leather-lined walls of the capsule's passenger compartment held them captive and from his position in the control cab they were not discernible.

His only distraction had been the view of Amynthia through the window, but once they had left the mountain at the centre of the city, their speed had increased and soon Mason's brain could not make much sense of the buildings and structures as they flew past. A sudden reduction in light told him that they were under the power-cells, the great ring of kites that encircled the conurbation, collecting the sun's energy and pulling it down to the city through the cables that anchored them to the ground. His eyes narrowed and he half smiled as he remembered working in the area, years before. He remembered the sound the cables made as they creaked under the tension of the kites. At the time, he had imagined he was walking through some great forest, the kite-canopy held on top of creaking steel cable-boughs.

And then they were out in the plain; the flat dusty belt of land surrounded by hills which separated the urbanites from the farm lands. Mason felt the weight drop from his body as the capsule stopped accelerating and he undid his restraint. He flexed his shoulders, pushing his body away from the padded vertical panel that had held him in a standing position. The capsule scudded along just above the dust and sand, racing toward a gap between a distant snow-capped mountain and a hill. He knew these features marked the route to the Trevelian holdings, but checked the readouts anyway to confirm their course.

'Mason, you busy?' The door to the cockpit was open and Jess was steadying herself against the frame with her arm.

He gave her a smile: 'No. Nothing to do but watch.' He tilted his head to the view through the front window.

Jess took a step into the cramped space and the door slid closed behind her. She put her hands on the console, its dials and readouts sitting in contoured panels that focussed them on the pilot's position. She looked out of the front window.

'We're already passed the Percival estate I'm afraid.' Mason nodded to the porthole directly next to Jess. 'But if you look carefully you can just make out the marker beacons for the approach.'

Jess did not look out through the porthole.

'Father says I'm ready but I'm not so sure.'

'I'm with Nicholas. You're more than ready, Jess Nichola.'

His use of her new name made her look across at him. He gave her a closed-lipped smile and raised his brows. She smiled back.

'I think your father's been looking for a way to give you rank for a while now.'

'But this is so much. To take on the running of another estate, and like this, with all this going on.'

Mason leant toward her. 'The size of the task is irrelevant. It makes no difference if it's large or small. You know that. In life, you'll always hit a point where you don't know what to do next. The trick is to find a way through. I've watched you do that many times, as has your father.'

'I know, but it just feels like more than I can deal with.'

'Your father doesn't agree.'

'I know he doesn't. But I'm not sure that he would've put me in quite so deep or quite so soon if Council hadn't ordered it.'

'Jess,' Mason waited until he had her full attention: 'do you really think that your father couldn't have dictated any agenda he wished to Council? I've no doubt that he told you the truth; that this was their decree, but if he'd felt this was beyond you he certainly wouldn't have allowed it. He knows you can do this. So do I,' he lifted his chin slightly and pushed his head forward in emphasis, 'and so do you.'

Her body relaxed a little and she smiled at him.

'I think your father's been looking for an opportunity to give you your second-given for some time. This is that opportunity and he's grabbed it. He knows you're capable of this. He knows you can handle yourself. Putting you into the Percival's is the perfect move. It'll stretch you, challenge you for sure, you'll have to find your traction with the Percival staff. It'll be hard but you'll succeed and it'll be the making of you. Your only real problem is your own self-doubt.'

Jess turned and leant her back against the console, looking back at the cabin's closed door. Some of the tension unwound from her shoulders.

'The reason I came in was that I'd like you there with me, Mason. To help me get to grips with things.' She paused and tucked a loose strand of hair behind her ear. 'I'd feel so much better about it if I had you around. Popos…I mean The Patriarch, wants to ask you about it himself though.' She flicked her head towards the door: 'Can you join us?'

Mason smiled at Jess and raised his eyebrows, prompting her to open the door to the cab and lead the way. Once there was room he slid his back along the support panel. His large frame, though advanced in years, was agile and nimble enough to allow him to twist through one hundred and eighty degrees so that he didn't have to enter the passenger compartment arse-first.

'Come and take a seat, Mason.' Nicholas indicated the place facing him across the table and Mason slid his body onto the bench-seat next to Jess.

'Jess and I have been discussing her move across to the Percival's and I'd like you to accompany her. Help her get to grips with it.'

'Of course. Wherever and however I can serve the Family.'

Nicholas's lips tightened across his mouth for a second.

'I want to give you an opportunity to say no to this one, Mason.' He looked directly into Mason's eyes. Mason gave a slight shake of his head, not understanding the issue.

'It'll mean you working closely with Dovac.'

Mason threw back his head and laughed, the penny having dropped. He looked directly at Nicholas.

'Not a problem Sir, not in the least.'

'You're sure?' Nicholas paused, searching Mason's face for any hint of anxiety. 'There are other ways to support Jess.'

'Not a problem.' Mason shook his head. 'Honestly, not an issue. I think I can keep my temper around him,' he looked across to Jess, 'besides, it'll be fun watching this fledgling flounder around and louse things up.'

Mason's large face was suddenly overrun with huge teeth as his mouth stretched to a grin, prompting Jess and Nicholas to laugh out loud.

The master, the Mistress and the trusted servant shared a rare moment as father, daughter and surrogate uncle in the privacy of the red and silver bullet as it shot across the plain.

***

'For their glory'.

'For their glory'.

She ended the transmission and sat back in her chair.

How easy it had been.

Once she had learned of his weakness, of his devotion, she had simply taken him by the hand and led him where she chose.

She allowed herself a smile. Her prominent cheekbones and narrow chin gave her face an almost perfect symmetry. At over sixty years of age she still had the ability to cause men and women decades her junior to hold their breath. Their compliments had never seemed to matter. Her intellect would not allow it.

The years that had passed since the end of the war had been long and frustrating but her ascendancy was underway at last. She was the only remaining saint to have taken office immediately following the war. The other two had each been appointed in the last few years, following the deaths of her peers. A young woman and a man, a boy really, whose heads were full of the fictions of the Holy Union. She had always hated mediocrity and when it had become the currency of her office she could stand it no more. To be fettered by the baggage of these two fools had been the final provocation.

Soon her agent at the Percival Chateau would be whispering and nurturing discontent, and the bond between the Families, already weak, would surely break.

.

CHAPTER SIX

The girl lay on her back, her eyes wide open. She wondered why she had no urge to get up and work alongside her cousins, why she was so content just to lie in her bed.

As the sun moved to the horizon, it coaxed the shadows of the plants growing on the outside of her window across the ceiling. The girl watched. She had no sense of time passing. She just observed as the shadow-fingers pulled themselves across the beams and hop flowers, until eventually she slept.

***

'Do you know what happened?'

Jess Nichola Trevelian spoke to the woman sitting next to the bed of the sleeping girl. Her voice was gentle and soft so as not to disturb her.

'In truth, Mistress, I'm not sure. We arrived at the Primrose section as normal and the group were assembling in the yard. I was still in the transport when I was summoned. The poor thing had collapsed.'

Jess nodded and put her hand on the woman's shoulder. Her eyes were drawn to the scar that ran down the girl's face. The reds and blues of healing and bruising still interrupted its pale symmetry.

'If you please Mistress, I'm to blame.' Jess looked back to the woman, whose eyes searched Jess's, looking from one to the other, pleading. 'Let the record show that this was my fault. I put her to work too soon. It was where she saw her cousins die, it wasn't her fault. Please Mistress.'

As she spoke, the woman squeezed the fingers of her left hand in the fist of her right. Jess knelt in front of the woman, taking hold of her hands and looking directly up into her eyes.

'It was not your fault. You are not to blame. She expressed a wish to return to work and, until yesterday, she had done so without incident. There was no restriction placed on her work patterns and you couldn't have foreseen this.'

'No Mistress, please. She's young, I'm to blame, please Mistress. She's young, too young, do not....'

Jess squeezed the woman's hands. 'There's nothing here that needs to be recorded. Nothing.'

There was silence as the woman held back her tears in relief. She nodded a grateful thank you, her eyes holding Jess's.

'Our community is blessed indeed to have a Mistress with so great a compassion for her namesakes. One who would go to such lengths.' She dropped her head and eyes. 'May each of The Three Living Saints bestow their full blessing upon you, Mistress.'

'Go and join your cousins.' Jess stood and motioned the woman towards the door. 'I'll stay with her.'

The woman gave a bow of her head, not in deference but in gratitude, as she got up from the bedside and left.

Jess turned and looked out at the window-framed blackness of the evening. She placed her hands on the sill, breathing in the scent from the flowers growing around the glassless window.

She tightened her lips, worried that her decision, her first decision as Jess Nichola Trevelian, had been the wrong one. Any period in which a namesake was unable to work must be recorded on the panel outside her cell. She knew the rules, but it had felt so very wrong. The girl had already had a period of convalescence and her community had accepted this. But further episodes could see her cast out by her cousins and once that happened there would be no place for her. The rules were quite clear and she should be following them.

She looked up at the ceiling, stretched her slender neck, and ran a hand from its nape up through the hair on the back of her head, pulling out the band that held her ponytail in place. It felt wrong that this should count against the girl. She had been trying to work after all. She had been caught up in something dreadful, something not of her making. But to be Mistress-of-Trevelian, to take on a second given name, that meant not shying away from difficult decisions. Had she done the right thing?

She let out a long breath and stared into the blackness outside.

'Thank you, Mistress.' The girl's voice made Jess jump. She turned to the bed and found herself held in the gaze of the girl's deep brown eyes. She was staring directly at her from where she lay. For a moment, Jess was at a loss.

'How do you feel?' she said, regaining herself a little.

'My not being able to work should count against me in The Record,' said the girl, ignoring Jess's question. 'Thank you, Mistress.'

'Can you remember what happened?' Jess's voice was gentle.

The girl stared at her for a moment and then turned her head to look up at the ceiling.

'I remember having breakfast. I was seated with one of my younger cousins,' the girl smiled to herself, 'she wouldn't stop talking.'

'What did you talk about?' asked Jess, happy that the girl seemed to be finding her ease.

'Oh, I'm not sure. She was just chatting away about nothing.' The girl's eyes focussed on a point on the ceiling. 'I told her about a dream I'd had.'

The girl stopped speaking as she remembered The Menace, with his blue blue eyes and his face leaning over her, almost touching. She remembered how it felt to be paralysed with fear. And then she thought of how she shouted and light came from her mouth and how The Menace could not escape the torture. How she had conquered him.

'Do you dream, Mistress?'

Jess smiled at the girl but said nothing.

'I've dreamt before, but not like this,' she continued. 'Why do you suppose you remember some dreams but not others?'

'I've no idea.'

The girl sat up, put her feet on the floor and looked around for her clothes. Jess picked the girl's tunic from a hook on the back of the door.

'I'm glad you're feeling alright,' she said as she handed it to her.

The girl took the tunic, threw it over her head and tied the rope belt around her waist.

'Thank you, Mistress.'

'Do you remember feeling ill?'

The girl walked over to the window and looked into the darkness.

'When I got out of the transport... it was a lovely morning. I could smell the dampness in the soil. It was the same on the morning…of the…. the accident. It smelt like that then too. I think that's what made me remember. The smell. Such a beautiful smell. It was stronger that morning because we were turning the soil when it happened. Their bodies…' The girl folded in half and sank to the floor. She wept uncontrollably, her face in her hands. Jess knelt beside her, putting an arm around the girl's slender shoulders.

'They were good people,' she sobbed, 'they were good people, why did they die?'

Jess pulled the girl's head to her chest, rocking her as she cried. She could feel the wetness of the girl's tears on her hand as she swept her hair away from her eyes.

'Shh.' She held her tightly to her own body as the tears came and came. Eventually there were no more to give.

'Mistress?' The girl pulled away from her and they looked at each other, both still kneeling on the floor.

'What if I can't go back to work? What if I feel this way again?'

Jess looked into the girl's face. They both knew that Jess would not be able to excuse the girl every time she was unable to work. It would have to be recorded and if it became a regular occurrence there would be no place for the girl in the community. She would be euthanized.

'If I can't serve the family, if I can't honour the Living Saints… I'm nothing.'

Jess stood and looked at the floor for a moment. She folded her arms across her body and held herself as she thought.

'Can you read?' she asked.

The girl looked at Jess: she seemed not to understand the question.

'You can read?'

The girl did not move: 'Yes, Mistress, I'm a strong reader and completed all my lessons by my first coming of age five years ago.'

'Then you're well suited to the work I have for you.'

CHAPTER SEVEN

Charles Edwin George Percival sat in his office. The strands of his grey beard were no longer braided and they fell untidily into one another. A shadow of white stubble showed across his scalp.

The chair in which he sat faced across the room towards an ornate wooden door. To its right was the stone fireplace that would try to tame angry logs during the cold winter months. There was no fire today, only an exquisite arrangement of dried flowers framed by the carved stonework of the mantle. To the left of his chair were the doors which led to the garden. By the time the sun was up he would normally have reviewed the day's tasks and used these doors to take a stroll across his private lawns. Today, as had been the case for many mornings, he simply sat. The glazed doors that led from his office to his gardens were open, but if the cool sweet morning air entered the room it did so without the knowledge of its master.

He drew in a long breath. The moment had come. He could not delay any longer.

'Dovac,' he spoke into the empty room.
'Sir.'

'Would you come in here please, I need to instruct you.'

'Sir.' The intercom clicked.

Charles took another long breath as he waited for his head-of-household to attend.

'Yes Sir.' Dovac closed the door behind him and faced his master, his thin hands clasped behind his back.

Charles stood, walked over to the double doors and looked out across the lawns.

'Dovac… Dovac as you know, members of the Trevelian family are due to arrive today to take over the running of the estate.' Charles kept his back to Dovac as he spoke. 'They'll arrive in the next few hours.'

'Yes Sir. Everything is prepared, the Patriarch will be billeted in the east wing, I arranged for it to be opened and aired yesterday. All is in hand Sir.'

Charles dropped his gaze to his feet.

'Dovac. The Trevelian party will not be headed by Nicholas Alexander Michael. His daughter has been made Mistress-of-Trevelian and she is to oversee things here.'

Dovac flexed the muscles in his jawbone. 'Yes Sir, I see Sir.'

Charles turned to face him: 'And Mason-of-Trevelian will be accompanying her.'

Dovac's eyes widened.

'I know the two of you have…history…, we all do, but we must put that to one side for now.'

Dovac's hands knotted into fists behind his back. First the indignity of having the estate placed into the hands of the Trevelians, now the news that they would not even be commanded by a full Patriarch but by his daughter, and this, the final insult: Dovac would be forced to report to Mason. It was more than he could stand.

'Absolutely Sir,' he said. His voice quiet, his smile obsequious.

'I should have said something earlier, Dovac, I know. I'm sorry for that.'

'No. No Sir. Not at all.'

'I should have. I've known since Trilogy.' Charles walked the two paces to the bench where he would normally stand to work. He ran a hand across the console that no longer responded to his touch or voice. It remained closed, inert. 'I've been preoccupied as you know, but still, I should have spoken with you about it.'

Dovac watched him for a moment.

'Is there any news of the young master Sir?' he asked.

Charles's eyes focussed on some point in his past, not seeing the physical world in front of them.

'No. No, there's no news. I've no idea where he is.'

'I'm sure that's good news Sir.'

'They'll track him down soon enough and have him in detention. At least then I'll know he's safe.'

Dovac gave a nod. 'Yes Sir.'

'God only knows where he is,' said Charles under his breath.

If Dovac had a reaction to Charles's unguarded reference to The One true God, to the world before the Church of the Holy Union, he did not let it show.

'Will there be anything else Sir?' Dovac broke into the silence.

Charles shook his head and Dovac clicked his heels, tilted his shoulders forward, turned and left.

Charles returned to his chair. As he sat there, alone, his soul was held in the soft embrace of his faith. He had felt a tangible pain when The Authority announced that Adam was to be arrested. His son. His life. But even from such a bleak place as this Charles secretly reached out to his God, to the God for whom he had fought and commanded armies during the wars of The Conflict. And his God answered. 'Have faith. Take comfort.'

***

'We shall have to find you a name,' Mason spoke to the girl as she looked out of the front window of the capsule. He glanced across at her. Even with the scar on her face she was pretty, he thought. Good genes and a healthy life-style. He allowed himself a smile.

The girl's attention shifted from the view out of the window, her brown eyes turning toward him.

'A name?' she smiled back.

'You're part of the household now. Someone in the service of the Family should be "-of-Trevelian"'.

The girl looked back out of the window, waiting to catch her first view of the Percival holdings.

'I'm not sure I want one,' she said after a while.

Mason's brows dipped.

'That's a strange thing to say. Why?'

'I don't know.' She tilted her head to one side as she thought, 'I suppose it takes me further from the community of my cousins.'

Mason looked at the girl's profile. Remembering.

'You're about to enter a different world to the one you've known,' he said. 'You'll have to leave your community behind. I'm not sure how you will find the change.'

'I'll adapt to it,' said the girl with no hesitation.

'I hope so. It'll be different though. I'm not talking about where we're going, the Percival Family perform the same function of food production as our family. You won't find them so very different. But you'll be moving in different circles now. Your Mistress might meet with a member of the elected council or someone from Seminary. It'll be different.'

The girl looked across at Mason.

'Seminary?' she asked, 'might I see a Living Saint then?'

Mason smiled at her.

'It's possible,' he said.

The girl turned back to the window, her eyes wide.

'I might meet a Living Saint?' she said, 'but how should I behave? I couldn't do that.'

'Just follow your Mistress's lead. The focus will be on her not you.'

The girl relaxed and smiled back at Mason.

'She's a fine person isn't she, Mason-of-Trevelian; the Mistress I mean.'

'She is indeed little one.'

He was surprised to have used such a familiar term but the girl did not react.

'Mason,' the intercom came to life with Jess's voice: 'how close are we? I'm afraid I've rather lost track of our progress.'

Mason spoke into the air: 'We've passed through the mountain range and are about two hundred kilometres from the Percival Chateau, Mistress.'

***

Jess was sitting alone in the passenger compartment.

She placed her hand on the brick-sized console in front of her. It glowed blue-green as it came to life.

'Connect me to my father's private office.'

A triangle of light floated above the console, balancing on its point, and Jess waited as her father's image walked into it and sat in front of her.

'Jess. You must be almost there.'

'Popos…Father I mean.' She shook her head. 'Yes, we're a couple of hundred out.'

'Good.' The green dots making up his grainy image wriggled liked tiny insects, blurring the edges of his face. He smiled. 'What's on your mind?'

Jess sat back in her seat; the triangle of light responded by tilting itself forward a little.

'It's just that…I've been going through the Percival logs and there are a couple of things, technical issues, that need some urgent attention. It looks like Charles Edwin George has let things slip a bit.'

Nicholas's image gave a shrug. 'I think in the circumstances that's understandable don't you? What things?'

'One of the sectors is flooded; seems a reservoir wall has failed. And a seed bank has lost some of its contents.'

'Presumably a failure in its environmental system.' The image waited for more but Jess remained silent. 'That it?'

Jess nodded.

'OK so these are things you'll need to get to grips with. But they're nothing you haven't dealt with back here. What's the problem?'

Jess ran her fingers through the hair above her left ear.

'It's not that. It's not the technical stuff.'

'What then?'

'It's… I'm not sure how to go about keeping The Patriarch on my side?'

Nicholas's image became fractionally smaller for a second as his body moved slightly. He nodded.

'Right,' he said, 'here's the thing. You don't need anything from the Percivals. You have the mandate of Council, that's all you need. And you've Mason there. You know what needs to be done, just go ahead and do it.'

'I know. I know all that. But the job will be much easier if I can bring Charles and his people along with me rather than order them about. It'll make the whole situation much easier.'

The flat green image smiled: 'You're going to do a much better job at the Percival's than I would have Jess. You've always had the emotional intelligence that I lack. I guess that was your mother's gift. You're going to be a better leader than I ever could.'

Jess smiled back.

'I wish I could remember more about her,' she said.

'Well. So do I.'

They looked at each other through the triangle for a moment before Jess continued.

'Thing is, I don't know how to go about it, how to conduct myself with Charles. He's known me since I was a baby, how can I get him to take me seriously?'

Nicholas's image was silent for a moment.

'If you think about it, you already hold the stronger position. Charles may be many things but he's no fool and he'll understand how the land lies. You have the mandate, you've the rank, and you have the technical competence. He won't push against that and if he has any sense he'll be grateful if you reach out to him. And if he doesn't, he doesn't.'

'I'm just not sure how to reach out I suppose.'

'That's your first test then, Jess Nichola Trevelian. Show me, show yourself that you can find a way.'

This was something new. Her father had always been keen to lead her through whatever options were on the table when she brought problems to him. But this time he was leaving her to have the ideas. She leant forward.

'Well,' she said after a while, 'one thing I do know is that I'm not happy playing political games with people. My instinct tells me to be open and straight forward with Charles.' She nodded to herself. 'I'll explain the situation and how I feel about it and simply ask him for his support.'

The door from the control cab slid back and Jess looked up to see the girl standing in the opening. She seemed unsure as to how to proceed. Jess nodded at her but held up a palm, asking her to wait.

'Thanks Father.'

'Sounds like you have a plan,' he said, 'send me comms when you get a chance. I'm here.'

'Thanks,' she smiled and nodded. 'End transmission.' The triangle faded from the air in front of her and she raised her eyes to the girl.

'Sorry Mistress, to interrupt you, I…thought I might ask if you needed anything before we arrive. Mason-of-Trevelian says that we will be at the Percival Chateau in twenty minutes.'

Jess smiled at the girl. 'I'm fine, but I'm glad you came in, I'd like to talk to you.' She nodded to the seat facing her and the girl sat down.

'Things've moved pretty fast for you haven't they?'

The girl smiled.

'We've not really defined what it is I want you to do.'

The girl smiled again and said, 'My understanding is that I shall serve as your private steward.' She straightened her shoulders and recited, 'I shall accompany you at all times unless you tell me otherwise; I shall be mindful of your needs and comfort; I shall endeavour to put around you any measures that will support your wellbeing and allow you to carry out your duties.'

Jess smiled: 'Mason has obviously briefed you very well.'

'No Mistress, if you please, Mason-of-Trevelian has not presumed to educate me in this. These are my own deductions based on what I've read in the Trevelian Articles.'

Jess processed this for a moment.

'Well, your deductions, as you put it, are quite correct. As you perhaps already understand, I've been asked to take control of the Percival holdings, and I'm going to need plenty of help. Your task is to make sure I can concentrate on this work. That I'm not distracted from it.'

'Then I will do my very best in that Mistress.'

'I'm sure you will.'

Jess smiled at the girl. She looked unsure of herself as if she had something more to say.

'Was there anything else?'

The girl took in a deep breath before answering. 'Just that, that I'm very grateful to you for, for asking me to serve you in this way.'

Jess nodded. 'This is a change for me too.' She looked out of the window at the blur of sand-browns and blues racing past. 'And I'm going to need all the help I can get.' She was silent for a moment before turning back to the girl. 'I suspect it'll be me who's grateful to you before too long.'

The girl returned her smile. Jess was struck by the way it seemed to overcome the scar on the girl's face. It shone through it, conquered it; the scar was still there but invisible.

'I think we should get to know each other a little,' she said. 'We're going to be in each other's company for quite a while.'

The girl looked confused.

'I'm Namesake-Trevelian, Mistress. You know everything there is to know about me.'

Jess felt foolish. How did she expect one of her namesakes to react to such a question? She thought for a moment, not knowing quite how to backtrack.

'Well, for example, tell me why the community haven't used the new glasshouse that we erected last year. It's been empty for an entire season, why?'

The girl fidgeted slightly in her seat before answering.

'It's, it's not that we're not appreciative of the Family's efforts to give us the means to tend the land. It's, well, it's that the new glasshouse is not so suitable as the older ones.'

Jess sat back in her seat.

'Really? But it incorporates the very latest technology.'

'It's not that we're not grateful, Mistress.'

Jess shook her head, 'I know, I didn't mean to make you feel uncomfortable, it's just that the new glasshouse was designed to improve the land's productivity. I'm just curious as to why you don't think it does.'

'It's the windows, Mistress.'

'The windows?'

'We can't open them.'

Jess shrugged. 'But they work automatically. They open and close when the environment within the glasshouse reaches a certain humidity and temperature. They work automatically. You and your cousins know that.'

'No, if you please, Mistress. They do work automatically, but not according to what is required. Sometimes they do, but often the air becomes too damp or too hot or too cold. The needs of the soil change from hour to hour. In the old 'houses we can open windows according to the soil's needs.'

'So, you have abandoned the new glasshouse in favour of the old ones because you can open the windows yourselves?'

'No. We did so because the new glasshouse doesn't care for the soil. It wouldn't serve the Family to use it. The crops would not prosper as they do when we care for them ourselves in the older 'houses.'

Jess leaned forward and furrowed her brows.

'But if you had brought this to my attention, I could have seen to it that the algorithms controlling the new glasshouse were adjusted. They just need a little fine-tuning.'

The girl dropped her eyes to the table, no longer able to look at Jess.

'I'm sorry, Mistress. I truly am, but it's not the place of a namesake to instruct a member of the Family.'

Jess reached across the table and touched the girl's hands.

'Hey,' she said.

The girl lifted her eyes from the table and looked back at her.

'There's no need to apologise. The community did what they're supposed to do, make the soil work. It's down to me if the tools aren't suitable, not you.'

There it was again, the girl's smile.

'Do me a favour though,' said Jess.

The girl nodded.

'From now on, if you see something that you think looks out of place or doesn't make sense to you, let me know.'

'Mistress, I couldn't...'

'It's what I need from you. Amongst other things. I need you to speak up if something doesn't look right, OK?'

The girl nodded.

'Yes, Mistress.'

'This is a change for us all, but perhaps most of all for you. I'll try to be explicit in what I want from you and one thing I want is to know what you think. I want you to speak your mind. That's what it's for.'

The girl nodded and got up from the seat. Jess watched as the door to the control cab sealed behind her. She shook her head.

'I'm an idiot,' she said under her breath. How could she have not spotted that as soon as the new glasshouse was built. She had lost count of the times she had admonished her father for not paying attention to the expertise of the Family's namesakes. And here she had made just that error.

She looked out of the window, hoping to catch a glimpse of what would be her home for who knew how long - at least a couple of seasons. She could feel the capsule begin to decelerate, they must be well within the estate now. The moment when she would have to assert herself was coming perceptibly closer; in just a few minutes she would take control of The Percival Family's holdings. The conversation with her father had reassured her: the fact that he trusted her to find a way to make it work. Still, as she sat in the capsule waiting for the moment to arrive, she felt a little sick: a ribbon of anxiety mixing with the excitement running around her veins.

***

Mason adjusted the two chrome levers, his hand movements subtle and careful. The transport's engines responded, slowing to a soft rhythmic thumping as the craft came to a stop and hovered just above the ground. The capsule moved in response to Mason's hand, gently tilting and edging its way through the security field to the landing bay at the rear of Charles's private gardens. He cut the engines and slid back into the passenger compartment.

'I'll go out first,' he said, 'smooth the way.'

Jess looked up and nodded. She was being dressed by the girl and had been watching as she struggled to fasten the silver buttons running down the front of her formal cloak.

'We'll be along in a minute or two,' she said.

Mason stepped down onto the landing bay. It was located behind two hedges which ran one behind the other, cleverly shielding it from the Chateau. He walked between them and into the garden. It was quite beautiful: lawn to all corners with a central walkway of gravel between two rows of trees holding beautiful pink blossoms, the occasional petal floating in the air. To the sides of the walkway, knee-high hedges framed small formal displays of flowers, each square dedicated to a different colour.

Mason stepped onto the path and made his way towards the sharp thin figure standing on the patio, its back to the open double doors which Mason knew would lead to the Patriarch's office. The figure made no attempt to meet him half-way or extend a hand. It stood tourniquet-tight, allowing Mason to do the work, the air around it crackling.

Mason stepped up onto the patio.

'Mason-of-Trevelian. A long journey well-made is ended.' The figure gave the subtlest of nods.

'Dovac-of-Percival.' Mason returned the nod. The two former comrades observed each other for a moment before Mason continued, '...been a long time.'

Dovac's narrow lips offered what was barely a smile in agreement. He placed his hands flat to his side and made a polite bow.

'Charles Edwin George Percival, Head of the Family Percival, awaits Jess Nichola Trevelian, Mistress-of-Trevelian within.' Dovac's lips and nostrils sneered at the difference in rank as he turned and extended a wiry arm to the door behind him.

'Mason-of-Trevelian, welcome to the Percival Chateau.' Charles had appeared in the doorway and Dovac's body straightened slightly. 'Dovac, see to it that Mason-of-Trevelian knows where everything is and that all the arrangements are to his liking.'

Dovac acknowledged his master's bidding and began to lead the way.

'That won't be necessary for now Sir.' Mason glanced at Dovac. 'The Mistress,' (he emphasised the word) 'wishes to discuss certain matters with you Sir.'

'Of course,' said Charles, 'Dovac, please make sure our guests' apartments are ready.'

Dovac's thin face grew thinner as his lips met and disappeared into a pencil-thin line. He nodded to his master and then to Mason and disappeared into the office. The two men waited until they heard the door close behind him.

'You must forgive him,' said Charles. 'You must forgive us both. This is not a situation I had ever anticipated.'

'Quite so Sir, none of us could.'

The sound of feet on gravel made Mason turn. Jess, her long cape now fastened from neck to waist and showing the Trevelian crest in gold across her chest, was making her way up the path, the girl following a little way behind.

'A long journey well-made is ended,' said Charles, stepping down from the patio to meet her. He touched his right hand to his chest and bowed his head slightly.

'Thank you, Charles Edwin George Percival.' Jess returned the bow and continued with the formalities required of her, 'I am Jess Nichola Trevelian, first heir and Mistress-of-Trevelian. In accordance with my Office and with Council edict eight of this year I have come to oversee and take control of the Percival quotas and holdings until further notice is given.'

Charles smiled. 'In other circumstances I would be filled with joy at your acceptance of a second given name. Please accept my sincere congratulations on your becoming Mistress-of-Trevelian.'

'Thank you, Charles Edwin George.'

'Jess Nichola, I appreciate your use of my given names when you address me, but I think, given the circumstances, and if you're comfortable, that I should be happy if we were to limit ourselves to one-given.'

Jess smiled and nodded, hoping this meant acceptance as a peer and not reinforcement of his memory of her as a child.

'Jess then.'

'Charles,' he responded with a small bow.

After a moment, Jess said, 'I'd like to map to your systems straight away if I may.'

Charles turned and led Jess into his office. He gestured to the workstation.

'It won't work for me of course,' he said, 'but I assume it's been coded for you.'

Jess placed her console, folded up like a clam, onto the top of the workstation. Immediately it came to life, a blue light running laps around its edges and spreading like a spider's web to the workstation, aligning the estate to Jess's authority.

'I assume that you have an up-to-date picture of my, that is to say, the Percival holdings,' he said.

'I believe so Charles Edwin…,' she stopped herself: 'Charles.'

'You'll no doubt wish to take a tour to each of the sectors.'

'I would, but first I'd like to speak to the namesakes who are overseeing the seedbanks. I'd like this to be the priority.'

'I can see that the Percival holdings are in competent hands Jess.'

'Charles, if I may speak freely?'

Charles shot a glance towards Mason and then back at Jess.

'I know this must be a difficult situation for you,' she said, '…to have me across here in control of things. But that's Council's decree and that's how it is. What I want to say is that…' her hands tried to explain her point in front of her belly as she spoke, 'that I hope…that is, I think that the best thing for the Percival holdings would be…if we could find some way to keep you and your staff engaged in the management of the estate under me. What I mean is, I've plenty of experience in managing and fulfilling quotas and will work hard to make sure the Percival sectors are maintained in a good and productive order. I'd very much appreciate your support in this.'

Charles's white eyebrows lifted and his kind eyes looked at her.

'Jess, it's true to say that I was much angered when your father convened Trilogy. And I cannot deny that I felt insulted by his demand that I submit to a cell-line comparison. But it seems that he was justified in his accusation of my son. You are, I can see, a safe pair of hands. I and my staff are quite at your disposal.' He paused for a moment. 'Perhaps a place to begin would be to get you all settled in your quarters. Dovac,' he spoke into the air, 'would you come and collect our guests.'

Jess appreciated the spirit of hospitality but the label "guest" felt somehow wrong. She was now the controlling mind at the Percival Chateau and the term made her feel that there was work to be done to fully establish this fact with Charles. She recognised the seed of self-doubt in the thought and determined to weed it out before it took root. She picked up her console from the workstation, the synchronised light-show between it and the office terminal having long finished.

'Thank you, Charles, that's thoughtful.' She held the console to her chest and patted it. 'I'll review the latest data sets and then I'd like to take a trip out to the seed stores with the relevant namesakes.'

'Of course. Dovac,' he turned to his servant who was entering the office, 'would you please see to it that the namesakes are assembled at the seed banks in, shall we say two hours?' He looked across at Jess, who nodded. 'And please place my land transport at Jess Nichola's disposal. Have it brought around to the archway.'

CHAPTER EIGHT

His blue blue eyes stared into her face, they peeled away the skin, uncovering everything she was. Transfixed, unable to look away, made naked by the stare that held her tight, she stared back. The skin of his face, pale and lined, was framed by the folds of his hood. He stood over her body, held still by the bindings that bit her ankles and wrists, making her part of the wooden chair on which she sat.

He looked around for his own chair. It was in the corner of the room; the hot airless room where she had waited, immobile, for the hours before he had arrived.

A single lamp had burned dimly in the ceiling above her head, its light unable to reach the walls. She had not been able to tell if she was alone as she had waited there on the seat for him. For some time, she had thought that others, many others, were sitting in rows just out of sight, staring at her from the shadows. These others were not held prisoner as she was, but were spectators, gathered to watch a show. Waiting to see what she would do.

When the light flashed into brightness as the cloaked figure entered, she found that she had been alone after all. Alone in the centre of a featureless steel-walled room with no window, just a door in one wall and a chair next to it in the corner.

She could not remember how she had got there. She could not remember any moment in her life. Not who she was, nor whom she knew, nor where she had come from. It was as if her life had begun in that room, in that moment.

The figure walked to the corner and retrieved the chair, carrying it to where she sat and placing it carefully and silently in front and to the side of her. Close. When he sat down his knee touched her right thigh. She felt the restraints cut into her flesh as she tried to move her body away from his. She struggled until she felt the sharpness of his blue blue eyes on her face and then she stopped struggling. He placed his hands on her hips and leaned in toward her face. She wanted to vomit.

He looked at her for an age, looked into her eyes, bringing his face to within an inch of hers. With each breath she took in he exhaled, so that she was forced to draw in his stink.

He smiled and sat back in his chair, taking his hands with him.

'So my dear, you must answer my questions and we will see what is to become of you.'

The dreaming girl could now see the young occupant of the chair begin to cry. As she slept, the dreaming girl could not hear the questions that The Menace was asking. She could only watch as the prisoner writhed and cried and shook and shouted. On it went.

Question.

'No no no,' shaking head.

Leaning in. Question.

'Please!' cries, tears, sharp-edged restraints cutting into flesh.

Question. Question. Question.

At last The Menace leaned back in his chair. He made a subtle signal with his hand and shook his head. There was a loud report and blood gushed from the girl's forehead. It ran down between her eyes, down the bridge of her nose. As the dead head of a six-year-old girl slumped to the side and a red river ran across her cheek, missing her mouth and shoulder and pooling in the drain by her feet, The Menace stood, leaving his chair where it was, too close to the rag dead doll.

As the girl awoke, she could remember every detail of the dream. But with each inch that she moved into wakefulness, the dream receded by a mile back to its own world. When her eyes were fully open and focussed, there was little left other than a sense of unease.

***

'You are a fool.' Adam Charles Percival slammed his hand onto the table.

Citizen Owen looked at him from the shadow. The Head of Civil Security knew Adam would struggle to see his face but even so he did not react to the outburst.

'To suggest that I could've had anything to do with bringing about the deaths of the Trevelian namesakes. My entire thesis is that we should be granting these people their freedom. How can you possibly think that idea compatible with any course of action that could result in me bringing them to harm?'

The Citizen did not answer. He looked at the young man sitting opposite him. So self-righteous and full of passion. Arrogant.

Adam swept his blond shoulder-length hair behind his ear; a strand fell back across his face.

'My detention is nothing less than an outright attack on The Right to speak one's mind. I'll see to it that this abhorrence is given a full and very public examination.'

Citizen Owen took in a long deep breath. His body ached, just as it had for many years. He exhaled and, with some considerable effort, straightened the curve in his back. He placed his forearms on the table and let them take some of his weight, leaning in, his face visible to Adam under the light, his nose casting a shadow across his mouth.

'You will be in no position to publicise anything at all so long as you are detained here.' He spoke slowly and clearly: 'and you will be detained here so long as my judgement dictates.'

Owen watched the anger flood into Adam's face. One more push and he would break.

'Your family cell-line was found at the scene of the Trevelian attack, at the very site of the explosive devices. So, either you handled them, or it was your father. Now,' he paused, giving a polite smile: 'do you suggest that your father handled the explosives?'

'No, of course I do not "suggest my father handled the explosives".' Adam slapped the table a second time.

'If not you or your father, then how do you account for the presence of your family's cell-line?'

Adam's face became red with rage as he shot back his response: 'I have no idea, no idea at all. Someone put it there, obviously!'

'Everything I have points to you, Adam. Your cell-line at the site, your rank gives you the means of obtaining the explosives. Your motivation is a little more difficult, but I think you seek publicity and that you consider the loss of a few namesakes a price worth paying for the liberation of their cousins.'

Owen allowed a silence to hang in the air that separated them, a gap in which the accused might offer a confession or more often make some ill-conceived comment that would become a trip-wire later on. It was a technique he adopted almost unconsciously, one honed in the many interrogations he had conducted in his work, in his journey to becoming Head of Civil Security. Once learned, never forgotten. But he was not surprised when no confession came. He sat back in his chair, retreating into the shadows. A place where one such as he should feel more at home.

'Convince me then,' he said, his right hand open and palm up: 'convince me that you would not do this thing.'

Adam looked back across the table, his eyes unable to find the Citizen's.

'OK,' he said, 'my position is this: our use of the namesakes is an anachronistic abhorrence. I say that to hold property in our fellows is disgusting and must be ended. You call this my "motivation", that I want publicity for this, but killing them makes no sense. I want them to be free, to be properly treated.'

Adam altered his body's position slightly, sitting more upright as he spoke, his tone calm, his words now those of the intellectual in debate, rather than the accused under interrogation.

'Look, we've built our society on the back of enforced servitude. Oh, in the beginning we maybe had no option. The soil needed to be tended and that needed to be done by hand. But this is hardly a justification. My argument is that we are obliged to change this, to find a way to do this without reliance on a slave-class. It's not enough to say that it's a kindness to rescue our foundlings and orphans from the streets, to lift them from their poverty and deliver them to our communities of namesakes. We move them from a life of freedom to one of slavery when we do this. It's no more than holding them in property for our own advantage. It's slavery. It's not right, it's not moral. We must find a way to give each of them a free and proper life.'

The Citizen watched as Adam became more animated, voicing what was obviously well-rehearsed rhetoric.

'Now, you may say the namesakes have a good life. We give them a place to live and they have their comforts and are given purpose. They're well looked after. And yes, you're right. We do do these things for them. But their lives are lived without choice, they're lived on our terms not theirs. No matter how well we treat them this can't be correct. They must have their freedom and they will. In time, they surely will.'

Owen listened and watched while Adam spoke. Yes. Here was a young man of conviction. A fool perhaps, but one who believed his own words. It would be quite clear to any who heard him, that Adam would neither condone nor participate in any act that could result in the death of a namesake. He would have to make quite certain that his voice was never heard.

'Yes yes yes,' said Owen, waving his hand in front of Adam's face, 'that's all very fine, but I still have before me an individual whose cell-line is all over what remains of a bomb-site. I can draw only one conclusion: that you're guilty of this act and must be incarcerated accordingly.'

Adam's mood changed from orator back to firebrand in one beat.

'You Sir are an outrage! I know that you don't believe I could've committed such an act. You're unable to find the guilty party so you seek to hide your own inadequacies by incarcerating the innocent. You can't find the true agent behind this act so you find it convenient to settle for me. I demand that you allow me to present my case to Council.'

Owen leaned forward into the light and looked Adam directly in the eye.

'I will not,' he said calmly. 'You will be detained whilst I complete my investigations,' and then with a smile, 'no matter how long those investigations take.'

Adam sat back in his seat and glared at The Citizen. They both knew that he could take as long as he wished in his "investigations".

'Once they are complete we will see who is an outrage.'

Owen watched Adam's face. But where he had expected to see defeat he saw defiance. Adam leaned forward and spoke quietly.

'I demand examination by The Curate.' The words hit Citizen Owen, bringing him to a full stop. 'I demand to be interviewed by The Curate, by the cleaner of souls. His methods will bring the truth to your eyes in a way even you'll be unable to ignore or deny.'

Owen had not anticipated this request and was silent for a moment.

'But, Adam Charles,' he used his two given names in an attempt to change the shape of the space between them, to slow Adam's anger and encourage him to reconsider, 'the risks associated with an examination by The Curate are significant and the consequences grave. An adult could lose his mind during the process. If the technique were unsuccessful there would be nothing recognizable of the man left after the test.'

Now it was Adam who leaned forward. He paused before speaking in a quiet but assertive voice.

'The risk is mine to take. I wish to be examined by The Curate.'

***

'I have no choice but to acquiesce.' Citizen Owen stared at the comms unit as he spoke.

'There is always a choice and there is always a consequence.' The words came slowly, the voice quiet, almost too quiet to break through the static of the transmission.

'But his presence here will soon be known. I can't ensure that his isolation is robust. His father is an important man and he'll be sure to want to visit with him. I can't avoid that, not even for the glory…'

'Careful with your words Citizen.' The voice, stronger now, assertive, aggressive even, cutting Owen to a stop.

Silence. No words. Just crackles.

'I must allow the examination,' said Owen.

Silence. Thought. Wheels within wheels.

'It's of little matter.' The voice decisive, its words no longer hidden in the hisses and static filling the ether between there and here, but riding on top of them. 'The examination is more than likely to result in his end. In which case, we have no issue to deal with.'

'But if the examination should deliver a verdict of innocence…'

'Should a pronouncement of innocence be made by The Curate, Adam can still be made use of. I have certain strategies in motion that will generate a further option for us. They're a little more extreme but….in the name of….,' the voice in the speaker trailed to silence before announcing its decision, '… allow The Curate's examination.'

'Amynthia: roots of reason.' Prof. E. Fuller

The word "seminary" seems originally to have referred to the constitutionally defined component of the state whose task it was to hold a moral compass to the noses of its elected governors. However, in common usage the word had changed its meaning and come to refer to a place, a district where Amynthia's officials lived, worked and studied: the many buildings and gardens located within a walled area inside the great city.

Sitting at the foot of The Step, the hill from which the Chambers of Trilogy looked down upon the city, the tiny streets of Seminary wound their quiet and quaint ways to and fro. From above, the only things visible would have been the overhanging balconies and roofs thoughtfully created by long-dead architects in order to provide shelter from the rain and the sun. The people who walked these streets were a mixture of the district's inhabitants, the Seminarians, and those city dwellers who lived near enough to its walls to steal a few moments of its tranquillity.

The majority of the great city had been re-built in the decades following The Conflict, the century of wars that had brought humanity to its knees. Seminary, that is the district, was different. It alone had been almost untouched by the fighting. Partly, we think, because of its location, drawn into the protective skirt of its mother hill, and partly because it had been heavily defended as the centre of religious observance and power in those dark and distant days. Whereas the 'new' city of Amynthia radiated out like a tsunami of grey blocks and nearly-ordered grids of streets, the old district looked, felt and smelt different. The bricks that made up its structures were warm and red-brown, and of varying sizes, crafted and placed by skilful hands confidently asserting that their work would stand the prolonged test of time.

The buildings nearest the walls separating the district from the rest of the city originally housed gambling halls and brothels. These had been frequented by the less "religiously inhibited" members of the clergy who at that time resided in the district. Such pursuits had been confined to the history books long before the end of Conflict, and there seems to have been no desire to recreate this aspect of the old world after the war. The buildings in this area were now dedicated to the nobler effort of housing the city's higher arts. Traditional theatres, art galleries and small and intimate concert halls now had the right of occupation in these buildings, along with food halls and restaurants catering for their audiences.

A great green arc separated these venues from the central and oldest part of the district. The parks had been carefully restored during the reconstruction that followed the war. Mature trees had been saved where possible and saplings planted where the damage had been too profound. One imagines ornate ponds stocked with decorative fish and colourful plants being tended day and night by an army of volunteers from beyond the district's walls.

During the daytime, citizens would wander the parks and copses, enjoying the taste of the air or the feeling of space they seemed able to offer even when crowded. By sundown the parks were mostly deserted, the plants and animals left to their own devices.

The central area, cut off from the theatres and bustle of the majority of the district by the green spaces, was the only area still used for anything close to its original purpose. Here three square buildings named Desolation, Hope and Redemption, each three storeys high and two hundred metres in length, formed three sides of a huge square. Each building's corner almost touched that of its neighbour. There was enough space for perhaps six people to pass between them shoulder to shoulder and enter the almost empty courtyard that was their focus.

Children would arrive in the great square on the day after their seventh birthday, no doubt in a flurry of proud fathers, tearful mothers and bemused siblings. They would initially take up residence in the building called Desolation. Their lives were then spent studying the canon of scripture that defined and directed The Church of the Holy Union. As their years advanced, so would they, first to Hope Building and then to Redemption. These were the places where the Seminarians lived, learned and laboured.

A fourth, much taller building, named Salvation, completed the square, its black facade in stark contrast to the warm red of its three neighbours. Salvation Building contained the offices and living quarters of the senior Seminarians and The Twelve: the representatives of the pantheon of gods drawn from their ranks. Salvation was the seat of power.

Reproduced from the essay 'Amynthia: roots of reason' with the kind permission of the estate of Prof. E Fuller.

CHAPTER NINE

Demeter looked down from her rooms in Salvation Building. She was wrapped in the brown and white robe worn by each of The Twelve; a small blood-red poppy neatly embroidered on its left side was hers alone to wear as the Living Saint of Famine. By sunset the large empty courtyard below would be full of the crush and excitement of those waiting for her blessing, but for now her eyes took in the large square, empty but for the central dark red monolith.

She knew that by now the carnage had begun. Far away from the city, lives had been taken. She had taken them. There was no stopping it.

'The new beginning,' she thought out loud.

She looked across at the timepiece that sat silently in the corner of the room. In a few hours, the trumpets and drums of each of the residential districts of the city would begin to play. The young men of each community would take it in turns to carry the huge wooden floats supporting effigies of goddesses, gods and God, through the twists and turns of the city's streets, arriving in the courtyard below at midnight. It would all be over by then.

She thought again about how, when one does something truly dreadful, something whose consequences are dire and cannot be undone, that when one does such a terrible thing, one changes. Some part of one's insides changes forever. She felt again for the numbness inside of her. For the binding that had wrapped itself around whatever it was that used to define her, and prevented that part of her from looking back at what she had done, at what she was about to do; the magic that stopped her from screaming out loud or sobbing or speaking of it. The thing that gave her strength.

Her attention was drawn back to the courtyard by the sound of the large bell sitting in the frame on top of the red monolith. While its chime echoed around the walls of the four huge buildings bordering the square, the doorway in the building called Hope opened and its occupants filed out into the courtyard. Like a leaking bowl, the square spat them from its tight corners into the neighbourhood beyond. Off they flowed to join the processions of the communities from which they had come.

Hate was a strong word, but Demeter hated the Seminarians, all of them; holders of the moral compass and guardians of the great lie that was the Church of the Holy Union.

She stretched her neck, raising her chin towards the ceiling. She rolled her shoulders, shaking off her stiffness and, turning from the window, she picked up her bag and left.

***

The girl enjoyed the feeling of the cool air in her lungs as she marched quick-step from the Percival living quarters to retrieve a coat for her mistress. She liked the way her breath made little clouds when it was like this. It was something she had never experienced back home. The air was different here, cooler. She wondered what this meant in terms of the demands placed on the land and the relative merits of various crops. She would ask Mason.

As far as she could tell, their work was going well. The Percival estate was similar to her own Family's. The land was divided into sections, each growing a mixture of crops such that should one section fail others would make up any shortfall. Each section was served by a self-sufficient compound much like the ones in which she had worked. Water, seeds and equipment were all managed within each section, as was the production of soil from the barren dust and sand. If she overlooked some minor details in layout and style she could easily imagine herself back at the Trevelian holdings.

As for the Percival namesakes, she had not seen where or how they lived, only how and where they worked, but they looked and behaved much like her own cousins. It was only in the detail - the style of their dress and way they set their hair, or the sublime music which they made - that distinguished them from the Trevelian namesakes. Their sense of purpose and cohesion made her long to be back with her own community, to work and worship among them, to praise the saints, to take a seat in the hall and drink their caldi and share their food. But she knew that her life was here now.

She slipped through the gap in the hedge to the landing platform to find the capsule's hatch open.

'Is the Mistress with you?' Mason turned to the girl. He was standing in the passenger compartment, his console open on the table in front of him.

'No, Mason-of-Trevelian, she's talking with Charles Edwin George Percival.' She looked at him for a moment, his eyes on her but preoccupied; elsewhere. 'I understand that there's news of the Patriarch's son,' she said.

Mason's attention had returned to the console. She waited in the silence which seemed to grow out from him.

'He's been arrested.' She thought the information was significant but he did not react. She watched him for a moment more before asking, 'Is there some problem?'

He looked up at her.

'I don't know. Probably just some glitch in the comms route to the Trevelian estate that's all.' He looked back to the screen and spoke to himself: 'I don't know if the problem's with my console or some issue with the Percival uplink. Jess is much better at these things than me.'

'I'm sorry that I can't help. The consoles are new to me. They seem very complicated.'

'In fact they're very simple to use,' Mason's eyes were buried in the display as he spoke,'…when they work. You simply need to learn how to operate them.' He looked up at her and smiled: 'I'll show you when we have some time.'

His smile felt genuine and warm to her and she smiled back.

'You're very kind to me, thank you,' she said.

'My pleasure.' He turned from the console and stretched his neck and shoulders. 'Did you say Adam Charles has been arrested?'

She nodded.

'I wonder how Charles is taking it. I guess he knows he's safe at least.'

His eyes dropped back to the console's display screen and retreated beneath his oversized and now furrowed brows. The girl moved to the rear of the capsule, retrieved her Mistress's coat, and was about to take it to her when she heard her coming up the steps.

'Mason. Have you had any contact with our Chateau today?' asked Jess.

'No. Is it right that Adam's been arrested?'
'No contact at all?' she said, ignoring his question.
Mason shook his head.

'No, I haven't been able to establish a link all morning. I assume there's some incompatibility between our consoles and the Percival uplink.'

'I don't think so,' Jess's voice was a little breathless and her words came quickly, 'I've had a robust link since we arrived but this morning, nothing. Not even from the unit in Charles's office. I think the problem might be back at home.'

Mason's head nodded almost imperceptibly and his lips tightened.

'Let's try the capsule's on-board transmitter,' he said.

He pushed his console to one side, led Jess into the control cab and they stood in silence as the transmitter woke, its slow-glow warming through yellows to orange.

'This is Mason-of-Trevelian for the Trevelian Chateau.' He waited a few seconds for the transmission to be acknowledged but no response came.

'This is Mason-of-Trevelian calling the Trevelian Chateau, respond please.'

Still no life from the speaker.

'Come in please Central, this is Ma...'

The speaker clicked and Mason was immediately silent. All he could hear was the sound of breathing.

'Come in Central, this is Mason.'

'Mason, this is Luther. Do you receive?'

'Luther, what the hell's going on?'

The voice took another breath. Tired. Laboured. Choked with emotion. Its words came slowly.

'There has been another attack, Mason. We're still assessing...' The voice weaved around static, '... explosions in several...the Mistress that...'

'Luther, repeat your message, your signal is poor, say again, repeat your message'

The words came and went, spoken from lips close to a microphone so that they held the intimacy of moving directly from mouth to ear.

'…over the fourth…on now going…fix…,' and then the signal was lost.

***

By the time Demeter had entered the courtyard it was almost empty. Three of the Initiates from Hope Building were standing together in quiet but earnest discussion by their doorway. 'Why can't they just leave,' she said under her breath.

Unnoticed she left the square through the gap made by the corners of Hope and Redemption buildings and made her way through the busy streets to her rendezvous. She covered the short distance to the small walled olive grove in just a few minutes. She had chosen the location to allow her meeting to be inconspicuous by its openness.

Ares and Hermes were sitting in silence on the low brick wall of a well, enjoying the shade of one of the ancient trees. They were each dressed in a knee-length white tunic tied at the waist by a cord, Ares' blue and Hermes' a subdued dark red. When he saw Demeter, Ares stood and approached her.

'We're missing Procession, what do you mean by calling us here?'

Her dark brown, maternal eyes stopped him in his tracks. She spoke softly: 'Be calm, Ares.'

He walked along beside her, hissing under his breath: 'You cannot simply summon us to you like this. You may have rank, but we're part of The Twelve and you should not treat us so.'

Demeter seated herself on the wall next to Hermes, looked up at Ares and without shifting her gaze from him said, 'And what do you say, Hermes?'

The youngest of the three stared mischievously up at Ares.

'If your cause is just and the gods will it, it shall come to pass,' he quoted confidently.

Ares' cheeks flushed slightly at this.

'I said I know that you have rank. I only meant that we too have position…' He looked from one to the other. 'Today is Procession…we have obligations; we must honour our districts.'

'Sit down please, Ares and stop pouting.' Demeter spoke and Ares obeyed. She turned her body towards his and looked down into the well. It was dark and deep but she fancied she could see the occasional flash of reflected sunlight that had somehow fallen into the water and now fluttered about like a bird trapped in a cave.

'You're both too young to remember the days of The Conflict.' Ares followed Demeter's stare down into the darkness of the well as she spoke. 'Plans often don't run as one expects Ares, but don't worry, you shall still honour your neighbourhood in Procession. In fact, you shall lead it directly to the Fields of Elysia.'

Ares looked up to find Demeter smiling at him. He swallowed.

'You would give me that honour?' his voice a whisper.

'The gods yearn for the devotion of the faithful, Ares, those of a pure faith. It is time they were honoured. An important and sacred task. One that can be entrusted only to the devout. Can you be relied upon? Are your hearts pure?'

Hermes seemed not to have been listening to the conversation. He had been leaning back, his eyes closed and his back arched, enjoying the dappled morning sunshine and the sound of the breeze in the olive leaves.

'I told you, Ares,' he said, his eyes still closed, 'show a little faith. The gods favour us.'

'I don't need a lecture in faith from you!' spat Ares, and then quietly to Demeter: 'Our hearts are pure. We're ready for the honour you bestow.'

'Here.' Demeter reached into the open cloth-sac slung across her chest and removed a small leather-bound rectangle. She made a fist of her left hand and pressed the disk of the ring she wore on her little finger to the box's longest edge. A thin blue light drew a ring around the box and then spread across the leather surface like a cobweb. The light show was subtle and when it was over Demeter stroked the small rectangle and it slid apart into two identical blocks. She leaned forward and placed one device into Hermes' bag and handed the other to Ares.

'Obviously, you need to avoid being searched.'

'Obviously,' said Hermes as he pulled his satchel closed.

'I've contacted our friends and someone will be waiting for you at your temples to make sure the honour of carrying the standard is yours.'

Hermes stood, his broad beautiful body every inch the god for whom he was named.

'For the glory of the pantheon.' He looked directly into Demeter's eyes as he spoke and she felt the stirring of sensations she had not experienced in many years. He turned and headed towards the opening of the walled garden.

Ares was silent, staring at the box he held in his cupped hands, not knowing how to ask the obvious question.

'Because the gods will it,' said Demeter.

He looked up from the box.

'The gods have given you this task, Ares. You'll be feasting with them tomorrow.' She reached out her hands and held his face. 'You've been chosen, Ares. You have been chosen to travel to the west. To live eternally in the company of the gods.'

She watched as the doubt left his eyes and his fingers wrapped themselves around the device which gave him the power to change the world.

'Sacred Demeter, it's an honour to play my part. To assist you.' His eyes stayed with hers as he tucked the box into his tunic.

'Thank you.' She smiled. 'Ares, I relinquished the right to call you son when I took the name of the Goddess Demeter, but you have a mother's thanks.'

'An honour,' he said, and left.

***

Mason spent a few moments turning the receiver's dial, searching for a voice amongst the fizzes and crackles of the ether.

'That's it,' he said, 'the signal's gone.'

Jess could not get her mind to work. She knew she must act, but she could not think. The sound from the little speaker had shocked her into inaction. The broken message from the Trevelian estate, the tension in Luther-of-Trevelian's voice. And what of Popos? Was he safe? Injured? It felt as if her mind were full of cogs and wheels that had become jammed together and would not move. She could not think.

She was suddenly aware of Mason, of his gaze. She could feel him looking at her. Was he waiting for her to make a decision? Of course he was. She was Mistress-of-Trevelian. She was of rank. It was for her to assess the situation and decide on an appropriate course of action. But what good was she when her brain was like this? She clenched her fists and her jaw. She willed her mind to think think think. What should she do? Another attack? What of her father, what of Popos? She must see him; he must be alright. She felt as if hands were pressing against her chest, crushing her, crushing the air and the life out of her. She turned toward Mason; his eyes were studying her face.

'Take a moment,' he said. His voice was calm and level. 'You feel trussed up, your brain won't work, you can't think. This is normal in this kind of situation. Take a moment and let your brain catch up with you. We will sort this.'

She nodded and took a breath.

'I'll be in the back,' he said.

She watched as he moved out of the control cab and into the passenger compartment. He said something to the girl that Jess could not quite catch. She was so glad that Mason was here. He had a skin that could cope with any situation. She took the moment he had given her and used it to steady her breathing before following him, taking a seat so that she faced him across the table.

'I think we need to split up,' she said, 'we need to keep a presence here and we need to get back home to find out what's happened, to help.' She looked across the table at him. His eyes met hers, kind eyes; not soft but kind.

'OK,' he said, and then, 'I agree. How do you want to play it?'

She felt the tension drop from her shoulders. If he said that he agreed, then he meant it. She trusted Mason to speak his mind. Her self-confidence started to return. Slowly the wheels and cogs began to move inside her head.

'I'm not sure. I'm worried about Popos, about my father, I'd like to be the one to go back there.'

Mason shook his head.

'No, I should be the one to go back. We've no idea what you'd be walking into, we can't risk your safety, and overseeing the Percival holdings is more fitting a task for the Mistress-of-Trevelian than for one of its servants. You should stay here and I should go.'

Jess considered the position for a moment. Her lips pursed slightly and her eyes narrowed.

'Let's keep trying the comms,' she said. 'If I can talk to father and get a better sense of things back there, I think that'll help me make the right decision.'

'OK, may I make a suggestion?'

'Of course.'

Mason leaned forward and put his hands, palms down, on the table as he spoke.

'I agree that it'd be helpful to get a better picture of what's going on. But things sounded pretty serious so I also think we need to act quickly. So, my suggestion is this: I'll leave now and keep trying the comms from the capsule while I'm on the move. You should go and tell Charles that there is some problem back home. I'll contact you as soon as I get any information and we can change our plan if necessary.'

Jess felt a certainty flow into her body.

'No,' she said. 'I do think you're right about leaving straight away but here's what I want to happen. I'll go back home and you'll stay and update Charles.'

Mason took a breath before nodding.

'OK,' he said. 'I'll show the girl how to fly the capsule. She can pilot it and you can concentrate on using the transmitter while you're on the move.'

'Sounds good,' said Jess, 'thanks Mason.'

***

Demeter knew she was taking a risk. She knew that she had placed her life in the hands of others, that her survival was dependent on their skill. She knew this but still she took her place next to the Living Saint of War and the Living Saint of Plague on the balcony of Salvation Building.

She took up her position and looked down on the square that was beginning to fill with the faithful.

Some of the Deacons, those Seminarians over the age of twenty-one who had made permanent lives here, had arranged themselves at their windows. Others had elected to watch the arrival of the processions, and the giving of the blessing by the saints, from the square itself. There was no demarcation within the square but, in accordance with some unwritten tradition, the Deacons confined themselves to tightly packed groups strung out in front of their own building, their black ankle-length cassocks making them look like colonies of flightless birds jostling for precious space in which to make a nest.

The children under twelve, the youngest of the Seminarians, were being led from Desolation building by their house leaders according to an agreed schedule. For them a guaranteed front row: they would be close enough to touch the processions as they passed around the square and spiralled to the monolith at its centre. The Initiates, from twelve to nineteen years of age, were noisily finding places here and there wherever they wanted. Demeter could smell the street food cooking on trolleys dotted around the square. The excitement building within the crowd was palpable.

It was nearly noon. In a few minutes the distant noise of drums and trumpets would be heard from the surrounding districts. Their processions would wind and meander through the narrow streets toward the square where, at midnight, she and the other Living Saints would bestow their blessing on the assembled. But this year there would be no blessing. This year a greater glory awaited and in twelve more hours it would be done.

***

As Ares entered his district's temple, he was swallowed by the crowd that had been gathering there since the early morning, drawn back to their home district like salmon up a stream.

He pushed his way through the people and incense toward the altar at the temple's centre and looked up at its effigies. Procession was the only time the statues could be touched and seen close-up, not through the blackened iron bars of the gates which normally confined them to the temple's holy-place. The beauty of their carved faces, swathed in flowers and surrounded by tall white candles, their flames cupped in glass, stole Ares' breath and held his heart. He had led the district's procession twice, but never had he felt the presence of the gods as he felt them now. This year he would truly honour them by his glorious deed.

'Call to assembly,' the disembodied voice of the Principle Celebrant shouted the words. 'Call to assembly.'

Bodies jostled and pressed one into another as the crowd made its way out into the midday sunshine. The young women of the district were already assembled in front of the temple. The white tunics of penance covered their bodies from neck to foot and tall conical hats holding masks which barely allowed their wearers to see the corporal world, transformed these women into strange ghostly figures. The tributaries of people disgorging from the temple formed a river which in turn split and flowed around these white rocks, particles of spray breaking free and scattering to find their own vantage point along the route of the procession.

Ares made his way to the centre of the shrouded figures, to the point where the district's standard was waiting for him. He took the staff in both hands, lifted it from its stand and turned to face the temple. He stood and waited, heroic, as the ghosts formed ranks in front of him, six abreast, their eyes watching him through the tight ornate lace of their masks.

'Company of drums!' shouted the Celebrant.

Ares drew in a deep breath and closed his eyes. He could feel his body resonate to the immense sound coming from the six large drums held on the chests of their beaters. One beat for every two of his heart.

He opened his eyes and watched as the effigies swaggered out through the temple door in time with the drum beats and took their place behind the women. Young men, eager to take a turn at carrying the immense weight of the float on their shoulders, crowded around its edges.

'Company of trumpets!'

Procession began with a chorus of trumpets so loud that Ares imagined they were shaking the buildings around him into the ground. He turned and let the Women of The Penance flow past him, forming an unyielding wave of white that washed the streets clean so that he and the effigies could walk in their purity.

A soaring, deafening soundtrack filled Ares' soul, joining his emotions to those of the crowds lining the route, sweeping them all into an enthralled ecstasy.

As he wound his way through the streets and pathways of the district, toward the square at the centre of Seminary, he was unaware of the hours as they passed, or of the pain in his shoulders and legs. He thought only of the small box sitting in his tunic, next to his heart, blessed and ready to sing to the glory of the pantheon through the death of the unholy. The striking of a righteous blow at the heart of the Church of the Holy Union. The liberation of the pantheon of gods from the shackles of 'The One'.

This would be the end of the aberration of peace by the doing of violence that would bring him to paradise.

***

It was approaching midnight when the first procession entered the square with Hermes bearing its standard aloft. The cheers of the crowd spurred the district's band to ever greater heights of pitch and volume.

From the balcony, Demeter watched.

As Hermes led his float toward the centre of the square, a second procession entered the space. Demeter was conscious of her heart pounding in her chest. She moved half a step back on the balcony and as the third procession, led by her son, her beautiful son Ares, entered the square, she looked up to the sky and exhaled slowly and deeply.

The bright orange flash filled her senses. She thought perhaps she could feel the heat of the blasts but could not be sure. There was a great noise and then she was floating backwards from the balcony into the preparation room. The marble floor, gentle and waiting, caught her and ushered her back, allowing her to slide across its smooth cool tiles to the rear wall of the room.

She was aware of glass and debris suspended in the air around her, of being unable to breathe. Her final emotion before losing consciousness was that of surprise; she could not hear a sound, it was all so peaceful.

*"And as she stood before the water,
A great fish appeared and took her into its belly,
and it bore her under the sea to paradise"*

The Second Book of Eve

CHAPTER TEN

The image of The Authority hung in the air of Charles's office.

'Where exactly?' he asked.

'In the central square, just as the first processions were arriving. Many lives have been lost Patriarch. Many lives.'

Charles made no response. He looked into the eyes of the image: little more than a girl, ill-equipped to deliver such a message.

'Patriarch, I must inform you that material recovered from the area contains your son's cell-line.'

Charles's face folded in disbelief.

'That's not possible,' he said.

'Patriarch, is your son with you?'

'How can he be? You have him in custody. You already have my son.'

'Adam Charles Percival escaped from the custody suite two days ago.'

Charles reached out his hand to steady himself on the armchair beside him.

'Please would you ask Jess Nichola Trevelian to join us, I have a message from Council that you both need to hear.'

It took Charles a moment to process and respond to the request.

'That won't be possible, Authority. She's returned to her Family's estate. Mason-of-Trevelian is now her proxy.'

'Why?'

'There had been some incident at the Trevelian estate yesterday. She's returned and Mason acts on her behalf.'

'Then please fetch him.'

Charles nodded to the image and spoke into the room.

'Dovac.'

'Sir.' His servant's voice responded immediately.

'Go and find Mason-of-Trevelian. Ask him to come to my office straight away.'

'Sir,' the speaker clicked.

Charles looked at The Authority, her young eyes floating in the ether in front of him. She looked frightened.

The door opened and Charles turned and nodded at Mason.

'Sir.' Mason closed the door behind him.

'Mason, I'm in transmission with The Authority, and she informs me that there's been an explosion at Seminary, at the central square during Procession last night.'

Mason's eyes widened and he looked over to the image of The Authority as it hung in the air.

'Mason-of-Trevelian,' the image nodded, 'The Patriarch tells me that your mistress has returned to her holdings and that you are acting for her here.'

Mason nodded.

'What I have to say I must say to you both. Material recovered from the blasts at Seminary during Procession contained Adam's cell-line.'

'I see,' said Mason, looking across at Charles.

'The Authority has just informed me that my son escaped custody two days ago,' said Charles.

The two men looked at each other.

'Patriarch.' The image turned to face Charles: 'I must ask you again, is your son with you?'

Charles let go of the chair and straightened his body.

'No. He is not.'

The Authority seemed to stiffen, as if a silver thread running through her body had been pulled tight.

'In the light of Adam Charles Percival's escape, Council has sanctioned me to station an octave of cherubs at the Percival holdings. Once they've made a search of the Chateau and grounds for your son they'll remain on the estate. If you or any of your household are contacted by Adam Charles, you are directed to make this known to a cherub immediately.'

Charles did not react to the imposition of the war machines on his estate. He did not care. All he could think of was that Adam had escaped.

***

Dovac's office was too large.

His notices of rank, each one held in a silver frame, were on obvious display on the wall opposite the door: the wall that any visitor would see immediately upon entering the room.

Mason stood in front of the platform on which Dovac had his desk.

'It's just a transport, Dovac,' he said.

Dovac did not look up, but raised an eyebrow in anticipation.

'...of-Percival,' said Mason completing Dovac's title.

Dovac smiled and slid the fingers of his right hand across his desk, tracing the woodgrain that swam beneath a deep dark varnish. His fingers came to rest against an ornate silver ink well, the only object on the desk's surface. He picked it up and examined it.

'A gift from The Curate himself,' he said, 'for services rendered. Services that etiquette demands must remain undisclosed.' He smiled as he carefully put it back in its place.

Mason placed his arms behind his back fighting the urge to run at Dovac, put his hands around his neck and squeeze. He spoke softly, calmly.

'Dovac-of-Percival. I am of course entirely in your hands in this matter but as you know, my Mistress has had to return to our Family's holdings and she has taken the Trevelian transport capsule. You will appreciate that I need to get back there. I need you to lend me one of the Percival transports.

Dovac smiled. A thin-lipped, mean-spirited grimace that spoke of spiteful intent. A cat playing with an injured fledgling.

'A transport is a valuable item Mason-of-Trevelian. Surely I don't need to explain to you of all people that it's my duty to ensure that all properties of my Patriarch are properly cared for and looked after.'

'I will of course ensure that it's returned promptly, duly serviced and pristine.'

'Well I don't doubt it Mason-of-Trevelian,' his teeth now visible through his lips, 'but what of mishaps and what of liabilities? There's much to consider and it would not do for one to lack due diligence in one's duty to one's master. At Percival, we take our responsibilities in such matters extremely seriously.'

Mason took two steps towards the desk.

'Come on, Dovac, it's just a damn transport capsule. Surely you can see something's going on here. First the Trevelian holdings are attacked, then Seminary. Now you've got a full octave of cherubs on the way and I'm willing to bet that once they arrive you'll be locked-down tight. You'll never be rid of me. You don't want me here any more than I want to be here, Dovac. Lend me a damn transport and I'll be gone. I need to get back to my Family.'

Dovac slowly adjusted the position of the ink well on his desk. He stood up and leant forward, putting his weight on his fists.

'Your *Family* is not worthy of the rank. It never has been.'

Mason's eyebrows lifted. 'So, this is what it's about is it? Still?'

Dovac pushed his chin forward but did not answer.

'You still carry it around with you, don't you? After all these years,' said Mason.

Dovac stood up, folded his arms across his chest and turned to look out of the window.

'You never could see the bigger picture Dovac. You couldn't see it then and you can't see it now.'

Dovac shot Mason a glance. 'And you could never follow an order. If I'd had my way you would have been….'

'What? Shot? Executed as a traitor? This is exactly why Nicholas was chosen to lead a Family over you Dovac. You have no vison. You're no leader, you never were and you never will be. All you ever achieved during your command was loss of life.'

Dovac's face flushed, Mason could see that his point had found its target. Perhaps he had gone too far. He could see Dovac's jaw bone flexing under his thin-skinned cheeks as the anger flowed through his body.

'Take the thing,' said Dovac through gritted teeth, waving his hand towards the door; 'take it and may your journey be well-made.'

***

The girl stood in the cockpit of the Trevelian transport capsule. She had found it surprisingly easy to operate: Mason had shown her how to set the destination on the control panel and how to initiate the machine's movement. At first, she had felt nervous to be in charge of so much power, but it soon became apparent that the capsule essentially operated autonomously, much like the agri-machines she had worked with for most of her life. A machine that was sophisticated in its design but uncomplicated in its use.

She was enjoying the view from the window, the sight of the landscape rushing towards them only to flash past in an instant. It was exciting, the feeling of speed and power. She imagined taking hold of the manual controls in front of her, the two near-vertical bars which controlled their speed and direction. She could see how they worked as they twitched and rotated in an echo of the route that the capsule followed. It took her mind off the dull persistent ache she could feel behind her eyes. She leant against the back support craving a jug of caldi. If she had one here she would keep it all to herself; drink it down in one go. She closed her eyes, remembering the moment that she last tasted it, back at the Trevelian estate, imagining the warm liquid running down her throat to her stomach.

Her mind floated back to the music she had heard at the Percival Chateau. Her Mistress had been involved in a detailed discussion with the Dovac creature. She had been engrossed and the girl could see no way of contributing or of assisting her Mistress. In fact, she had felt that her presence in Dovac's office was an unwelcome distraction so she had taken herself off to wander through the pretty private gardens. An unfamiliar scent had drawn her towards a tightly manicured hedge hidden behind three fruitless trees. She remembered the small white flowers, the shape of elongated bells that covered the top of the hedge. She had breathed in the sweet delicate scent of those flowers and there it was, sitting in the air around her: music. Music made by voices that held and supported one another in a way that the girl would not have thought possible. In her own chapel, she and her cousins would sing the morning praise, or the thanks for a good harvest, or the praise of the Three Living Saints, but their song was not like this. Their song was plain, each cousin singing the same notes as her neighbour. The music that had drifted through that hedge had been quite different. This music was made from several melodies sung together at the same time. Each line was a tune in its own right, and each magically combined with the rest to create a sound that made the girl want to weep and rejoice at the same time. Each voice was perfectly balanced with the rest. It was as if each melody held the next in its arms. It was breath-taking. She had never in her life heard anything as beautiful as that music.

She was suddenly aware of the capsule slowing down and her attention snapped back to the present. They were within the Trevelian estate and the Chateau was clearly visible in the distance.

It took a moment for the girl to realise just what she was looking at; to process the destruction in front of her.

***

Jess could smell the smoke even before the door of the transport was fully open. She almost fell to her knees with the sight that met her eyes as it swung open. Throughout the journey, she had thought of little else than her Popos, willing him to be safe, to be unharmed. She had tried again and again to re-establish contact with the chateau. Tried and failed. But the scene in front of her pushed even thoughts of him from her mind for a moment.

It was quiet, the only sound was the soft crackle of smouldering fires that had not burned themselves out. The area was almost unrecognisable. Instead of the order and neatness of the familiar landing platform, there was twisted metal and ripped hardstanding.

Jess stepped down from the capsule and walked along its side, steadying herself by drawing a hand along its smooth curved surface, pristine and shining in contrast to its surroundings. On the far side of the landing area she could see the sides of a large crater, the soil thrown up and over its boundary like torn flesh. The sickly-sweet smell in the air caught in her mouth and chest and she felt her knees weaken. Then she could feel an arm around her waist and the support of a shoulder. The girl was taking almost all her body weight and was moving her towards the damaged entrance to the Chateau.

'Thanks,' she said, standing up straight and releasing herself from the girl. 'Thank you, I can manage. We must find my father.'

'The entrance looks serviceable, Mistress.'

Jess nodded and led the way through the debris to the door leading into the rear of the Chateau. It was scorch-marked and slightly ajar. She pushed at it, swinging it back into the dark corridor.

'Power must be out,' she said, leading the way.

They entered the lobby and stood waiting for their eyes to adjust to the darkness.

'Mistress, what's that?'

Jess followed the girl's gaze and made out a shape lying neatly at the side of the corridor: a young face growing from a blanket which covered a still and inanimate body.

She looked along the corridor. Three more petite and shrouded remains were resting toe to head along its length.

'No,' said Jess, her left hand moving involuntarily to her mouth.

The girl brushed past her shoulder and knelt by the nearest figure. It was that of a young Trevelian namesake, perhaps ten or twelve years of age. The girl reached for the child's hand and brought it to her cheek, sharing her quiet tears with the cold skin.

'We were talking about dreams one morning. She was a sweet girl.'

Jess nodded, but said nothing, not knowing what to offer by way of comfort.

The girl looked up at Jess. 'Why is this happening Mistress? Why are my cousins dead? What value is there in any of this?'

Jess looked into the girl's face for a moment.

'I don't know. I just don't know.' She was struck by the tangible strength sitting behind the girl's eyes.

'Mistress!' The voice came from a silhouette framed by the doorway leading into the Great Hall: 'You're back.'

'Where's my father?' asked Jess, looking up at the shadow. She walked toward the voice, her pace quickening with each step, her feet creating a brittle bow wave of sound that bounced around the corridor.

'Mistress, I'm so sorry, we've done all we can.' As Jess approached, the owner of the voice reached out and cupped Jess's right hand in hers.

'Where is he?' she asked again.

'We've put him in his office Mistress, we have made him as comfortable as possible.'

Jess felt a numbness wrap around her head and body as she walked past the woman and into the Great Hall. She did not see the broken bodies lying on the tables, or the tapestries torn from the walls to be used as blankets.

She did not register the exhaustion of those tending to the wounded. All she could do was feel the need to be held by her father.

The damage to the docking area was not the only or by any means the most significant inflicted on the Trevelian Chateau. As she and the girl entered the administrative area of the building, instead of finding a darkened corridor they were hit by sunlight. It warmed the rubble mountain that was once the external wall of the building. Jess took in the damage but felt nothing. It was as if she were not moving her limbs but instead was floating in some magic cloud that navigated and moved on her behalf, insulating her from her surroundings.

There he was, laid carefully on the couch in his office, a blanket covering him from his legs to half-way up his chest. His skin was pale and he was so still, an otherworldly stillness seemed to surround him. But his eyes were open and when she entered the room they found hers immediately.

'Popos,' the word took on life in Jess's breast and pushed its way out of her mouth, almost a whisper. She crossed the room and looked down at his weakness, so different from her real father. No, it was him. The same eyes, holding endless love for her.

'Jess,' he breathed, 'my darling. I'm so sorry.'

She knelt by his side and picked up his hand. Kissing its back she held it to her cheek and began gently to weep.

He looked up at her and smiled.

'No, don't cry,' he said. ' "It is only by its impermanence that a life shows its beauty." '

Jess smiled back at her beloved father and squeezed his hand. They looked at each other in a precious moment that was theirs alone to live.

***

The girl stood in the doorway and watched as her Mistress knelt by the Patriarch's side. She could not hear the words they exchanged, but the Master was clearly very weak. She turned to the cousin who had followed them through the rubble.

'Will the Master survive?' she spoke in a low whisper.

'No. His injuries are too severe. He'd lost too much blood by the time we reached him.'

The girl could feel her heart beating, pushing the blood around her body. She was suddenly aware of the scar on her face; it felt hot, it stung with the heat. She did not understand how the world could be this way. How could a thing such as this happen? Why?

'What about the medical suite?' asked the girl.

'Destroyed. We've gathered everyone in the Great Hall. We're caring for them as best we can, for the injured and for those whose time is near. We thought it best to bring the Patriarch to his office. It was closer, and it seemed more fitting.'

The girl nodded and turned her face back toward her Mistress, a young woman in pieces. She must do something she thought. After a moment, she took her cousin's hand and led her back into the corridor so that they could speak more freely.

'Are any of the agricultural service pods in the grounds or are they all out in the fields?'

The woman frowned, not understanding the question.

'Most of the pods have a medi-tube in their inventory,' said the girl. 'Are any pods here or are they all out in the holdings?'

The woman continued to frown as she replied.

'All the pods are currently in the bays on the far side of the halls, none are in the field, but, there's no value in finding a medi-tube. There's no infirmary, the Master can't be saved. To prolong his life in a tube would be cruel. His time is here. It's fitting that the Mistress is with him. She can give him the final witnessing and bear witness that his hands were untied.'

The girl understood her cousin's point exactly. She was not so distant from her old life, from her community and upbringing. To prolong a life for its own sake, a life that could not foreseeably add any value to the community, this was not only unpalatable, but as the woman had described it, it was a cruelty. But the girl had caught a glimpse of another world. A world which operated in a way that was different to the one that had raised her. She had yet to understand it, but through the movements and shadows of that glimpsed world she knew that other rules might apply. She thought about how she might express this to her cousin. How she could make her understand.

'My duty is to my Mistress. I must look to her wellbeing and I know that she's not yet ready to lose her father. She'll be unable to fulfil her duty if he passes this day. Have a medi-tube brought here please cousin, have it done without delay.'

'But his time is here. Think of his memory. Think of how the Mistress will be scarred if she doesn't let him go.'

The girl placed her hands on the shoulders of her cousin and looked into her eyes. 'You remember the gentle generosity that the Mistress showed to me when I was still suffering. You know the debt I owe her for that.'

The woman nodded and dropped her eyes from the girl's.

'I know that my Mistress will suffer, no matter what this day holds, but I also know that it's not the right time for my Mistress to give the final witnessing. Please, go to the pods and see if any have survived. If they have, then fetch a medi-tube.'

The woman nodded and gave a small bow of her head, an almost imperceptible acknowledgement of the girl's newly found authority.

***

Mason's lamp lit his way as he moved along the entrance corridor and into the Trevelian Great Hall. Candles had been brought in to provide a little light for the namesakes as they cared for the injured. Mason felt the strength of bond they shared, one with another; it was something quite tangible. It was as if he were caught up in some religious observance in a great church. The women recognised and acknowledged him but he did not stop to help with the injured or to offer support, his place was with his master.

He picked his way along the broken corridors that ran between the Great Hall and the administrative rooms and paused in front of the door to Nicholas's office.

When he had made contact with Jess she had immediately told him of Nicholas's injuries. It had not sounded good, especially with no functional medical suite. He had gunned the engines of the borrowed transport, pushing them as hard as he could. He had felt powerless during the journey. He had wanted it to be over, wanted to be here, to see for himself and to help. But now that he had arrived he felt a great weight pressing against him, holding him back, preventing him from tapping on the door. He was about to knock when it opened, slowly, and the girl stepped out into the corridor. She stopped, pulling the door closed behind her without making a sound.

'Mason-of-Trevelian,' she hesitated; Mason could see she was surprised to see him. 'A long journey well-made is ended.'

Mason smiled and touched his hand to her shoulder.

'Let's not worry about formalities between the two of us,' he said, before raising his eyes from hers to the door. 'How are they?'

The girl exhaled slowly, sucking in her lips.

'The Patriarch is in a medi-tube. It's my doing. There's no hope for him but I couldn't see how Mistress could give the final witnessing. She's not ready. I know I should have let him go, his time is here but…I'm sorry if this was the wrong decision.'

Mason smiled down at the girl. Her face had a strength that he recognised from years before. But it held anger too.

'You know, I've seen death many times,' he said, 'too many times. Mostly it's been in the heat of battle, where you're cut off from the decision.' His eyes narrowed and his right hand waved in front of his chest as he explained. 'It's more that you've already made the decision by that time. You're committed to the battle and death is just part of that. It means you're insulated from it, from death, at the time it occurs at least. You don't have to feel it until afterwards.'

He thought back to the first time he had experienced death, what it had felt like. He thought too of the last time he had known it; he certainly hadn't felt isolated from it then. He knew its rawness, what it could feel like. The girl reminded him of it.

'The situation you faced, it's about as difficult as things get. Death is a very difficult thing to look in the eye and you did that and you made the decision to put him in a 'tube. To defy death, for a little while at least. I'm certainly not going to second guess that decision. You were the one here when it needed to be made, and you made it. I'd probably have done the same, I'm not sure I'm ready to lose him just yet either.'

The girl nodded. She was a survivor, he thought.
'How's Jess?'

'She's with him, she seems at ease now.'

The girl opened the door and the two of them crept into the dark room, silent and careful, not wanting to disturb the shadows cast by the candles over by the far wall.

Mason looked across the room. Jess was sitting next to the medi-tube that now held her father, the line running along its length alternating between blue and green, indicating that its occupant was being held in stasis.

He felt an impulse to see Nicholas's face, to look upon the man he had served for so many years, to kiss his cheek and call him brother, but he knew that opening the 'tube was not possible. As soon as it had closed around Nicholas it would have consumed him: an intricate silk web growing around his body and connecting to his cardiovascular system. The 'tube would now be filled with an amniotic fluid; its surrogate placenta was all that kept Nicholas alive now. Opening it would be fatal to its occupant.

Mason touched the girl on the shoulder and nodded his thanks. He left her standing by the door and walked silently over to Jess. He knelt beside her and spoke softly.

'How're you holding up?'

CHAPTER ELEVEN

Rebecca Catherine Valerie de-Monte, Matriarch of the Family de-Monte, nodded as she considered what had just been said. She balanced on the dark red velvet cushion placed on the end of her four-poster bed so that she appeared to be standing as she took the weight from her feet.

Her private rooms were dark. Typically, the only light allowed to penetrate the sanctum would be from the small lamp which stood on the bedside cabinet, its dim rays creating an ellipse around the orderly collection of pain killing preparations. This evening a second source of light made the shadows grumble and squeeze themselves into the corner of the room. It came from the image that floated in front of her. Rebecca stared into the steel-blue eyes of the cleaner of souls.

'Curate. If what you say is accurate, we must prepare for the worst,' she said.

The two age-lined faces looked at each other: not identical but echoes resonating from the same drumbeat.

'I agree,' the image said, 'what do you suggest?'

Rebecca stretched her neck and rolled her shoulders to relieve some of the tension that grabbed at them. 'And you have no idea who within the Seminary is behind all this?'

'No. Only that it has to be someone with considerable reach and influence.'

'One of The Twelve then?'

'Perhaps. Or some senior administrator behind the scenes. Someone trusted. A Deacon perhaps.'

Rebecca gave a slow and thoughtful nod.

'Tell me who your source is.'

The Curate's image showed no emotion in its response.

'No. I'm sorry, I won't do that. There's too much risk even with an internal comms link.'

Rebecca stood and stretched. She knew that she could trust his judgement on this, just as she had relied on it all her life, and he on hers. But could there really be such a plot? She walked from the edge of the bed to the curtained window and touched the fabric, rubbing it gently between her thumb and forefinger, testing its quality. As the image of The Curate was pulled towards her, the light it gave made the hunting dogs depicted on the curtain appear to move in search of their prey as if they gathered around it for the kill.

'Very well,' she said, 'we must contact the Families and let them know what we know. We must warn them and determine a plan and above all we must do this in a way that will avoid detection.'

As she spoke she continued to face the curtain that kept her from the clean light of the day. She had hated and shunned it for more years than she could remember, believing that her many sins would be exposed by the honesty of the sun. Wrapped and cocooned in the shadows for as much as her duties would allow, the recent trip to Trilogy had been the first time in years that she had felt the sun on her skin. She had forgotten what it was like. She toyed with the idea of wrenching back the curtain, to feel that warmth on her face again. But she did nothing, preferring to stand in her blacked-out world.

'When do you expect the call to Council?' she asked over her shoulder.

The Curate answered immediately: 'Within the hour.'

'That decides it for us then don't you think,' it was not a question. 'There's not enough time to send word by courier. We must risk the external comms link even without encryption. We must act now. I shall contact them.'

***

Another word would have made all the difference. One more word and she would understand. The girl floated high above the heads of the people she had come to know over the past six weeks. She knew that she was dreaming, but she knew also that truth could be found within dreams. So, she watched and she waited as she floated. Waited to understand the truth this dream held for her. She was sure that the very second the next word was spoken she would know.

She was in a seated position, floating in the air perhaps ten or fifteen metres above the ground. It was dusk and she could smell the dampness in the grass below. To her right was a leafless mature tree. She was level with its highest branches and if she had chosen to turn her head she knew that she would have been able to see every detail of every twig and branch-end. Below, on the grass, and to her left were Mason-of-Trevelian, her Mistress, Charles Edwin George Percival, and Dovac-of-Percival. There were also two people she did not recognise and a tall and very thin figure dressed in white whose features were blurred by a white light that radiated out from its face. They argued. No, that was wrong, they did not argue, they were scared and were all talking at once. All except the two figures she did not recognise and the figure in white. These were to the side of the others, in a group of their own, watching. One of the figures she did not know was looking up at her, and it was his or her next word that the girl waited for. All she needed was this one word and she knew it would all make sense. She could recall nothing of the strands of the discussion she had heard up to this point in her dream. This did not seem to matter. All she needed was one more word and it would be clear.

And then water closed in over her head and she wasn't floating in mid-air. Her senses were no longer filled with the scent of the grass. When she breathed in all she could taste was the heaviness of water. But she did not choke or cough, and it did not make her struggle or gasp for air. She could breathe quite comfortably.

As she sank, the light that had tasted of grass when she had been floating, became monochrome; blacker and darker until it seemed to press against her eyes. As hard as she stared, there was no way she could push her vision out from her eye sockets.

And then there was a great sound of swirling and a great feeling of being twisted and thrown about. She could not breath, and started to feel fear and panic bite at her toes. She would die. She could hear her own heart beating, faster and faster, it came to fill her head. To die, to die, to die, it shouted from within her chest, thumping so hard that it made her entire body shake with each beat.

And then. And then calm. She lay on her back. She lay on the grass, the same grass she had floated over before, but she knew this time that she was alone. She lay there, wet-through from her ordeal, but not cold. Not at all cold even though she knew it was night-time; even without opening her eyes she knew it was dark. She lay there, alone, on the grass, beneath that old old tree. She lay there with no other words to hear and slipped from dream-sleep to sleep.

***

From above, the city of Amynthia took the form of a wheel and at its centre was The Step: the hill on which The Chambers of Trilogy grew as if they were flesh clinging to stone-bone. Seminary District formed the hub of this wheel, its arc of green parks isolating the hill from the rest of the city. Four great spokes ran from this hub to the wheel's rim formed by the forest of steel trees tethering the city's solar collectors to the ground. Each spoke of the wheel marked the boundary of a quadrant of the city; a wide paved road that its citizens would follow into Seminary District and wind their way to The Step to witness the spectacle of mock democracy. They would pass into the hill itself through one of four great stone arches, the words 'Grain', 'Peace', 'Truth', or 'Faith' held in stone above.

Each entrance led to a dark tunnel whose curved stone ceiling became lower as its sides became narrower. These vessels spat citizens, one by one, into the amphitheatre that filled the cavernous space in the centre of the hill. The citizens would take up their places on the upper rows of seats, the front row being reserved for The Families and their staff and the next rows for the members of Seminary. Today, the cavernous public gallery was empty save for one lone figure sitting in the shadows in the upper rows.

From its vantage point the figure watched the small raised platform that formed the focal point of the amphitheatre. It was just large enough to accommodate two adults whose fingers would touch if they were each to stretch out their arms. Four tables formed a semicircle facing the platform. Each table held a place for a Council member, three from each quarter of the city such that representatives from the same quarter could never sit together or communicate in whispers.

The figure watched as the bureaucrat stood in the centre of the platform facing the members of Council, waiting for them to take their seats at the tables. The brightly lit bureaucrat wore a black robe over a simple white tunic tied at the waist with a black belt. The robe hung over his shoulders and did not meet across his front. Its elaborate gold brocade flowed down its entire length indicating the high rank that rested on the shoulders from which it hung. Once the members had taken their seats, he recited the formal words which signalled the convening of the Council of Amynthia.

'The Council serves the citizens. Members will speak only the truth. All opinions will be heard.'

He let a moment pass and then asked, 'Who amongst you stands as The Authority?'

Nematona stood, her small frame delicately clothed in a simple white floor-length dress gathered at the waist with a red cord.

'I currently stand as The Authority for Council by virtue of the lottery drawn the first day of this year.'

'Do any members of Council wish to challenge this appointment?' The bureaucrat left the question hanging in the air for just a moment: 'Then this Session of the Council of Amynthia is hereby convened under The Authority of Council member Nematona of district two.'

With the formalities over the bureaucrat moved to the rear of the platform and took up his seat to the left and rear of the chair that Nema now approached. Once she had taken her place she began the business of the session.

'Council members, you will of course be aware of the reason for this session of Council having been convened, namely the attacks that have taken place in the last few days. One attack took place at the holdings of the Family Trevelian, and one in the central square of Seminary during Procession. I know that you've all received the report of the preliminary investigation carried out by our head of civil security, Citizen Owen. In case you haven't had time to digest its contents, I've asked him to provide us with a summary of his findings in person before we discuss in detail what action we need to take.' Nema gestured to a position on the front row: 'Citizen. If you would be so kind.'

Citizen Owen eased himself from his chair and climbed the two steps onto the speaker's platform. He was not old, but his movements were, his shoulders rounded and his head bent to face the floor. As soon as he began to speak he disappeared behind a slowly rotating image of rubble, destruction and shockingly lifeless bodies.

'Honoured members of Council. What you see before you is the aftermath of the explosion that occurred at the height of Procession two days ago. As you can see, the damage is extensive. Loss of life is estimated to be between five and six hundred souls. An accurate figure should be available within the next seventy-two hours. Two blasts occurred simultaneously.' Shrinking circles appeared on the image as it rotated, pinpointing the positions of the blasts.

'The explosions occurred at the entrance to the square and, as you can see, close to the central monument.'

The image changed to show an aerial view of the Trevelian Chateau. The damage to the transport dock was clearly visible, but it was dwarfed by a huge crater on the other side of the building, perhaps fifty metres across. It had swept away most of the buildings that housed the Family's namesakes and a significant proportion of the Chateau itself.

'Here you can see what remains of the Trevelian Chateau,' he continued. 'As you can see the structural damage is extensive.' Again, two shrinking circles indicated the location of each blast as Owen spoke.

'We've been unable, as yet, to visit the holdings, but Jess Nichola Trevelian, recently appointed Mistress in accordance with this Council's wishes, has reported that her father, Nicholas Alexander Michael Trevelian, has been seriously injured. In all, only three of her staff survived the blast not including Mason-of-Trevelian who was with her at the Percival holdings at the time of the attack. She reports that eight of the Family's namesakes survived.'

The display faded and the members of Council were left staring at the good citizen. He folded his arms and let his weight fall onto his back foot in anticipation of a question. A member of Council stood, a thin young man with high cheekbones, his blond hair cut short at the sides and back but left longer on top and swept back from his forehead. Nema, The Authority, spoke.

'Council recognises Fideil Wras.'

'Citizen Owen.' The young man nodded to the Citizen as he spoke. 'We've seen the images of the devastation at Procession, so we're aware of the havoc, but what of the cause? What can you tell us about who's behind this and what do you know of their motives?'

The Citizen waited for the young man to return to his seat. He nodded and adjusted his glasses as if to acknowledge the legitimacy of the question.

'Honoured members of Council, our analysis of the residues that survived the fire in Seminary Square strongly suggests that our own military grade explosives were used. But as to who or why, at this stage we're keeping an open mind. The presence of this material points to the involvement of someone with a senior security clearance, or someone who has obtained clearance illegitimately by some means. Whether the parties carrying out the attacks are within the city, or are feeding some external party with the material I cannot say. In any case I must conclude that there's someone of rank involved. Our military stocks are under close surveillance and I've taken steps that will prompt the play. Should the perpetrator show their hand, I shall have them.'

He paused for a moment and waited for Wras to give a nod of understanding.

'In the meantime,' he continued, 'we must move to protect our food supply. The Trevelian holdings are, as you have seen, unable to function, and both they and the Percival holdings are vulnerable to further attack. It would therefore, I suggest, be prudent for us to put measures in place to "a" protect each holding, and "b" do what we can to support the Trevelian estate in bringing itself back into a state of full production.'

He paused to allow the members of Council to process and take ownership of the direction of his argument.

'I therefore recommend that Council authorise the deployment of four octaves of cherubs to the Trevelian holdings, and three additional octaves to the Percival holdings to augment the one already there. We must place each Family in the arms of the state for their own, and for our, protection.'

The young man stood again.

'Council hear your proposal Citizen and will vote on it in due course, but I wish to press you further on the matter of who may be behind this. You have made reference to "external parties". Is there a possibility that some surviving faction from outside our city has coalesced and is intent on attacking us? Could this be a resurgence of some malignant religious group attempting to rekindle the fires of The Conflict?'

Owen watched as faces looked one to another and the idea began to take on a tangible shape in front of him.

Another member of Council rose to her feet. She was perhaps in her sixties, with long hair that was a mix of jet black and silver.

'Council recognises Agneta Smetna,' said Nema from her chair at the back of the stage.

'I think the existence of any coherent force from outside the city extremely unlikely.' Smetna's tone was accusatory.

Citizen Owen took in a silent and deep breath; there was still work for him to do.

'There is an unanswered question before us Citizen,' she continued. 'What of the link to the Percival cell-line? Council is aware that Adam Charles Percival was implicated in the initial attack at the Trevelian holdings some weeks ago, and that this was the reason the Percival first-born was taken into custody. Into your custody. We hear that his cell-line was found at the site of the Seminary blast and we understand that he's escaped and at large. You are I assume aware of this?' The last comment was rhetorical and barbed.

Owen gave a slow single nod.

'Well,' she continued, 'it seems clear that we know both the "who" and the "why", and any suggestion of some force outside of the city is quite redundant. Adam Charles has made no secret of his opposition to the use of namesakes. Clearly, he has stepped from the light of free speech into the darkness of direct and violent protest. Surely there's no need to "keep an open mind" as you put it. Adam Charles is the obvious guilty party and the suggestion that others may be behind these attacks seems to me little more than an attempt to distract from the inadequacies of your custody suite.'

Smetna turned to her fellow members but her words were still directed at Citizen Owen.

'What is your plan? What are you doing to track this man down, to apprehend him, to prevent him taking more innocent lives and causing more harm? It is your custody suite from which he has escaped to carry out this attack. What will you do to put things right?'

Owen, the small and unassuming man, the person who, if met in the street, would be easily ignored or pushed aside, raised his eyes to the honourable member of Council and stared at her. He dared her to continue in her tone of political indignance. He dared her to say one more word. She did not. Instead she sat down into her seat, hoping for nothing more than for those eyes to find another target.

'Honourable members of Council,' Owen spoke in the same matter of fact way in which he had narrated the moving images: 'Adam Charles Percival did not escape from the custody suite.'

The members looked at Citizen Owen and at one another, not comprehending.

The Authority spoke from her chair behind Owen, causing him to turn to face her.

'But Council received word of his escape from your own office Citizen. You and I spoke of this matter and I've communicated with Charles Edwin George Percival and told him of his son's escape. Council sanctioned the allocation of a full octave of cherubs to the Percival estate to apprehend him.'

'Forgive me, Authority. I have made use of you and of Council.' He turned and bowed his head slightly to those seated in front of him. 'Yes, Adam Charles Percival was arrested following that initial attack on the Trevelian holdings. His arrest was prompted by the discovery of his cell-line at the scene of the blast, this too is true. But he protested his innocence from the moment his detention began. He insisted that the taking of a life was an abhorrence and that he could not live with such an accusation. He asked to be subjected to an examination by The Curate.'

The citizen allowed a moment to pass by way of emphasis. Every member of Council was aware of the risk to any individual who undertook such an examination. The Curate's unofficial title, "the cleaner of souls", was built upon the countless young namesakes whose minds had been irretrievably damaged by his work. Looking deeply into a mind, discovering its motivations and exploring its darkest corners, required a battery of chemicals that could rip that mind open, leaving it blank, "cleaned", its owner simply an empty vessel, fit for nothing but euthanasia. For the Percival first-born to volunteer for such a risky examination could itself have been taken as proof of his innocence.

'I sanctioned the examination.'

Owen paused for the benefit of the imagination of those present. None would have seen The Curate at his work, but each would have in their mind their own grizzly image of what was involved.

'The Curate conducted his examination in a comprehensive and robust manner and was able, quite unequivocally, to state that Adam Charles Percival was entirely without guilt.'

Owen's eyes scanned from left to right across the faces of the members of Council sitting before him.

'It was therefore my conclusion that the Percival Family had been the subject of a plot to incriminate them. I am, as yet, unclear as to who is behind this plot, though I have some candidates under scrutiny, and so I judged it would be useful to let Adam Charles Percival "escape" to give certain parties the opportunity to show their hand to me. Regrettably this plan has necessitated a degree of secrecy and I have been unable to be fully open with Council until now.'

His explanation complete, he turned to face The Authority and made a small apologetic bow.

'It was a necessary deception, but one for which I owe you each a sincere apology.'

He turned again to the tables and bowed his head a second time. Then he stood as straight and erect as he could as if braced for an assault.

There was silence for an age. Council was the highest and most respected organ of governance in Amynthia. It was held in universal high regard. To feed its members untruths was unprecedented. Fideil Wras, the thin young man, remaining in his seat, made the point that was in each of their minds.

'Citizen Owen. Your record of service to our city has until this point, been exemplary. You are held in the greatest respect by those present today and by those of the wider community who interest themselves in matters other than The Ruck. But to deceive Council is to set your shoulder against our society, to court expulsion from the city. Indeed, your actions may even have precipitated this attack.'

The good citizen bowed his head.

'If other options had been available to me I would have taken them. My action and my deception was, regrettably, necessary.'

Again silence. Consideration, weighing of words.

'But the Percival first-born is not in the custody suite is he, Citizen?' It was The Authority who spoke now, 'I don't believe even you could keep his continued detention a secret. He's not there, is he?'

'No Authority, Adam is not in the custody suite.'

He turned again to face The Authority, the wide-open eyes of the young girl Nema searched his face for answers.

'Then where is he?' she asked the question almost under her breath.

Citizen Owen continued to look at her as he half twisted his shoulders toward the members of Council. Keeping his eyes on Nema he extended his right arm to the figure hidden in the shadows high above the tables.

'He's over there.'

***

'I think you should reconsider.' The image of Rebecca Catherine Valerie de-Monte's torso and head floated in front of Jess and Mason as it spoke: 'Our medical facilities are up to the task and your father's convalescence will go better away from the city. We can offer him and you the tranquillity that Amynthia lacks. Besides there's no value in you remaining at your estate for the time being. There's little you can achieve in such depleted numbers. Others can be found to do the work.'

Jess smiled and answered quietly. 'I thank you for your offer, Rebecca Catherine, but I feel my father will be better served if we can get him into the city. He was terribly injured and there may be need for specialist medical care. It's a kind offer and…'

As Jess spoke, the image of Rebecca looked down to her tunic and adjusted it, letting her left hand come to rest under the emblem embroidered on its front. As she did this, Mason leaned forward and touched Jess's arm.

'If you will allow my interruption Mistress,' he said.

Jess stopped speaking and nodded.

'Rebecca Catherine Valerie de-Monte's offer is a generous and wise one. We should accept her hospitality. We should take The Patriarch to the de-Monte Chateau. Their medical suite will serve him.'

Jess's eyes narrowed as she looked at Mason. A second before the comms link had come to life with the grainy image of Rebecca, they had been prioritising the arrangements necessary to take her father's medi-tube to the city. Mason had been quite animated as to how they would need to ensure specific senior medics were on hand. Now, following no more than a polite and sympathetic offer from Rebecca, he was counselling a move to the isolation of the de-Monte estate.

'We should all go,' he added.

Jess stared at Mason, registering the emphasis.

'Very well, Rebecca Catherine,' Jess turned back to the image as she spoke, 'I would be honoured to accept your kind offer.'

'Come at once.' And with that Rebecca's image abruptly disappeared.

Jess disabled the comms link and turned to face Mason, raising her eyebrows in lieu of a question.

'She knows something,' said Mason, 'she knows something but doesn't want to share it in a broadcast.'

'Why do you say that?'

'Did you notice her hand?'

Jess shook her head.

'Have you ever noticed how each Family's crest is depicted on the city's shield? Trevelian and Percival on either side, the de-Monte crest in the centre with its wings extended over and behind the other two?'

Jess thought before she replied.

'It hadn't really registered before but yes, of course, I've seen it many times. What of it?'

'When the three Families were established after the war, the de-Monte Family was set apart from the Trevelians and the Percivals. They were given very specific duties, one of which was to protect us, to protect our two Families. The shield depicts this, their duty to protect us.'

Jess shook her head. 'But why?'

'It was Rebecca's idea. She was, is, a great military tactician. Always seven moves ahead of everyone. I guess she saw the city's vulnerabilities: if it lost its food supply it would be a catastrophe. Whoever controls the farms controls the city. She could see that the Families running the farms might need protection, so took it on herself to offer this.'

'And you think that Rebecca is doing this now? Based on what? I can't see how you make a meal from two pots of nothing.'

'I think that Rebecca was pointing to the shield on her tunic. The shield in which the Trevelian and Percival Family crests are held by the de-Monte crest. She was telling us that her offer was not one of hospitality, but one of protection.'

Jess's consideration of Mason's logic was academic, she implicitly trusted his judgement. When he had interrupted her with his suggestion that they should all go to the de-Monte's estate, she had immediately acquiesced, sensing something of his motivation. How could she possibly fulfil the duties of Mistress-of-Trevelian? Without Mason, she would be lost. Without Mason.

'We need to get organised,' she said, snapping herself out of self-doubt, reminding herself, in a phrase from the epic poem that sat in her childhood, that "life was earned before it could be lived".

'There are fourteen of us in total. We could all travel together but something tells me we should split up and use both transport capsules.'

Mason nodded. 'I agree. How do you want to play it?' he asked.

'You take the three members of staff. I'll take the namesakes and father.'

Mason pursed his lips slightly and said, 'If I may suggest: you and your father shouldn't travel together. I'll take your father's medi-tube. At least then there's a little defence in depth.'

'No Mason. Your advice is sound of course, but I'll take father. He and I will travel together. You will take the staff and I the namesakes.'

Mason gave a nod. 'Absolutely. Understood.'

'Make the arrangements,' she said.

***

The members of Council turned and looked into the darkness of the chamber. Their eyes searched the shadows in the area indicated by Citizen Owen's outstretched arm.

Adam Charles Percival remained motionless and invisible for a few moments. Calm, confident. He knew that his insistence on submitting to The Curate's scrutiny had bought him credibility in the eyes of Citizen Owen, making an ally of him. And now he had that same currency with the members of Council. He was innocent, he knew it and they knew it, and he had been the victim of a gross miscarriage of justice. He had their attention, and now, thanks to The Citizen, he had a platform.

The eyes of each of the members searched the shadows but could not find him until he began to move toward their tables. He was dressed in a dark-red hooded cloak, lent to him by the good citizen to cover the oversized tunic and knee-length skirt that he had been issued with whilst in the detention suite. As he approached the members, some of whom were now standing, he dropped his hood back onto his shoulders, exposing his newly shaved head and allowing them to see the marks left on its temples by the retention ring that he had worn as part of The Curate's questioning. The two red sores still wept and glistened slightly as they caught the light.

Eyes followed him as he walked past the members of Council and stepped up onto the platform next to Owen. He made no effort to turn and address the Council members, but instead faced The Authority.

'Hello Nema,' he said, 'did you miss me?'

The Authority made no attempt to hide her tears.

'I'm glad to see you,' she smiled.

Adam smiled back at her and turned to face the assembly.

'Members of Council,' he turned to Citizen Owen and gave a nod, 'Citizen. I'm aware that my views on the liberation of the namesakes are considered perverse by many of you. I'm aware that you may even consider my opinions to be dangerous and a threat to our society. But you can no longer think that my views have led me to perpetrate these acts of violence. I was unjustly accused and wrongly detained. I have submitted myself to examination by The Curate and as you've heard, he found me to be innocent of any such crime.'

Adam looked from face to face as he spoke, looking for any sign of challenge.

'You are aware that as first born of the Family Percival I have the right to address Council at any time. I do not claim this right. Instead I request that the honoured members give me leave to make a submission based on the injustice of the detention into which I was placed.' Adam clasped his hands to his abdomen and waited for a response.

It was Councillor Smetna who spoke.

'Council is a place where opinions can always be voiced. This is the place where The Right to speak can be exercised without fear or favour. I think we owe you that opportunity. You've been ill-treated and if there's no objection from the other members,' she looked to her left and right but no objection was raised, 'please go ahead.'

'Thank you honoured Councillor and Council.' Adam gave a small bow of his head, and moved his hands, clasping them behind his back; at the same time he widened his stance, taking on the appearance of a soldier standing at ease.

'It's not my place to give Council a lesson in history, but I feel, in order to give members a full understanding of what I want to say, I must provide a little context. Throughout recorded history, our society, and those which preceded it, have thrived on the backs of the slave classes…'

'Please, Adam Charles.'

It was an older, grey-skinned man who interrupted, taking to his feet as he did so.

'Please, let us not hear your tired arguments for the abolition of our namesakes. This Council has had to sit through your theorising and arm waving on at least two occasions to my knowledge. The namesakes are leagues away from the slave classes of history to which you refer. We have them because we need them. Their welfare is guaranteed as you well know, indeed your own Family plays an integral role in its provision. We don't need to listen to your soliloquising. You may be the first son of a Family...'

As the man spoke, Adam dropped his chin and eyes to the floor and swept his left shoulder and leg away from the members of Council, pivoting his body towards the bureaucrat who had been sitting silent and invisible throughout the proceedings. The bureaucrat stood.

'Gwayne Wilson,' he said, 'Adam Charles doesn't make his statement as the First Born of the Family Percival, he has been quite clear, as has Council, that he exercises The Right as a citizen who has been unjustly accused and detained. He may exercise this right with any topic he chooses, regardless of what he may have brought to these chambers previously.'

Gwayne clenched his jaw, realising the trap he had been lured towards, and returned to his seat. Adam nodded his thanks to the bureaucrat and continued.

'The slave classes were central to the survival and success of our forebears. They provided the labour to build their cities, to run their houses, to feed and even to entertain them. For centuries, our ancestors thrived by keeping property in their fellows. And then came The Conflict and the world changed.

'There were no slaves or masters. Only those who honoured the pantheon of gods and those who honoured The One. For the first time in our history, the hub and the rim of the wheel, the master and the slave, had the same status. They were united in the endeavour to crush the opposing world-view. There were those who believed in the multitude of gods, and there were those who believed in The One. That was all that mattered.

'Murder and persecution was carried through the world on the backs of the feeble-minded, the radicalised follower of each cult. No one was safe, and no place could offer sanctuary.'

Adam lifted his chin, allowing his voice to reach back into the empty shadows of the chamber.

'As the bloodletting gathered momentum it prompted exodus and transcontinental migration. The innocent desperately tried to escape from the chosen. Borders were permeable, people were displaced, starving, homeless. Those that had, feared those that needed; those who believed, killed those who did not. Slaves and citizens were united, they felt this fear together. They were bonded, both in these acts of terror, and in the feeling of terror itself. Slave and master fought alongside one another.

'The war had brought us despair and destruction, but it had also been the catalyst for innovation. Through the sheer need to kill we had developed technologies that previously could only have been dreamt of. Machines that could move under their own volition, that could think for themselves. Machines that could reason, that could destroy our enemy, machines that could protect us from them. Machines which accelerated us towards the very brink of destruction. But, machines capable of so much more. And when it was all over, these machines became our most powerful tools and allies.

'These great new technologies that had been the by-product of war were able to labour on our behalf: to give us shelter from the cold and the heat, to transport us, to provide us with power. But, the one thing we were unable to hand to them was the production of our food. Specifically, we couldn't automate the creation and care of fertile soil, or the nurture and propagation of our seed-stocks. These tasks needed the careful touch of our hand, not the sterile kiss of our science. And so, we needed to return to our reliance on a slave class. But how? From where?'

Adam held his hands out, palms facing forward, as if to catch the answer as it swam toward him through the air.

'And so we see the creation of a new strata in our society, a reinvention, a re-imagining of the slave: our namesakes.' He paused and smiled.

'Foundlings. Young people. Children lifted from poverty. Given a purpose. Gifted to one of the Families and tasked with the repair of soil made barren by war. Given the duty to care for the soil and nurture the seeds of our new society. Our survival was secured through nothing less than the enslavement of these children. We needed them to work our dust into fertile soil, to raise our seeds to young plants and to move them to the fields and onto our tables. The need was seen as justification enough for their abuse.' Adam considered his feet for a moment before looking back at the Council members and adding, '…for abuse is what it is.'

He paused again, taking a moment to study each face in turn.

'Honoured members. It's no secret, as has already been noted,' he nodded politely to the grey-skinned man, 'that I've long spoken out against what I maintain is an abhorrent abuse of life. But I speak my mind because that's what I think it's for. To subjugate a person in such a way, to commit them to a life of servitude, whatever the wider benefits, and however well we say we treat them, cannot be justified. Surely we cannot continue to have property in our fellows.'

He took a breath. He had painted this picture more than once, but never had there been such a canvas and never before was such a palette at his disposal.

'These recent attacks force our hand, honoured members. The attack on the Trevelian estate has left them unable to adequately fulfil their production quotas. The efforts of my own Family will not be sufficient to make up the shortfall. Food shortage is what awaits us. How long, honoured members, will it be before these shortages become the spark that ignites our citizens to protest and to violence? For this is surely what's ahead of us.'

Adam let his audience consider this point.

'But there's a way through this. A way not only to restore food production, but to increase its efficiency. And most importantly, in my view, it's an opportunity to leave our past behind us. To safeguard our food supply and to confine the abuse of our namesakes to history.'

The chamber was silent for a few long moments. It was Gwayne who voiced the Council's question.

'But without the namesakes, how do you propose our soil is made fertile? What's the alternative? Our technology can't perform these functions, as you've already noted. You're arguing against the use of namesakes, surely you don't propose to press citizens into service on the land? How can the soil be made fertile without the care of the namesakes?'

Adam took a cloth from inside his tunic and gently dabbed the glistening residue coming from the sores on either side of his head.

'You're question cuts to the issue,' he said. 'We have, step by step, automated our food production in the decades since the end of the war. Our machines can plough, plant, irrigate and harvest. Our only need for the namesakes is the production of soil. This is the last vestige of an old and morally bankrupt world. This task is all that remains, all we need them for is to turn our war-damaged dirt into soil.

It's the only thing that anchors us to our despicable use of namesakes, slavery in any honest language.

'The reason I've asked for my words to be heard by you today, is that I've learned that our reliance on these people for the production of fertile soil is no longer needed.'

Adam gave his audience a smile.

'I pledge that my words honour the tenants of Council to "speak only the truth", when I say I've recently learned that we now have the ability to automate the production of soil.'

Adam shot a glance at Citizen Owen.

'The chemists of Seminary have come to our aid. The addition of certain biological agents in the right quantities and at the right times can turn the dust that's under our feet into the rich fertile soil that we need for our crops. We no longer have a need to dirty our hands. Chemistry, simple chemistry can make our soil and I know for a certainty that the technology to automate this process now exists. A machine is capable of mixing chemicals and turning the dust until it becomes soil. And it'll do it all day and all night with more precision and consistency than any namesake. These chemical agents can be administered by machine as easily as by the hands of our slaves. Better in fact.'

Adam paused for a moment, allowing the echo of his last words to die. He continued in a quieter, more measured tone.

'I submit to Council that we have an opportunity to make a clean break with this remnant of the old world. This is the moment to make a change that will set us on another course. To leave behind the use, the abuse, of our namesakes. *You* could be the Council who takes this brave step; who frees the namesakes, who returns them to liberty and lifts our society to the moral high-ground to which it has always aspired.'

He nodded toward the Citizen.

'Citizen Owen has highlighted the very real vulnerability each Family faces to renewed attack: the perilous situation we now find ourselves in with respect to our food supply. He has suggested that war machines be allocated to each estate to afford them protection. If Council sees fit to endorse the Citizen's recommendation of placing each Family's holdings under the protection of the state, then why not, at the same time, decree the cessation of the use of the namesakes? Replace their efforts with that of Seminary's scientists and engineers. Allow our technology to free the namesakes. If you choose to do this thing, you'll not only liberate our fellows from their lives of servitude, you'll free our society from its reliance on an anachronistic abhorrence.'

Adam allowed some space into the room.

'You will secure the production of food for the city, and you will better our society. *You* will have done this.'

Adam took a deep breath and exhaled slowly and silently.

'I thank the honoured members of Council for allowing me to speak. And I request they consider my argument.'

He gave a short bow, nodded his thanks to Citizen Owen and turned to The Authority, repeating his bow. Before he left the platform he and sweet Nema looked into each other's eyes. Her smile held them both in a moment.

There was silence as Adam Charles Percival walked from the platform and disappeared back into the shadows.

CHAPTER TWELVE

Demeter used her left elbow to raise herself up from the mattress to a semi-seated position. She shuffled her backside up towards the headboard until her shoulders were level with the top of the bed's frame, her muscles stiff and aching. The effort was exhausting and she closed her eyes for a few moments when she was done. She could hear the rain on the window. Like a million whispered conversations just an inch from comprehension, or like a distant crowd-roar anticipating an imminent score in The Ruck.

The medics had got to her quickly. She had known of course that she and the other two Living Saints would have been the priority for the emergency team. But still it had been a risk. At some point she had learned that Apollo, the Living Saint of War, had died, either in the blast or from his wounds. She could not remember which. But Dionysus, who held the position of the Living Saint of Plague, had survived.

The years of The Conflict had equipped society with the technology and knowhow to mend bodies broken by battle, and she and Dionysus had benefited from this.

Demeter had known that if she survived the blast, and provided the medics got to her quickly, she would be saved. She would be loaded into a medi-tube where she had fallen and taken to a place of safety. If she made it to a 'tube, the danger would be over for her. That was really the only wager she had made with the gods. Once sealed inside she would be safe. Her cell-line would be analysed and within minutes her cardiovascular system penetrated by a web of organic material through which the medi-tube would stabilise and sustain her, holding her body in its womb, placing her in a coma, a stasis, as she was transferred to the medical suite. Once there she would be removed from her cocoon and held in the arms of an azrapone, the cool blue light pulling her muted brain-waves into synchronisation with its own glowing and dimming rhythm. The Seminary lavished its graduates with the very best training, and those who expressed an interest in medicine and showed a talent for it were fully indulged. Once she and Dionysus were sedated by the azrapone, the medics would work their brands of magic.

Yes, she thought, the only gamble had been the time it would take for them to get to her. She smiled to herself. It had worked. Twenty-four hours from the blast, here she was, conscious and convalescing.

She opened her eyes and waited for the blurred image of the room to coalesce in her mind. She found the beaker on her bedside table and with only a little discomfort drank some of the liquid. It was sweet and citric and its coolness soothed her throat.

Had it been worth it? she thought to herself. She would know soon enough.

***

The girl opened her eyes and stretched. She felt relaxed and fresh despite her lack of sleep.

They had congregated in the Great Hall for the night, tired and anxious souls gathering around the fire that some of the namesakes had made in the great hearth.

Mason-of-Trevelian had spent some time in conference with the other members of the household, directing their activities. Throughout the night, items of use for the trip to the de-Monte holdings were sought out and retrieved, and much effort was focussed on diverting what power they had to charging the engines of the two transports that would take them there.

The girl had sat apart from her cousins, away from the light and warmth of the fire, choosing a seat near the door. She had watched as they busied themselves with various chores throughout the hours of darkness, taking it in turns to sleep, to feed the fire and to patrol what remained of the Chateau's corridors. She felt no urge to join them, instead she had sat and watched from the shadows. Apart. Separate.

Jess had not joined them in the hall. She had stayed with her father. The girl had periodically checked on her, creeping along the corridor to the office where each time she found her Mistress sitting on the floor next to the medi-tube that encased her father's unconscious injured body, her left arm across its top. On one occasion, she could hear her Mistress speaking, her voice low and earnest. During each of her visits the girl stayed at the door so as not to disturb daughter and father. She observed in silence, considering what she might do to comfort her Mistress, each time concluding that there was nothing she could offer, and slipping quietly back to the hall. On her final visit, perhaps an hour before the dawn, she had found Jess asleep, her head slumped across the 'tube. She had crept into the room, removed her own coat, and laid it gently across Jess's shoulder. She had lingered for a moment. The young woman at her feet was feeling the mortality of her father for the first time and the girl felt her own compassion turn to passion and then to anger. An anger rooted in the needless and cruel destruction around her. She had left Jess sleeping and returned to her chair and her shadow.

When the dawn arrived, the girl looked down from her chair at the sleeping bodies radiating out from the fireplace. She knew that when they awoke, her cousins would drink caldi and sing the morning praise, but she did not want to join them. Something in her stomach twitched and tightened at the thought of giving thanks to the saints after what she had seen.

She stepped over and between the sleepers, and made her way out of the hall to the transport bay. The fresh dawn air met her as she opened the door. She drank it in. It was a little cooler than normal for the season, a remnant of the rainstorm that had rattled through their shallow valley during the night. She could smell the fields, still damp from its gift, and could feel her body open to it like a flower.

As she stood alone in the crisp new-day light, she could feel tears pricking the corners of her eyes. Not tears of sadness. Tears driven out by an anger. Tears that made her want to launch a primordial scream into the still air of the morning. The rubble of the transport area in front of her; the ruins of what had been her home at her back; the still-remains of the dead in the corridors this morning and the bodies of her cousins in the nursery tunnels those long weeks ago. These facts hit her fully in the chest. They hit her that very moment. But unlike the time she had returned to the fields and fainted away, when she had felt weak and helpless, the feelings that flowed with her tears now were feelings of strength and resolve. This time she felt a cool hard determination enter her body, like a strong powerful snake coiled tightly inside her belly, unwinding and moving out through her veins until her skin bulged with the tough strength of her reptilian body. Invincible and otherworldly. She recalled images of bodies and pain through the unblinking eyes of the snake that she had become. Now she understood anger.

All her life she had known her place in the world, not simply accepting it but rejoicing in it. As a Namesake-Trevelian, she and her cousins had purpose. Theirs was the joy of work and of worship. The care of the soil was their charge, and their own community of cousins was their sustenance. Their faith set them free and that faith was placed in the laps of the Three Living Saints. But when it counted most, the Church of the Holy Union, in which she and her cousins found meaning and morality, had decided not to protect the faithful, not to listen to their prayers. When they had needed them most, The Twelve and The One hadn't cared for them. No miracle had arrived.

The anger inside her chest spiked as the serpent flexed and moved her coils.

She heard footsteps approaching and recognised them as those of Mason-of-Trevelian. They stopped behind and to her left. She did not turn to him as she spoke.

'How could this happen? How could people do such things? How could those that cast themselves as holy and good let such terrible things happen?'

Mason stepped forward so that he was beside her, close, almost touching. They looked together at the wrecked transport bay in front of them.

'Why have the holy deserted us, Mason? Why have they allowed this to happen?'

The question sat in the air between them for a few moments before the girl continued.

'If the gods see all, why do they allow such evil? Or do they see it but choose not to prevent it? In which case, they're not benevolent, they don't love us. Or do they not see the evil? If so, then how are they gods?'

Mason remained facing forward as the girl spoke, not looking at her.

'Every day of my life I've praised them with my cousins,' she said. 'Every day. Until that day, that day at the nursery. I haven't prayed since.' She turned to face him. 'I thought the Saints held us in their care. I thought the aspect of The Twelve gods protected us, I thought the aspect of The One true God loved us.'

'And now you think differently?'

'And now I think differently,' she said, her tone quiet, but hard with resolve. She turned back to face the wreckage.

The sun had begun to warm the air and the still-freshness of first light was giving way to a soft breeze. It carried the sweet scent from the augibot flowers that grew around the perimeter of the docking bay.

They stood in silence. The girl's tears, angry and hidden until now, ran from her eyes making her scar sting. Silent, sincere, adult tears. She felt Mason's arm around her. She turned to him as he pulled her close to his body. She clung to his chest, her small frame lost in his torso. She buried her face in his tunic and sobbed.

For only the second time since the explosion in which she had nearly lost her life she allowed emotion to escape. Her body shook, and Mason was there with his great arms to protect her whilst she was vulnerable. She felt a warmth in his embrace that she had not expected. It felt right, natural. Protection. Safety.

After a long moment, the girl pulled herself away and wiped her face with the back of her hand.

'I'm sorry, Mason-of-Trevelian, I no longer know how to serve,' she said. She did not look up, but turned her head away from his as she spoke. She had not noticed Mason's own tears.

They stood side by side once again and stared at the broken ground in front of them. It was Mason who eventually broke the silence.

'Walk with me,' he said.

***

Mason led and the girl followed. Walking across the landing bay he took her into the thinly wooded forest that spun out from this side of the Chateau. This was one of only a few areas not left poisoned and barren by the war; its trees and plants reaching back to a time before The Conflict. Mason had not walked these paths for many years, but knew them and recognised individual trees that he had met in his younger years, his first years at the Trevelian holdings.

After ten or perhaps fifteen minutes, walking silently one behind the other, the pair came to a clearing bordered by twelve large stones. The stones formed a circle and were surrounded by a slightly raised embankment perhaps twenty metres in diameter. Eight of the stones were vertical, their feet rooted into the ground and standing at different heights, but all of them taller than Mason. The other stones had toppled and lay sleeping where they had fallen, wrapped in moss for warmth. Just inside the circle there was a large flat stone, its height level with the girl's waist. Its top had once been smooth but was now pitted and scarred by time. Mason pointed to the stone and indicated to the girl that she should sit on it.

'Can you tell what this place is, or what it was?' he asked.

The girl looked about her. The sleeping stones were to her right, the two standing behind her were taller and closer together than the others, the rest equally spaced around the perimeter. She shook her head.

Mason turned and leant against the flat stone, so that he and the girl faced into the centre of the circle.

'This place, and others like it, were temples dedicated to one or more of the pantheon of The Twelve gods. You can still make out the shape of the temple.'

The girl looked around at the stones again.

'The entrance would have been directly in front of you.' He nodded towards two of the standing stones.

'Representations of the gods honoured here would have been placed on ledges running around the walls, and there would have been a vaulted wooden ceiling above us.'

The girl sat motionless, taking in Mason's words, creating an image of the temple in her head.

'This temple was created several thousands of years ago, but only fell into disuse during The Great Conflict. It only became a ruin during the war.'

The girl was silent for a moment. 'You're showing me this place to convince me that the Church of the Holy Union has stood for all time. You want to convince me to continue in my devotion to it.'

Mason breathed out and shook his head.

'You didn't listen to what I said.' He turned to look at the girl, raising an eyebrow and tightening his lips.

The girl shook her head, not understanding his meaning.

'This temple is very old,' he emphasised the word "is", 'but it has nothing to do with the Church of the Holy Union, at least not in the way you assume. What did I tell you about its purpose?'

The girl thought for a moment.

'That it was dedicated to one or more of the pantheon of The Twelve.'

'And?'

The girl tilted her head to the side slightly as it dawned on her.

'You mean that only The Twelve were served here don't you? That there was no place for the aspect of The One true God. You mean that the Three Living Saints were not honoured here.'

'Not only were they not honoured, the Saints didn't even exist. And as for the aspect of The One true God, for the people who built and used this temple there was no such thing. For them, there was only The Twelve, there was only the pantheon of gods.'

'So the aspect of The Twelve is real but the aspect of The One True God is not?'

'No, that's not what I mean.' Mason pushed himself away from the stone altar piece by flexing his back and taking a pace forward.

'What do you know of The Conflict?' he said, still facing away from the girl.

'What I was taught, what we're all taught: that it was a battle between fanatical soldiers who aligned themselves with devils, and that it was ended when those faithful to the Church of the Holy Union prevailed. But I don't believe that any more. I don't believe that the Holy Union is a force for good or of truth.'

Mason turned and smiled at the girl, a kind and gentle expression that allowed her to stem the tears and anger that she could feel welling.

'You're right,' he said, 'the war was a battle fought by fanatics. But they weren't devils, they were believers in truth and in justice and in morality. The trouble was that each side held its own version of these noble virtues to be uniquely correct. The world can't hold more than one truth which says all others are false.'

He walked to one of the stones and ran his fingers down its rough edge.

'Here, and in temples like this, the pantheon of gods, The Twelve as you know them, were revered and worshipped. Their stories were told and their deeds celebrated. Temples had their holy days and rituals. And elsewhere, in lands far from here, churches were filled with the faithful who held their One true God to be the reality. Men and women lived, loved and died under whichever tradition they were born. And then, a little under a century ago, these two worlds collided.'

Mason had the girl's undivided attention.

'Each side believed that their gods or God were the truth. Both believed the other's views to be heresy, evil. They each believed that their God or their gods wanted to be fought for, wanted martyrs and would reward their warriors in their respective versions of the afterlife. The rhetoric of religious leaders increased and was adopted by the political class. The war spread and spread. Innocent people were caught up in it. There was a great tide of desperation pushing refugees through the world's borders until they were plugged. The initial compassion of host nations receiving the refugees turned into hate. There was forced repatriation and more violence. Fear fed the faithful, and their faith allowed them to escalate the violence, to do dreadful things. On and on it went. For over eighty years it continued. Each generation more committed to their holy cause than the last. I'm ashamed to say I played my own part in it as a young man.'

Mason looked up at the sky for a moment and took a long slow breath.

'I was there when it came to an end. But it wasn't because one side won and the other lost. The Conflict ended because we had no fight left inside of us. Neither side did. There was no one left with the strength or the desire to take another's life. We were utterly beaten. All of us. It was over.

'Then, people like the Patriarch, people like Rebecca Catherine Valerie de-Monte, they had the strength and the vision to say "no more", to say "it ends here". They built a new society, the society we have today.'

'But if neither the followers of The Twelve or The One, triumphed....'

'Where did the Holy Union come from?'

She nodded.

'They created it. Those that had the strength sat down together, and created the Church of the Holy Union.

They knew that deep in every heart there are two overwhelming urges: to have purpose and to be part of something, to belong to a tribe. They knew that if these urges weren't satisfied, sooner or later people would gravitate back to their old religions. They would resurface. They came to understand that this would inevitably lead back to war. As it says in The Telling, "The world was a beast with two heads, and such a beast cannot be led."'

The girl frowned at Mason, not understanding his reference.

'Forgive me little one. I forget that your upbringing was that of a namesake. "The Telling" is a poem. It's a record of the first decades of The Conflict that's handed to each generation in their childhood. It's intended to serve as a warning.'

Mason's casual dismissal of the girl's past-life hung in her consciousness as he continued to speak. It was clear to her, that no matter what the future held, their shadows would always fall on different ground, even if they were to stand shoulder to shoulder.

Mason looked at his feet for a few seconds before continuing. 'They decided that a religious tradition, one that could be controlled, was necessary to maintain the peace. So, they took bits and pieces from the polytheist and monotheist canons, so that the new religion would find traction with survivors from both traditions. They created the idea that each was one "aspect" of a greater truth: the "aspect of The Twelve", the "aspect of The One". The Seminary was created and given the job of maintaining religious rule. It appointed twelve people to represent each of the pantheon's gods. The Curate was the title given to the earthly representative of The One true God, and the two traditions were joined together by three of the pantheist Twelve being designated as Living Saints and given to the service of The Curate.'

'So the gods are a fiction,' she said, her eyes open wide to him.

Mason fell silent, clasped his hands behind his back and looked at the girl. He walked toward her, turned, and took up his original position next to her, folding his arms and tightening his lips before replying.

'Yes and no. The Church of the Holy Union is certainly an invention motivated by a political design, but it was based on two traditions each of which was drawn from ancient scriptures taken to be the revelation of truth to mankind. So, who is to say?'

As Mason spoke to her on this bright clear crisp morning, with the smell of the night's rain still in the air, the girl could feel her heart pound. The world did not function the way she had been led to believe. The Twelve and The One had not witnessed the destruction and done nothing to prevent it, allowing the suffering to unfold. No, The Twelve and The One were not there, they did not exist.

It had all been a lie. The prayers, the praise, the ceremonies. She felt the ground move under her feet and her legs weaken with the realisation. She thought she might faint. But then the serpent twisted inside her, lending the girl her strength.

'But how can we base our world on what we know or even suspect to be make-believe?' she said.

She could feel the scar on her face burn and sting. She wanted to hit Mason, to pound her fists into his chest. It was a lie. All of it. She, her cousins, had been used. She leant back against the stone, her palms down to take her weight. She felt wetness, cool and pure, around the fingers of her left hand. A wet sponge of moss. She looked down at it. Nature, she thought, always there, always finding a way to thrive. No matter what we put in its way.

'We should get back to the Chateau,' she said. Her voice was calm.

***

Nema watched as Adam walked into the shadows of the chamber, his footsteps making their way to a seat somewhere in the darkness. She could no longer make out the shape of his body, he was lost to the shadows, but she had the sensation of his eyes on her, and it made her feel that their history, which had for a while been confined to a tiny compartment in her heart, was spreading out through her body as it once had. She turned to Citizen Owen, suddenly aware that he was smiling at her.

The thin grey-skinned man again stood and addressed Council.

'If it's the case that Seminary have the technology to automate the production of soil, surely we must deploy it. Especially so if the automation is more efficient than the use of the namesakes.'

'Citizen Owen,' Nema was The Authority once more, 'do you have anything further you wish to contribute to this meeting of Council?'

'Only this, Authority. I don't comment on the morality of our society's use of namesakes, but I can confirm that The Seminary's scientists have indeed developed a method for the automated processing of soils. Adam Charles Percival was accurate in his statement that we have the capability to fully automate our production of fertile soils.'

Agneta Smetna rose from her seat.

'It strikes me that there is only one course which Council can now follow,' she said. 'If such science does exist we must surely make use of it. Amynthia's food supply must be guaranteed. The Trevelian holdings will struggle to fulfil their quota in their current state. We must do all we can to help them. We must make use of this technology. I suggest that we remove the burden of food production from The Families, and give this responsibility to Seminary.

The only issue for discussion is whether or not we can be confident of this science. If we can gain assurance that it will work, the only logical course of action is that we must make use of it.'

There was silence in the chamber for a few moments before Citizen Owen turned to The Authority to ask for permission to speak. She nodded.

'Councillor Smetna, your logic is quite sound. The technology has been extensively tested in the laboratories of Seminary, it's robust and it's workable. I'm convinced that it's reliable and if, as you suggest, we task the right people to oversee its introduction, it will work.'

'And by the right people,' The Authority asked, 'you agree with the Councillor's suggestion?'

'I do Authority. We should do as Councillor Smetna suggests and place both Families' agricultural holdings into the care of The Seminary.'

The Authority stood, a signal for Citizen Owen to leave the chamber. He gave a small bow of his head and made his way, slowly, down from the platform and across the floor. The Authority and Council members listened as he collected Adam Charles Percival from the shadows. Their footsteps could be heard moving up one of the aisles, their exit signalled by a brief glimpse of light spilling in through the doorway as they left the chamber.

The Authority remained on her feet as she addressed the members.

'Council, there would be a conflict of interest if this matter were to be decided through Trilogy. It is my view that this is a matter for Council alone to decide. I suggest that we formally debate the following motion: that the agricultural lands of Amynthia be placed into the care of The Seminary, that The Families be relocated from their holdings and that their namesakes be freed. Who will support this motion?'

***

The screen, mounted in the wall in front of Demeter's bed, held The Authority's image. Despite her medication, Demeter had not slept. She had lain awake waiting, hoping that a message would be forthcoming from Council, and here it was, her moment of truth. The planning, the plotting; the next few seconds could only hold the moment of her success. There could be no other reason for the call.

'Honoured Demeter.' The Authority's image gave a slow bow. 'My sincere condolences for your loss.'

Demeter gave a weak smile and slight bow of her head.

'Thank you, Authority.'

A silence sat between them for a moment.

'A mother should not have to grieve for her son,' said the image.

Demeter did not answer.

'Council are glad to see that you're making good your recovery. You're still bed-bound?'

'No Authority, I'm reasonably mobile though still in need of some rest. The Seminarians have given me the best of their care. I'm most fortunate.'

'Many wouldn't be as gracious as to count themselves fortunate to have been caught in such an attack. Your perspective speaks to your goodness.'

Demeter gave a modest smile.

'Thank you for your words Authority, they're warmly received.'

She allowed silence to develop. She wanted The Authority to make the request uninvited, to come to her.

'Honoured Demeter,' the young woman's image paused as if unsure of something, 'I hesitate to burden you with this matter in your period of mourning and during your convalescence, but the city has need of you.'

Demeter said nothing, she would offer no help.

'The recent attacks on the agricultural holdings have made our city vulnerable to food shortages. The Trevelian estate has been badly damaged and the Percival holdings have fallen behind in their quotas following certain domestic issues that I know you're familiar with.'

Demeter continued to give the image her polite silent attention.

'Council has been made aware of technology and science developed by Seminary to promote the formation of fertile soils. You are aware of this work?'

'I am,' she said slowly, 'though I'm not familiar with the details I'm afraid.'

'Council has been in debate throughout the night and has decreed that this technology be deployed to the fields forthwith.'

Demeter nodded at the screen.

'It's hoped that this will secure the city's food supplies.'

'I see.'

'Its implementation will be made the responsibility of Seminary, since it is they who developed it and understand it best.'

Demeter nodded as if taking in information that was novel to her, considering the message from a perspective of it being a new and unfamiliar idea.

'And what of the Families, their staff and their namesakes?' she asked.

'The Families are to be brought to their chambers at Trilogy where they'll be given various civic roles to fulfil. Their staff will be released from their obligations and allowed to take citizenship. Council has yet to determine the fate of the namesakes.'

'I see.' Again, she allowed a silence to fill the space.

'Honoured Demeter, these are troubling times, uncertain times. Council is nervous of lending its trust. It not only needs someone capable of overseeing the transition of the farms to Seminary, but someone it can trust, rely upon.'

Here it comes, thought Demeter.

'You've not only been caught up in this latest atrocity but you've lost a son to it. Council has come to the view that your integrity and loyalty is beyond doubt. It's Council's wish that you be entrusted with the task of overseeing the transition of the Families' holdings into the care of Seminary.'

The image paused before asking: 'Is your health and wellbeing such that you'd be willing to undertake this task?'

Demeter took a moment as if to consider her position.

'Certainly,' she said, speaking the word slowly, as if it had formed through a process of weighty thought.

The Authority gave a single nod of thanks.

'I'll transmit the Order of Council to your personal code. Please keep us updated on your progress at the holdings. And, Honoured Demeter, Council thanks you.' The image bowed its head and was abruptly gone from the display screen.

Demeter's mouth slowly expanded into a broad smile of knowing satisfaction.

'Here we are', she recited to herself, 'our feet on the road to paradise, our fists in the face of the devil.'

As she twisted her body toward the console at the side of her bed, she was hardly aware of the ache that ran across her shoulder and grabbed at her neck. Whatever pain had escaped the medication had no power against Demeter's will, strengthened as it had been by the success of her plan. She pulled the counterbalanced arm across the bed so that her console was sitting directly in front of her. Immediately it came to life, the web that ran around its outer surface picked out by a glowing and fading blue light.

She exhaled gently, directing her breath across the blue-glow, and waited for it to recognise her, and like a clam giving up its pearl, it opened and revealed the Orders of Council, waiting there for her.

CHAPTER THIRTEEN

The girl got back to the Chateau before Mason. She had led the way along the path without speaking and he had lagged behind. Her head ached and she needed to think, to process what he had told her back at the stone circle.

She could hear activity as she walked up the dark corridor toward the Great Hall. Not voices but the sounds of organisation, of things being packed and prepared by her cousins for the journey to the de-Monte holdings. She knew they would have understood what needed to be done and would simply have organised themselves to do it. She realised that, as had been the case during the night, she felt no compulsion to help them, to join them in this duty.

The corridor became dark as Mason's large body blocked the natural light spilling in through the entrance. She turned and looked up at his silhouette as it approached. When he was near enough for her to see the features in his face, she took hold of his sleeve and drew him to one side; her voice sharp with anger but quiet so that only he would hear.

'What you said, about the Church of the Holy Union, about how it was created at the end of the war,' she looked up into his face, searching his eyes, 'that was the truth wasn't it?'

Mason nodded. She moved away half a step and felt the serpent tighten her coils.

'Why? Why Mason?'

He made no reply.

'Why would you treat us like that? You feel no duty to us, you only want our loyalty so that you can use us. To you we're not people. We're just another machine to work the fields.'

'No, that's not true.'

'It is, it's the truth,' her eyes burned as she spoke.

'For us, faith is everything. It's what binds us together. It's what gives us freedom. But it's not real. It's a lie. It's just there to control us. The Twelve and The One are a lie. They don't exist. There's no beauty in faith, no freedom, it's not real, it's nothing less than a prison. Faith doesn't set us free, it keeps us in chains.'

Mason shook his head. 'No.'

'We must tell the others the truth.'

She began to move toward the Great Hall but Mason took a firm hold on her upper arm and pushed her to the wall. She looked up at him, she could feel the anger burning in her scar.

'Let go of me. They need the truth,' she said.

'No.'

She glared up at him, her muscles tight, pushing against his arm.

'We can't tell them.' His voice was calm, kind.

'Think about it. Think about the situation we find ourselves in. I told you what I told you because you needed to know. You were already part way there. I thought you were owed that much.'

'My cousins are owed just as much.'

'They will hear the truth, but not yet. I'll let you decide, but think about this first.'

Her body relaxed as he released his grip on her arm.

'There are difficult times ahead,' he said, looking into her eyes, 'difficult for all of us. Ask yourself how you feel knowing what you now know. How do you feel knowing that The Church was an invention? That your faith was based on this invention? Ask yourself how your cousins will feel if you tell them. How will they react? Will it help them? Will it help them through the next few days and weeks? You said yourself that it's faith that binds them together, well, there's a saying, "Faith is real if it's felt in the heart". Right now, your cousins need their faith. Don't take it from them. Not yet. Let them keep their faith for now.'

She looked into Mason's eyes. She couldn't reconcile the kindness in his voice with the lies he had been a part of. She felt betrayed by him but she knew he cared for her. She stared at him, studied his face. He was a good man, she could see it, she knew it. The moment ended when the door from the Great Hall opened. She turned to the woman who emerged.

'Cousin, where's the Mistress?' asked the girl.

The woman was carrying a small cube containing a portable power cell. The girl knew that it must be heavy for its size.

'She's using the communicator in the Trevelian Family transport,' she said, her words held back by the weight in her arms.

The girl turned on her heel, and without waiting for Mason, walked back out to the landing bay.

***

Jess was sitting in front of the comms unit in the capsule's passenger compartment, her hands on the table, fingers interlinked. She listened.

'… you are to wait at the Trevelian holdings until we arrive. For the transition to be efficient we'll need an accurate description of each of the agricultural sections from you; their status, any damage, progress reports, up to date gap analysis.'

'Of course, Honoured Demeter,' said Jess. 'Do you have an estimate of when the representatives of Seminary will arrive?'

Demeter's image smiled.

'Four octaves of cherubs have already been despatched and should be with you within the hour,' it said.

Jess felt a chill run through her body. Mason had been right. Rebecca Catherine Valerie de-Monte had meant to warn them. Somehow de-Monte had known that the Trevelian Family would be under threat. She must be careful not to let Demeter know this. She must appear neither concerned nor complacent.

'Cherubs, Honoured Demeter? I took your meaning to be that the Seminary would simply be overseeing the work here. What need is there for war machines, and in such numbers?'

Demeter's cold emotionless image regarded Jess for a moment before replying.

'I've been asked to ensure that our agricultural supplies are secured, and it's my judgement that in the light of recent events the allocation of cherubs is a prudent measure. As you can see from the Order of Council, this is within my gift.'

Jess nodded as if she could see that this was a reasonable and sensible precaution. The imminent presence of cherubs on the estate meant all was lost. They would not be able to leave for the de-Monte's. But she would not let Demeter see her unease.

'So what, if any, provision do we need to make for the Seminarians? As you know, our living spaces have been significantly damaged.'

'There's nothing. I'll personally attend the Trevelian holdings in the morning to oversee the transition. I'll have with me only a small group of technicians and we'll bring an accommodation unit with us which will suit our needs very well.'

Jess knew that she must be careful. She must not arouse suspicion, she must ask her next question without asking.

'Could I make a humble request on behalf of the namesakes-Trevelian?'

Demeter gave a regal nod of her head: 'Of course.'

'Their Chapel was all but destroyed. Would you be able to include an artisan in your work team? It would mean so much to them to have their place of worship reinstated.'

'Don't concern yourself with the wellbeing of your former namesakes. Provision has been made for them. The cherubs will see to it.'

Jess felt a chill run down her back.

'I look forward to receiving your reports,' said Demeter and then her image was gone.

Jess sat for a moment staring at her own reflection in the black screen before becoming aware of a shadow spilling across the floor of the capsule. She swivelled in her chair to face the silhouette of the girl in the doorway.

'She means to euthanize my cousins doesn't she?' said the girl. 'She has no intention of allowing any of us to live.'

The girl walked toward her and took up the seat opposite, facing her eye to eye across the table.

'Let me take them to safety, Mistress. We have become a target and our presence will put you at risk. You and the remaining household should travel with Mason-of-Trevelian. Let me take my cousins in the other transport.'

Jess's eyes narrowed, surprised at the suggestion.

'You showed me a great kindness Mistress, back when I couldn't work. I'm grateful for that, for you taking me in. But my place is with my cousins, and you're safer if we travel separately. Give me one of the capsules and let me take them.'

Jess felt a strength in the girl's voice. A different person from the folded weeping body she had comforted in her cell.

'I'm afraid that won't do any good,' she said.

She turned to Mason as he entered the transport.

'Why?' he asked, 'what's happened?'

'Council have placed ours and the Percival's holdings under the care of Seminary,' she said. 'Actually, they've given the task to The Living Saint of Famine no less. Poetic in a way if you think about it. Demeter will be here in the morning but she's sent cherubs: four full octaves.' She raised her eyebrows at Mason. 'She must've anticipated Council's decision and despatched them some time ago; she said they'd be here within the hour.' She gave Mason a small familiar smile. 'You were right about Rebecca de-Monte wanting to warn us, but I fear Demeter has us boxed in or cut off whatever we do. Even if we leave immediately we'll be rounded up by the cherubs. We can't outrun them.'

Mason moved into the control cab: 'Let's see shall we?'

Jess followed and watched as he activated the console and waited for each of the three panels to turn from a dark chocolate brown to backlit yellow-orange as they powered up. He adjusted the two dials located at the bottom of the nearest panel and studied the display.

'No. She means to put us on the back foot and scare us into inactivity,' he said. 'If four octaves were an hour away, we'd be able to pick them up on the 'scope. There's nothing moving out there. No, she may have sent cherubs on ahead of her, but we've a few hours at least before they get here.'

Mason adjusted the settings on the scanner.

'There, it'll give us a proximity alarm if anything approaches within 500 kilometres. That's the best I can do from here.'

'So we have a chance.' Jess turned back to the girl. 'We'll split the household and the namesakes between the transports. Mason will take the Percival transport, you and I will take this one. The Family will be your shield.'

The girl did not respond.

'Have them bring father in here.'

The girl paused for a moment before giving a bow of her head. Jess waited until she had gone.

'Mason, what's happened? She seems changed somehow.'

He looked through the door after the girl.

'She's been through a lot. One moment she has her community around her, certainty, the next…not easy for any of us to have our world bent out of shape, but for a namesake…'

Jess studied Mason's face for a moment. There was more, she could see it. But she would not ask.

'Do you think that Seminary are sending anyone to the Percival holdings?' she asked.

'Good question. They already have cherubs stationed there so I think we must assume that whatever's in store for us has already happened at the Percival estate.'

Jess looked out through the front window of the cab.

'The Percival namesakes,' she said.

Mason placed his hand on Jess's shoulder. She looked up at him.

'We must try to help them,' she said.

'No. It's no use, they're already lost. That's not an option. We must get you and your father to the de-Monte's as quickly as possible.'

Jess turned her head back to look out of the window.

'That's not good enough,' she said under her breath, and then to Mason: 'How soon before we can leave?'

'This capsule shows a full charge and the Percival transport should be good to go. It was at sixty per cent when I arrived and it was put on-supply straightaway. We can go as soon as you give the word.'

The transport tilted slightly and Jess reached out with her hand to steady herself. She turned and looked up at the monitor in the ceiling: it showed the medi-tube that held her father being loaded into the cargo bay.

'Get everyone into the transports,' she said, 'I want us to be on our way in ten minutes.'

'OK.'

Jess watched him leave. She curled her bottom lip into her mouth and drew it back out, scraping it against the top row of her teeth. She turned back to the window and looked out across the pad, reconstructing the corners and places where she had played as a little girl. Where she had laughed and cried and loved, where she had grown. It was all gone now. Mason was right, the world had been bent out of shape.

***

The girl was watching from inside the cargo bay as one of her cousins made good the restraints around the medi-tube. The bay's floor was almost entirely taken up with it. A few crates of supplies and items salvaged from the Chateau were locked to the walls on either side, leaving just enough room to walk up and down the hold to secure the load. The woman worked silently and efficiently, pulling down on the ratchet that ate away at the cords running across the top of the container, making each of them tight before moving to the next. She was older than the girl by perhaps a decade and her hands, toughened by years of physical work, were strong and precise in their movements. As the girl watched, she felt set apart from this woman: still her cousin but somehow no longer connected in the way she once had been.

When each restraint was in place and secure, the woman looked across at her. Could she sense it too? thought the girl; the difference, the unfamiliar space between them? The woman gave her a single nod and walked down the ramp into the daylight. After only a few steps she stopped and moved to the side, keeping her eyes to the floor as her Mistress passed and entered the hold. The girl watched, the simple act of deference visible to her for the first time. It's not right, she thought, for my cousin to cast her eyes to the ground in this way. It's not right.

The girl watched as Jess peered into the darkness of the cargo hold, searching the shadows. After a moment, she walked up the ramp to stand beside her. They looked down at the 'tube; a blue light ran from head to toe, changed to green and ran back up to its top. Slow and measured, it indicated that its occupant was stable and safe. Jess leant forward, placing her hand on its cool smooth surface, and let her breath spill out across it, making it damp with condensation. The girl made as if to leave.

'The world seems to be unravelling in front of us doesn't it?' said Jess.

The girl stopped and turned to face her but made no reply.

'Two months ago, we knew who we were, where we fitted,' said Jess.

The girl looked into Jess's eyes, her pupils made wide by the shadows, sucking in the light. She looked at her Mistress and her Mistress looked back at her. There was a weight to the silence.

'What will become of the Percival Namesakes?' The girl's voice was quiet but held no trace of weakness.

Jess shook her head.

'If there's any chance that they're still alive, I would like to try to help them Mistress.'

The tangible strength in the girl's voice made Jess hesitate for a moment before she replied.

'I'm sorry, but I must look to the protection of those in the charge of the Trevelian Family. We must concentrate on getting our people and our namesakes to the de-Monte Chateau.'

The girl watched as her Mistress turned back to face the medi-tube. After a moment's silence, she kissed her hand and placed it on the surface at the point where her father's chest would be.

'I understand Mistress.'

The girl turned and walked down the ramp into the sunlight.

***

Mason stood to the side of the Trevelian capsule as it powered up. He could see the girl through the porthole in the cockpit as she flicked switches and studied the control panel. She was certainly a quick learner. He watched as she punched in the coordinates and lifted the transport from the pad, its sleek body slowly rotating so that he lost his view of her. Yes, he thought, a quick learner, and adaptable.

'I had to tell her. It was the right thing to do.'
There was no one to hear him, he spoke to himself.

He waited until the capsule carrying his Mistress and Patriarch began to move away, before turning and walking to the side of the compound.

'Control.' He spoke as he walked, and the smooth stone-grey slab responded by moving out of the shadows and approaching him. 'How many surveillance units do you have that are still operational?'

'Three, Sir, one airborne and two terrestrial.'
It waited while Mason considered his options.

'I want one of the terrestrials in the Great Hall, somewhere tucked away…up behind the rubble at the north end, and the other one in the corner of the Master's office. Get the airborne one on top of one of the outbuildings. I want it to scan the feeds from the terrestrials and relay the signals to my personal code. Clarification?'

'None Sir, your wishes are clear.'

'Do you have enough power for an EMF blast?' he asked.

The mechanical voice replied, 'Yes Sir.'

'I want you to wait at the side of the transport bay. As soon as the Seminarians arrive I want you to power down. Monitor for communications from myself or the Mistress but in all other respects I want you deactivated. Do not respond to commands given by any other party. Clarification? '

'None Sir, your wishes are clear.'

'Execute.'

A flying surveillance unit unfolded from the stone's flat body and launched itself into the air. The stone then moved away to deposit the terrestrials according to its instructions.

Mason walked over to the transport capsule lent to him by Dovac. Its mirrored outer surface reflected his image and as he approached, the curves distorted his broad muscular body. He walked up the treads of the ladder attached to the hatch folded out from the side of the vehicle, and pulled it closed behind him.

It was older than the Trevelian's capsule, its design more elegant. The passenger compartment was lined with dark woods inlaid with silver and enamel trees and flowers. Lamps, with glass shades in the shape of elongated flowerheads, secreted sedate pools of light onto four deeply varnished tables. He ignored the occupants who were seated ready for their journey, and moved his large frame through the doorway in the centre of the bulkhead separating the passenger cabin from the cockpit, sealing the door behind him.

The passengers rocked and shimmied as the capsule stepped from the ground into the air. As it rotated towards its direction of travel the sunlight moved around the cabin, illuminating first this face, then that body. The passengers were silent, sharing or avoiding glances, looking at the floor, staring through a porthole. They were tired. They were numb. They had been wrenched from the certainty of the past. They were frightened.

Mason held the control column in both hands. He did not punch in the coordinates of the de-Monte Chateau, he wanted to fly the machine himself for a time. For all his experience and a lifetime of scars, he too felt the pain of change and welcomed the distraction of activity. He pushed the column forward slightly to level the craft and pulled on the lever under the fingers of his right hand. The capsule accelerated, kicking up dust and detritus from the ground less than a metre beneath its silver skin and pushing Mason's back into the support that allowed him to remain standing as it picked up speed.

The sun was now directly ahead of them, although at a height that meant it was only just visible at the top of the thick glass of the viewing window. When the pace of the machine had quickened to what he felt was an appropriate speed, Mason released the lever and allowed his body to stand free of the back support. He leant forward and adjusted the scanner, tuning it so that it searched for the Trevelian transport that was somewhere ahead of them. He stooped to catch sight of them through the window. Yes, a plume of dust in the distance over to the right and ahead, that was them, good.

He studied the console to find the bearing of the de-Monte Chateau, and twisted the control column to correct their direction slightly. He could feel his muscles and his mind relax. He flicked a switch above his head to deactivate the cockpit lamp, preferring the mix of natural light and the yellow glow from the needles and dials in front of him. He stretched his powerful neck, ear to shoulder, first to the left and then the right. He pulled back the trigger, increasing their speed and reducing the view through the side portholes to a blur.

If all went to plan, both transports should be at the de-Monte's Chateau by nightfall.

CHAPTER FOURTEEN

Citizen Owen studied the young man sitting opposite him. How could such naivety find form?

'Thanks,' Adam said, leaning forward in his seat.

Owen gave him a closed-lipped smile and raised his eyebrows, a signal of openness.

'…for letting me take The Curate's test. For helping me make the case to Council. Thanks. We've made a difference. The two of us. A big one.'

'Of course,' said Owen, 'but as you pointed out, I really had no choice. It was you who insisted on being tested, and once you had… my Office is interested only in truth.'

'Nevertheless, you've played a part in something important, Citizen. This will be the end of the abuse of the namesakes. They will have their freedom. You and I did that.'

Owen watched as Adam leant back in his chair and stared at the ceiling. For a moment, he thought he looked like a decapitated corpse, the shadows cutting his head from his torso. Could this young fool, even now, not see where this was going?

'I'm going up front for a bit,' Adam said, getting up from his seat and heading towards the cockpit.

***

Dovac had just enough time to flick the intercom to "off" before Adam walked through the doorway.

'How are we doing?' asked Adam.

'We are making good progress Sir.' Dovac bowed his usual obsequious bow.

He kept his eyes on the young master as the capsule sped on. Adam had not looked at Dovac when he entered the cockpit and he continued to stare out through the front window, his hands held behind his back. Dovac thought his stance heroic.

Dovac had been "of-Percival" since the beginning, he had joined them before the birth of the young master. He had, from an appropriate distance, seen him grow, seen his father dote upon him, seen him indulged in a way befitting someone of his rank. He had never understood Adam's issue with the use of the namesakes, something Dovac considered to be consistent with the natural order of things, and he had shared in the pain it had caused his Master. He had also felt his suffering at Adam's arrest. Now he felt the joy of the son's return.

He looked down at the control panel, adjusting the pitch of the nose to minimise the buffeting of the bow wave of air reflected from the ground just beneath them. He could of course have left all this to the control system, but somehow he enjoyed making such adjustments by hand. It reminded him of his younger days.

After an age or perhaps just a moment, Adam asked, 'How is father?'

Dovac slowly moved the control column back to its automatic setting before replying.

'He is in good health Sir, particularly so since news reached him of your imminent return to the Chateau.'

Adam continued to look ahead and Dovac's attempt at a smile went unnoticed.

'If I may say so Sir,' he waited but Adam did not respond, 'it is a great relief to all the staff-of-Percival that you are coming back to us.'

He watched as Adam, his eyes closed now, took in a long breath and then slowly exhaled, pushing the spent air out from his lungs until there was nothing left inside of him.

'Would you like me to attempt to contact your father via the communicator Sir? We will be in range in a few minutes if we are not already.'

Adam opened his eyes and turned to Dovac for the first time.

'No. Thank you Dovac. Let's wait until we arrive. I think he and I need to talk face to face. A lot has happened, to both of us, and I think he and I need to talk face to face. Somehow conversing over the airwaves doesn't seem appropriate.'

***

Adam steadied himself against the side of the cockpit as Dovac executed a precise one-hundred-and-eighty-degree rotation and put the capsule down onto the Percival's private landing pad. He could see hints of the sandy-coloured stones of the Chateau through the green hedge which separated the platform from his home. Home. It had been a long time since he'd thought of it in that way.

He was suddenly aware of the capsule's engines. Their whine had sat outside his consciousness during the journey, but as they powered down the sound dropped in pitch, through lower and lower frequencies, so that he could feel the vibrations through his feet, connecting him first to the machine, and then to the earth on which it now sat. He looked out through the small porthole in the side of the cockpit. There he was, his father, emerging from the gap in the hedge as the dust settled.

Deep within, Adam could feel a spark of joy. As he moved into the passenger compartment eager for the hatch to open, that spark took hold. It burned away the years, allowing him to feel a son's love for a father.

'Give me a minute,' he said over his shoulder to Owen, 'and I'll announce you.'

He let the handrails lead him down the steps from the capsule. What began as a slow walk across the landing pad turned into a run and ended with his arms around Charles, pushing him backwards.

'Father,' he held the old man to his chest.

When he had been young, Adam had been sensitive and fragile. Wounded by the death of an animal or some perceived childhood unfairness. He found comfort in his father's arms now, as he had as a child. He did not attempt to hold back or hide his tears.

As he stepped away he drew back his hood, exposing his face and shaved head. Charles touched the scarred tissue on his scalp.

'What have they done to you?'

Adam shook his head, the joy of his father's concern bringing forward a smile for the first time in what felt to him like forever.

'Nothing. It doesn't matter.' He looked down into Charles's eyes. 'It's good to see you, Father.'

Charles's eyes dampened and he put his arms around Adam again.

'Yes,' he said.

Their embrace continued for a moment and then Adam took a step back. He half turned and extended his arm towards Owen who was watching them from the foot of the capsule's steps. The two men knew each other of course, but etiquette demanded that formal introductions be made.

'May I present Amynthia's Head of Civil Security, Citizen Owen.'

Adam waited as Owen bowed and shuffled across the apron toward them. He turned to his father when Owen was standing next to him.

'Citizen Owen, may I present my father, Charles Edwin George Percival, Patriarch of the Family Percival.'

Charles extended his hand and Owen held it.

'A long journey well-made is ended,' said Charles.

Owen gave a small nod of his head in thanks.

'I understand that I have you to thank for my son's liberty, Citizen.'

Owen gave no response.

'Come,' said Charles, 'receive our hospitality.'

Charles turned and led the way through the hedge. As they walked across the lawn to the open doors which led directly into his office, he took Adam's hand in his.

'It's good to have my boy back at my side.'

Adam did not reply.

'You've been gone for such a very, very long time. Not just your detention.'

Adam knew what his father meant.

'But to submit yourself to examination by The Curate. The risk. I can't think of it. It could have been your end. The way it could have left you. How could you have been so reckless?'

Adam let go of his father's hand and stopped walking. Charles turned to him.

'It was worth it father. It's all at an end now.' He smiled: 'It's all finished. The namesakes will be free now. They'll be free.'

Charles smiled back at his son and they continued, more slowly now toward the office. As they reached the raised paved area in front of the double doors, Adam was hit by the familiarity of the stones making up its surface. They were irregular and did not match, but had been fitted together with such great skill, that exquisite patterns flowed from their contrary shapes and colours. He remembered how as a boy, he would study them, making out the forms of dragons, dogs and trees. He was home.

***

'Please take a seat, Citizen.' Charles gestured to the sofa facing the empty hearth.

'Thank you once again for all you've done. The Family Percival will forever be in your debt. Would you care for something to drink?'

Charles crossed over to a small hexagonal table where several glasses and bottles had been placed, ready for the moment.

'Thank you no,' said Owen, 'if I may?' He gestured toward Charles's desk and terminal.

'Of course,' said Charles.

Owen walked over to the desk, placed a small rectangular box next to the terminal and watched as the blue web glowed and faded across its surface, synchronising, burrowing its way into the estate.

'You don't need my access signature?' asked Charles.

Owen did not speak, he kept his eyes on the box until the glowing lights faded and its lid slid open. He placed his thumb into the box and held it still.

Adam and his father exchanged glances.

Citizen Owen waited for the box to complete its scan before removing his thumb and turning to Charles.

'I am sorry,' he said.

'What is this?' Adam looked from his father to Owen.

The Citizen ignored Adam, speaking instead to Charles.

'Council have listened to your son's argument. He told them of the means to turn our dust into soil without the use of your namesakes.'

Charles was silent for a moment.

'I see,' he said.

He walked over to the door and looked out onto his manicured lawn. Owen carefully slid the lid of the box back into place using the thumb and forefinger of each hand. It closed with a crisp "click".

'The Order of Council has been uploaded to your systems and a cherub unit will attend to your namesakes. You and your son will remain in the Chateau for a while in case Seminary needs your input. Where are the namesakes now?'

Adam watched as his father crossed his right arm across his waist and used his left hand to massage his temples as he looked to the floor.

'No,' said Charles, 'I won't let this happen. The Namesakes-Percival are under the protection of my family and I will not let you harm them.'

Adam watched his father for a moment before turning back to Owen.

'Citizen... what exactly is to become of our namesakes? You led me to believe that you'd oversee their liberation.'

Owen turned to face Adam.

'No, Adam, I simply allowed you to infer as much.'

Adam pushed his chin forward and stared at him.

'What did you expect?' continued Owen. 'You made the case. You explained to Council they had no need of the namesakes, that the production of soil could be achieved without them. You showed them that they are not needed. Where, in your mind, was that argument going to take them?'

Adam stared at Owen, whose eyes met and held his. He swallowed hard and returned his gaze.

'But this isn't what we discussed, not at all!' said Adam. 'You told me about the Seminary's work so that we could free the namesakes.'

'As they say, "When the rains fell, the rivers found their own path"'.

'Don't quote scripture to me, this is real-life and it's a situation of our making, yours and mine!'

'No, Adam, it is a situation of your making.'

Adam continued, 'But my whole point was that the namesakes should be freed from their enslavement.'

Owen smiled as he continued with the quotation: '"and death was their freedom."'

Adam felt as if every nerve in his body had been squeezed and pulled and crushed, and each one was red-raw and screaming at him. The injustice that had been the focus of his adult life was, he had thought, within a breath of being righted. But, in that moment, the ground had shifted under his feet.

'You've used me!'

Owen's reply was calm and measured.

'You allowed yourself to be used.'

'You befriended me. After the examination, you took my side, supported me, guided me.

'Yes,' Owen smiled and gave a slight bow of his head in recognition of the compliment. 'Although I cannot take full credit, it was your own childish, feeble-minded naivety that made it possible.'

Adam covered the distance between himself and the Citizen too quickly to allow Owen to fully deflect the first blow. Owen's nose cracked and as his body recoiled he struck his head against the wall.

'I won't let you!' spat Adam.

Adam was considerably taller than the Citizen, but their eyes were at the same level. Adam had hold of Owen by his throat and had found the strength to lift him from the floor and pin him to the wall.

'You have used me.' As Adam squeezed, Owen's arms grasped at his hands and fingers, attempting to release the grip.

'Adam no, let him go, Adam,' Charles had taken a moment to react and was next to his son, pleading in his ear.

Adam could not hear his father's words. All he was aware of was the life he was about to extinguish. He spat as he spoke.

'You will not harm the namesakes, I'll kill you first.'

And then Adam could feel nothing but pain. It was so vivid and so crushing he could no longer breathe or see. His temples burned and he thought his skull would be crushed under the pressure. He threw back his head and his mouth opened in a silent scream. He dropped Owen and fell to his knees, his body convulsing, the veins in his scalp and hands standing proud under his skin.

Owen released the button he had found on the device located on his belt. He soothed his neck with his hand.

'You're a blind fool,' he coughed and cleared his throat, 'you and your father, both of you. You have enjoyed the privileges of your status for too long. The days of privilege are over. We have known the method of your undoing for some time, but the vehicle? We had to wait for you to come along to provide that.'

Owen smiled as he allowed a light pressure from his thumb to depress the button again.

Adam was thrown from his knees to the floor, his mind churning with the agonising heat.

'Useful little gadget isn't it? Those scars on your head were not left by The Curate's toys, they were my gift to you.'

'Please. Please, Citizen. Stop.' Charles was trying to still the writhing body of his son as he looked between him and Owen.

Adam's face was contorted and crumpled, his skin turning blue-grey, his lungs fighting for air; this was surely his end. And then the pain stopped and Owen was a crumpled sack lying across Adam's legs.

Adam and Charles looked up to see Dovac standing over them.

Sometimes a moment can last an age. Dovac was statue still and Adam did not breathe despite having been released from the grip of Owen's device. He stared at Dovac, unable to find his voice.

'I heard the interchange via the comms link in the capsule,' said Dovac, making no apology for his eavesdropping.

He extended his arm and Adam, kicking off the dead weight of the unconscious Citizen, took it and allowed himself to be pulled to his feet.

'Are you injured?' asked Dovac.

Adam shook his head: 'I'm fine'.

'Thank you, Dovac,' said Charles, taking his son in his arms and holding him close. 'Thank you.'

Dovac gave a modest bow of his head before looking over his shoulder toward the lawns.

'We need to leave. I assume The Citizen will not be best pleased when he recovers,' said Dovac.

Adam and Charles met his suggestion with silence.

'I've tracked the capsule that was loaned to Mason-of-Trevelian. It's following a route that'll take it to the de-Monte holdings. I assume the Trevelians have met with a similar set of circumstances and they're seeking refuge there.'

Charles nodded: 'Yes, the de-Monte holdings. We'll find sanctuary there, we must leave now.'

Dovac took hold of The Citizen's folded body and pulled it over to the desk. He removed the belt from Owen's tunic and used it to bind his hands and feet together behind his back. He then picked up the device that Owen had used to torture Adam and handed it to him.

'Get rid of this,' he said. 'It will have a limited range but in case he catches up with us.'

Adam stared at the box for a moment before throwing it out through the open doors into the garden.

Dovac picked up the box which Owen had used to access the Percival systems, dropped it onto the floor and smashed it with his foot.

'That should slow him down a little,' he said.

The three of them then set off across the lawns towards the capsule. As they moved Adam spoke.

'He asked you where the namesakes were?'

Charles shook his head; his breath was short.

'No use, it'll be too late. By the time we reach them a cherub will have found them. We must leave.'

'No,' said Adam, 'we must try to save them. We must.'

He quickened his pace to a run and was inside the cockpit before Dovac and Charles had reached the capsule's steps.

'Adam, it's no good,' said Charles as he climbed in, 'you must put aside this cause, it's time to let it go.'

Adam did not hear his father; he was already activating the controls. Charles followed him into the cramped space.

'It's too late for them Adam. We must get away.'

Adam's hands impatiently twisted and adjusted the controls for a few moments before he turned to his father.

'All my life you've taught me to be true to my principles. Today is not the day to tell me otherwise. If my principles had value yesterday, then they have value today. Where are the namesakes?'

Charles stared at his son for a moment.

'I don't know. At their work.'

Adam was looking at the data feeding into the console that he had been adjusting a minute before. 'It looks like there's something going on out at one of the compounds. We'll go take a look.'

***

The capsule lifted and spun to face in the direction of one of the storage compounds used by the Percival namesakes. Its entry hatch closed and sealed itself as the silver canister twisted and accelerated.

Charles grabbed and held the doorframe of the cockpit to prevent himself from falling. Once the capsule had reached a steady speed he was able to let go. He did not try to dissuade Adam but made his way unsteadily back to the passenger compartment and strapped himself into the nearest seat. Dovac was standing and using his hands to steady himself. He sat down opposite his master.

'Are we heading for the de-Monte holdings Sir?'

Charles shook his head.

'We're heading to the compound where Adam thinks the namesakes are congregated.'

Dovac considered this for a moment.

'Please excuse me Sir.' He headed to the cockpit. As he entered he could see that Adam was concentrating hard to manoeuvre the capsule.

'Sir, may I suggest we access the remote viewers at the compound to determine the situation there? We should be able to pick up a signal from here.'

Dovac did not wait for Adam to reply but adjusted some of the dials until an image appeared on the screen over their heads. It was split into four quadrants, each showing a different view of the same compound. He studied the figures on the screen. The grainy image showed the namesakes huddled together in one corner of the compound. A cherub stood guard in front of them, the silver hemispherical dome on top of its black bulk seeing everything around it, its stillness imposing, aggressive, preventing them from running. A second cherub was visible some distance from the first and in front of it the unmistakable image of dead bodies lying untidily on the ground next to one another.

'They have begun to euthanize the namesakes,' said Dovac.

Adam's jaw bone flexed in his cheek.

'Dovac, go and look after father. Make sure you're both securely strapped in back there. Once we have come to a halt, get Father to safety. This might be bumpy.'

Dovac understood what was in Adam's mind; he nodded and moved out of the cockpit and into the passenger compartment.

Adam did not watch him leave but concentrated on the controls, the capsule straining under his unpractised hand. When he was happy with the trajectory, he looked back at the screen and studied the view from the compound. Four more namesakes were making their way towards the second cherub. They formed a line some distance in front of it, there was a flash which made the screen opaque for a moment, and as the image returned, their bodies fell to the floor. At the other end of the compound the remaining namesakes were motionless, calm, some standing alone, some in pairs or small groups holding each other's hands. Another four namesakes were being ordered to leave the group and walk over to the area used for their despatch. Adam wandered what strange quirk of logic had prompted the two cherubs to organise their duties in this way. Surely it would have been more efficient simply to cut them down as a single group. If he did not know better, he would have suspected that the war machines were deriving some form of perverse pleasure by prolonging the executions and making the namesakes watch their cousins die.

He looked out of the front window and could see the walls of the compound racing towards them.

'60 seconds,' he shouted, '30...20...brace'.

As the transport entered the compound, Adam pulled back the throttle to reduce the speed and at the same time twisted the control column to cause the capsule to spin so that it was now travelling sideways. The first noise was the sound of the capsule slamming into the cherub that was carrying out the executions. The thin skin of the transport folded around its mass and punched it into the ground. The capsule rotated so that its pilot and passengers were lying on their sides. It continued to move across the ground, kicking up dust and debris as it skidded toward the second cherub.

The namesakes scattered in all directions and the capsule grabbed the bulk, shunting it across the compound and crushing it into the wall.

***

Dovac opened his eyes. He was disorientated and at an odd angle. He had been unconscious but judged from the sound of the engines still running down that this had only been for a few seconds. He pulled at the release mechanism of his restraints. As they opened, he fell onto his Master whose seat was now below him.

'Are you hurt Sir?'

Charles coughed and shook his head. Dovac found Charles's restraint and tried to release it, but his weight was pulling it taut and it would not open.

Suddenly he was aware of arms around him: slim female arms fastened around his torso; slender hands had reached around his thin body from behind and had grabbed hold of his coat at the front of his chest. He realised that the namesakes must have climbed into the capsule and one was pulling him free.

'No, not me, the master is trapped.'

As he was being pulled away, another of the namesakes pushed past him and began to work on the Patriarch's restraint, releasing him and pulling him out.

Adam was the last to be dragged from the wreckage, dazed but essentially unhurt.

The three of them sat in the dust looking at one another and at the crumpled transport. It was Adam who broke the silence.

'I had to,' he said.

There was silence again as the namesakes began to gather around them at a discrete distance, forming a semicircle with them at its centre.

'But what now?' asked Charles, 'what now?'

Adam looked at the faces of the namesakes staring at them. Silent and expectant. The broken capsule lying on its side was obviously beyond repair. What had he been thinking? He lifted his face to the sky and exhaled deeply.

'I have no idea,' he said.

Dovac stood and brushed the dust from his skirts.

'There may be a way,' he said, and then to the namesakes: 'How were you brought to the compound?'

One of the namesakes stepped forward, she was in her thirties and, like her Percival cousins, wore her long brown hair in a thick braid.

'Dovac-of-Percival, a land transport collected each work group from the fields and brought us all here.'

'Where is the transport now?'

'Once we had alighted it was ordered from the compound by the cherubs. I believe it's behind the southern buttress.' The woman indicated the wall to her right.

'Good. Two of you go and see if it's functional and bring it into the compound if you can.'

Two of the namesakes immediately moved from the semicircle and went to locate the transport.

Dovac turned back to Adam who said, 'But a land transport will never make it to the de-Monte estates, it's energy cell will be exhausted in a day. Even if it could make it that far it would be so slow that it could never outrun a skimmer or a cherub.'

'If they're undamaged, we can use the energy cells from the capsule, three out of its four will still be charged after the short journey here. And a land transport is much more difficult to spot and track than a capsule, especially if we pick a more circuitous route. It will be slow, but we may not have to outrun anyone.'

All three of them knew that slim though their chances were, Dovac's suggestion offered them their only opportunity for survival.

Charles Edwin George Percival stood up from the dust and, with the air of a man not quite in charge, grasped the lapels of his tunic with his hands.

'We will do as you suggest, Dovac. See to it please.'

Dovac gave a single bow of his head and then turned to the namesakes.

'We need the fuel cells from the capsule. Let's see if we can get at them.'

Without a word, a small group of the Percival namesakes followed Dovac over to the capsule and started to open the hatches that contained the fuel cells. Others went to the tool house to collect the equipment necessary to remove them.

After a short silence, a namesake stepped forward and addressed her Patriarch.

'Please Sir, we have fallen cousins.' She indicated the lifeless bodies at the other side of the compound. 'We must attend to them.'

Dovac, suddenly aware of the silence, looked up from his work. He could see that both Charles and Adam were at a loss as to how to respond. He walked back from the wrecked capsule so that he was standing at the focal point of what remained of the semicircle of women.

'Namesakes of the family Percival. Today you've been subjected to a terrible ordeal, you've seen your cousins slain and looked your own final moment in the eye. That threat is not yet passed. We may all meet our ends this day. We must leave your cousins where they have fallen and allow their passage back to the dust to take its natural course. We must look to our own survival.'

The namesakes were still, they did not react.

'I'm sorry,' said Dovac, 'this is the way it must be.'

CHAPTER FIFTEEN

The girl could see what she assumed to be the de-Monte estate on the horizon. She had remained in the capsule's cockpit throughout their journey; there had been nothing for her to do at the controls once she had set the craft in motion, but she had not wanted to join the others in the passenger compartment.

She understood her Mistress's position. If there were no hope for the Percival namesakes, then they must leave them to their fate. If there were no way of helping them, the only appropriate action was to save themselves. She knew her Mistress was capable of great compassion; she had felt it, benefited from it. Still, the girl wondered if she would have made the same decision if it had been members of the Percival household and not their namesakes threatened with execution.

No, she had not wanted to join the others, she had remained in the cockpit.

She could feel the absence of her faith. It would have given her comfort at a moment such as this, an anchor, certainty, but it was not there. It did not exist, there was only the space it once occupied. She felt the serpent in her belly tighten, first with anger and then with resolve.

Her attention snapped back to the view in front of her. The estate was close now and she could see that it was not at all like the Trevelian or the Percival holdings. She had expected to be travelling through concentric rings of fields centred on a Chateau as was the case at both the other estates. But there had been no sign of anything except dust around them throughout their journey.

It was difficult to judge the height of the wall they were approaching, but it was substantial. She could not see its ends as they curved away. She guessed that it must encircle the hill whose sides rose steeply behind it. Now she could pick out structures climbing one side of the hill: windows or balconies sitting one on top of the other in a spiral that climbed out of sight to the other side. As they got nearer she could make out details along the wall. It was built from a grey stone, its blocks of different sizes, fitted together expertly to form an imposing defence many metres high.

The transport capsule, still under its own autonomous control, slowed and headed toward the only visible interruption to the stonework; a huge arch four or five times the height of the transport and sealed with a substantial and solid looking wooden door criss-crossed with black metal strips.

'Not what you expected?' Mason's voice, made thin and nasal by the speaker carrying it through the air from the other transport, cut through the rumble of the motors and made the girl jump.

'No, Mason-of-Trevelian,' said the girl, 'this is not what I expected.'

The two capsules came to a gentle halt next to each other, kicking up skirts of dust in front of the great gate. The girl looked out of the side window of her cockpit and could see Mason making some adjustment to the controls in his craft. She saw his lips move and then a beat later his disembodied voice bounced out of the speaker in front of her.

'This is Mason-of-Trevelian, "…and the tree gave them shade, and they in turn gave it life."'

Mason turned to face her.

'A greeting,' he said over the intercom, 'so they know we've brought only friends.'

The gates in the wall slid back, producing a gap just wide enough for a single capsule to move through.

'This will be a test for you,' said Mason, 'you'll have to do this bit manually.'

She watched as he lifted his capsule from the ground and gently guided it through the opening. She placed her hands on the control stick and followed him through the gate, setting her craft down on the unkempt landing bay next to Mason's capsule.

'I knew it. You're a natural,' said the tiny speaker.

The girl felt a warmth flow through her body from the compliment, the serpent relaxing her grip. He had been part of the lie. But he had been the one to open her eyes.

She powered down the motors and folded the control column into the recessed panel, allowing herself room to turn and walk into the passenger compartment.

The space occupied by the landing platform was in shade. The height and proximity of the wall meant that the soft evening light that had shared their journey for the past hour was unable to join them. As the girl stepped from the vehicle she was met by a coolness in the air, the kind that persists in those places where the sun is unable to routinely reach. The girl, used to working in the open fields of the Trevelian estate, was surprised that she found the sensation to be a familiar one. Somehow, she knew that what she was sensing at the back of her nose was coming from the moss growing on the shaded stone wall and platform around her.

She had expected her Mistress to undertake the formalities of presenting their party to the Matriarch of the de-Monte Family as soon as they had arrived. Instead she watched as Jess followed a group of the namesakes from the passenger bay around to the rear of the transport. There was no room for anything else in her heart but her father, thought the girl.

Mason's eyes also followed Jess. He too could see the truth. He walked the short distance from the door of his transport to the girl.

'Come with me,' he said and set off towards a series of roughly hewn steps that were cut into the side of the hill leading up from the landing area.

***

The steps were steep and had wrapped themselves around tight hairpin terraces up and up to a small wooden doorway, its surface uneven and greening with damp and age. The girl turned to look down the hillside from the small paved area on which she and Mason now stood. She was just level with the top of the perimeter wall and could see now that it was several metres thick. How different this was from the Trevelian and the Percival Chateaux, so elegant and beautiful, surrounded by gardens and farmland. The de-Monte holdings had no such refinement and seemed not to extend beyond this great defensive wall. It appeared just to consist of the hillside.

Mason placed his hand against a small panel near the centre of the door. The sudden repeated banging noise it made as it opened caused the girl to jump and turn to watch. The door looked like it had not been opened in a while and the noise was made as its swollen wood repeatedly jammed and jumped under the force of a motor pulling it back into the darkness of the hill. Then silence, and the girl looked into blackness.

One by one, starting from somewhere deep inside the curved passage in front of her, arches of lights running up the sides and across the ceiling of the tunnel were activating. Each one burst into light with the sound of a gunshot that ricocheted up through the hill's throat. Before the arch nearest the doorway had fully illuminated, a small metal-wheeled trolley appeared from around the curve and slid to a halt in front of them on the tracks set into the floor.

The trolley was a simple carriage with no sides and had just two bench seats facing each other across a small platform. Each bench was upholstered in plush red velvet, was large enough to seat two adults and was close enough to its twin to force its occupants' knees to overlap.

Mason beckoned the girl to take a seat. She opted for what was to be the forward-facing bench and Mason took his position diagonally opposite her so that they did not have to encroach upon each other's space.

As the girl looked around for a control panel or some device by which the trolley could be activated it set off along the tunnel of its own accord. The sudden movement threw her back against the soft cushions of the bench and Mason smiled at her, his body rocking with the motion of their travel. She looked back to see the door closing behind them, sealing them into the hill, and then they had turned a corner and all she could see were the arches of lights racing past them. She leant back against the seat and let her hair blow about behind them. She could feel that they were moving up an incline. It felt good and she closed her eyes; a comforting smell, a familiar mustiness, filled her head.

The trolley began to slow and she opened her eyes. Mason was looking over his shoulder in the direction of their travel and he stood up as the trolley came to a halt next to a door cut into the side of the tunnel.

The girl followed him down from the trolley. Her view of the door was blocked by his body, and once it had opened she was unable to see the owner of the female voice which greeted them.

'A long journey well-made is ended, Mason-of-Trevelian.'

Mason's head bowed.

'Thank you, Rebecca Catherine Valerie de-Monte, on behalf of the Family Trevelian thank you for your generous hospitality.'

'You are most welcome, Mason. It has been a long time. And who is this you have with you?'

Mason turned to acknowledge the girl: 'One of our loyal and valued namesakes, ma'am. Recently appointed to the duty of individual service to Jess Nichola Trevelian.'

'Indeed,' Rebecca looked back at Mason: 'appointed to a position of "individual service", and to a Mistress of a Family no less.'

Her eyes turned to the girl again, a cold thin smile on her face: 'Quite something for a namesake to take on.'

Mason barely nodded.

'We must be doing something right after all,' she said.

Mason moved away, allowing Rebecca and the girl to fully face each other. The one, brown hair and brown eyes, the other, silver-grey and sharp blue. Not a match but somehow a pair. His eyes glazed slightly, seeing the past, remembering hope, remembering loss.

Rebecca reached out her hand and ushered the girl into the room. It was dark and warm but held no furniture. Tapestries hung on two walls, gold and brown backdrops to motifs of reds and greens. Narrow stone steps led up from an alcove at the end farthest from them. Rebecca stopped in the centre of the room and turned to look at the girl.

'So my dear, how do you find your duties?' Her tone was friendly, informal.

The girl was taken aback, at a loss as to how to reply.

'Quite a change for you I expect? Quite a different way of life?'

'Yes ma'am,' replied the girl.

'You have adapted? Coped with the changes, the new demands placed upon you?'

'I believe so ma'am,' she said, held by the scrutiny she saw in the woman's blue eyes.

'But you have yet to be given a name.' Rebecca turned back to Mason. 'One with such duties should be named "of-Trevelian" should she not? This seems careless of your Mistress.' Her eyes came to rest again on the girl's.

The girl felt a chill run through her. A chill that resonated deep inside, waking the serpent which tightened in her belly, making her strong.

'Madam, my Mistress has had more important issues to attend to.'

'Quite so.' Rebecca's demeanour changed. She turned to Mason, no longer interested in the girl.

'How is he?'

Mason pursed his lips slightly and shook his head.

'He'd lost a lot of blood before we arrived. The namesakes had made him comfortable but there wasn't much they could do. The medical suite had been completely gutted. This little one took the decision to transfer him to a medi-tube.' He nodded towards the girl as he spoke.

'Really.' Rebecca's eyes once again focussed on the girl, this time with an air of intellectual interest.

'Such a decision runs counter to your faith and upbringing does it not my dear? Where there's no hope of a life being able to make its contribution, should it not be allowed to fade? Has its time not come?'

Once again, the serpent tightened and the girl spoke freely.

'My Mistress was not ready. I judged it appropriate. A life can make its contribution in many ways.'

Rebecca considered the girl for a moment, holding her gaze. The girl did not look away.

'Your decision will have saved his life my dear,' and then to Mason, 'I've arranged for Nicholas to be brought to our medical facilities. He should be there by now.'

With that the Matriarch turned and led them up the narrow stone stairway.

***

The room was dimly lit to allow a clear view through the window into the medical suite. The girl slipped in as quietly as she could, not wanting to disturb her Mistress. Jess was standing with one hand against the glass, perfectly still, watching as her father's medi-tube was posted into the sterile environment. Her breath settled on the window in front of her mouth, drawing an opaque oval pattern on the glass.

The girl watched her Mistress. The daughter watched her father.

It would take some hours for the metal callipers and claws to open the medi-tube, allowing the man inside to be removed and his repair to begin.

The girl wondered what her Mistress was feeling. She thought back to the passing of her two cousins, cut down in front of her by the blasts in the nursery tunnel. She had been there when their lives had been taken, she had prepared the robes for their passing, she had walked in front of them in their procession and she had watched as they had been placed into the ground and given back to the earth. If she had acted more quickly, had been able to think more clearly, could she have saved them? Could she have brought them to safety? Could she have watched as they were mended and cared for as her Mistress now watched over her father? She reached her hand up to her face, tracing a small section of the scar with her finger.

The serpent made a gentle movement in her belly and spoke.

'No,' she whispered, 'they were already gone, already taken. There was nothing you could have done.'

She felt her body relax.

***

The girl was asleep. Somehow, she knew that she was. She felt a thousand hands around her body, holding her arms and shoulders, not in restraint but in love. A thin musty smell filled her nose and throat, it sank into her chest. It felt good.

To her left she could see a long dimly-lit tunnel. Its walls, where they were not in darkness, were decorated with red tongues of colour swirling on a white jagged background that came to a point where the darkness took over. In front of her was the passage through which she and Mason had entered the de-Monte hill, and to her right? She could not see what was on her right but instead felt that she was next to a thin wall with people talking on the other side. She could make out their voices but not their words.

'My dear one,' the voice came to her from beyond the thin barrier, 'my dear one.' No, not from beyond the barrier, from beyond the dream. The girl did not want to leave the arms that wrapped around her and held her so completely, but the voice was making them fall away, and as they disappeared the girl began to float up and out of the tunnel and back into the light of a room.

'My dear,' said the voice.

The girl opened her eyes. She had been sitting in an anteroom to the medical suite, awaiting her Mistress who was holding vigil over her father. The room was small, containing just three wooden chairs, and she found herself slumped across them as she awoke.

Rebecca Catherine Valerie de-Monte was standing opposite her by the closed door of the medical suite.

'I am sorry to wake you, my dear.'

The girl swivelled her body, sliding her legs across the seats and down onto the floor. She felt a little disorientated and her head ached. She stood.

'I'm sorry, ma'am, I hadn't intended to sleep.'

'There's no need to apologise, you must be exhausted.'

The girl suddenly remembered her Mistress and moved toward the door.

'Your Mistress is sleeping. In her chambers. I have just escorted her there and have returned to have a talk with you.'

'Talk with me?'

'With you.'

Rebecca took the seat on which the girl had been resting her head and beckoned for her to sit down. The girl hesitated for a moment, unsure of how to respond, and then sat down, leaving an empty seat between them. Rebecca twisted her body and looked at the girl, placing her hand on the back of the vacant chair.

'Mason has told me all about you.'

The girl said nothing.

'I understand that you were injured in the attack at the Trevelian nursery tunnels?'

The girl remained silent. She did not feel intimidated or too frightened to reply, only confused as to why she could be of interest to the Matriarch of a family that she had not been gifted to. She looked into the blue blue eyes that were watching her so closely.

'And your cousins, at your side one moment and in the arms of the Saints the next.'

The girl could feel an intensity in Rebecca's eyes, scrutinising her as she allowed this statement to hang in the air between them. Still the girl did not speak.

'I expect your faith has been a great comfort throughout these events.' It was a statement, not a question and Rebecca relaxed back into her chair as if finished.

'No,' the girl responded, not aggressively but with certainty, 'when we gave them back to the earth perhaps, but lately I find no comfort in faith.'

Rebecca raised her eyebrows and leant forward a little, pursing her lips in consideration, interested once again.

'But our faith is what sets us free,' she said. 'Without it, where is the meaning, where can truth be found?'

The girl did not want to recount the conversation that she and Mason-of-Trevelian had shared at the stone circle. The explanation of how The Aspects of The Twelve and The One had been brought together had torn at her and the wounds were still raw: her Church had been used to control and enslave her cousins. She did not want to speak of it. It was no business of this woman.

She felt an intensity in Rebecca's eyes, the silence between them becoming heavier and heavier, forcing her to speak.

'Meaning and truth have no place in the faith that I know,' said the girl.

She was surprised at the Matriarch's reaction, not angry, not even wanting to enter into debate or argument. She watched the Matriarch's eyes move down and squint slightly: her reaction seemed to be one of intellectual interest. The girl felt that she was being studied.

'Tell me, my dear,' the subject had changed: 'what do you make of the de-Monte estate?'

The girl frowned, uncertain of the question.

'What do you make of it? Is it what you expected?'

The girl answered slowly, carefully.

'It's very different from the Trevelian and the Percival holdings.'

Rebecca nodded and smiled, matching the girl's tone and volume: 'Yes, that's certainly true. How do you feel, being here?'

The girl was silent.

'Is there anything about your surroundings, anything about us that makes you feel uneasy or disturbed? How do you find us?'

'I'm quite comfortable, ma'am. You've been most kind and hospitable to my Mistress and her father.' She nodded towards the door of the medical suite.

'Quite so, but that's not my meaning,' her tone now slightly impatient: 'how do you feel, what is your reaction, your emotional reaction to your surroundings?'

'I am at ease,' said the girl, 'I like the way the air feels.'

The girl watched as Rebecca Catherine Valerie de-Monte's shoulders relaxed.

'But I was having a strange dream when you…'

'A dream,' interrupted Rebecca, 'you remember having a dream?'

The girl studied the Matriarch's expression: it was somewhere between surprise and disbelief.

***

The Curate listened intently to the conversation through the relay. How could it be, he thought, that a namesake could remember a dream? Did they all remember their dreams or was it just this girl? Was this girl typical or an aberration?

***

'Do you dream every night?' asked Rebecca, her tone soft again, intended to draw out data.

'No,' said the girl, 'not every night. But more so recently.'

Rebecca nodded: 'And do you talk about your dreams with your cousins?'

A strange question, thought the girl.

'No,' she said, and then: 'Sometimes with the younger cousins.'

***

The Curate sat back in his seat, staring at the ceiling as he thought, 'I wonder when she last drank her caldi?'

***

'If I may ask, ma'am, why are you interested in my dreams?'

Rebecca looked at the girl.

'I interrupted your sleep my dear, you must still be very tired,' she said, ignoring the question.

The girl stood instinctively as the Matriarch got to her feet.

'If you follow the corridor around to the left as far as it will take you, you will find your Mistress's chambers. Why don't you attend to her and if she is still sleeping, make yourself comfortable there.'

CHAPTER SIXTEEN

Dovac could no longer make out the features of the road through the front window of the land transport. He had to trust it to find its own way, to bump and plod, loyally following the route he had programmed six or more hours before. The Percival namesakes had made short work of removing the power cells from the wreckage of the capsule that had paid for their lives. They had connected one to the motors of the land transport and stowed the remaining two securely in its cargo bay. Within an hour of making the decision to leave the compound they had been on their way.

Before the sun had set, Dovac had kept an eye out for any signs of craft following them. There had been none. Presumably Citizen Owen would have initiated a search for them. Or perhaps they were no longer of any consequence to whatever plan was playing out around them. Now that the sun had gone there was no way to know; their first and only warning would be the arrival of search lights from vehicles that they would not be able to outrun. They had made their play and were committed to it. Dovac felt again the stirrings of long-lost emotions. He had felt them when he had struck the Citizen and he felt them now. The complicated mix of exhilaration and fear that had, for him, been the texture of war.

Adam and Charles sat in the observation platform alongside Dovac. They had stared out into the distance as they set off, but now that it was dark outside, they stared through their own reflections. Ghosts trapped inside the glass.

Behind and below them, the air in the passenger compartment was stale and unpleasant. The Percival namesakes sat in silence, their sweat filling the cramped humid space. A land transport such as this was intended to crawl between work areas, making trips of no more than an hour or so. It was not designed for extended journeys and was not equipped with any welfare facilities or even windows that could be opened. The only fresh water that was available was that which they had thought to carry with them, the only toilet facility was to stop and open the door, something they had not dared to do except when they needed to swap out one of the power cells.

It started with a single voice. One of the older women, her once brown hair turned to an exquisite silver, each strand paid for with years of loyal service, hard work and faith, closed her eyes, leant back her head and began to sing. Her voice, a rich dark contralto, grew from a resonance deep within her chest and entered the bodies of the namesakes seated on either side of her small body. As their voices joined with hers, counter-melody and harmony grew around the tune as others set their voices free, giving them to the choir that formed in the acrid and stagnant space that bumped its way into the night. The Percival namesakes sang and were cousins; united with one another and those left behind.

> '…and we share our light with you,
> Who must leave our sides and join with the earth,

We will not forget, we share our light with you.'

***

Mason stood in the semi-darkness of the cockpit. The day's light had long since left and the details of the deMonte compound outside were lost to the shadows. He did not reach out for the light switch. He stood wrapped in the darkness left by the fading comms screen in front of him, alone with his feelings, not wanting to process what he had just seen relayed from the Trevelian estate.

The years after the war had washed Mason in sadness. They had been painful, filled with anger and guilt. He had lost so much in the journey from then to now, that at times he had felt it almost unbearable. He had buried his feelings deep inside, in a place where they would not hurt him or slow him down. He had clung to the belief that he had survived to help build a better future. He had always believed that the long-game would deliver a promised land; a world in which religious faith would never be the catalyst for murder. It would never happen again. Amynthia, their great new city, would learn the lessons of history. He had allowed himself to believe that they had succeeded, that this promised land had come into being and that the work was done. But what he had just witnessed in the transmission from the Trevelian estate had swept that belief and that hope aside. He knew exactly what was coming. He could feel it in his stomach. A feeling he had not experienced in many years, but there it was. Unmistakable. The unrestrained violence directed toward those of difference. It had been his life as a young man and it was about to make itself known once again. He was now certain of this.

He wanted to be alone. He wanted to be on an island, the only person as far as he could see. He felt the dark hopelessness of the past like ice inside his chest. It was suffocating. Without hope how could he find the strength to continue? Tears came and he was still for a moment more, comforted by the darkness that folded around him. He was grateful for the blanket of night.

After some minutes, he took in a deep cleansing breath and stared straight ahead through the window of the capsule's cockpit. He was suddenly aware of a source of light behind the craft. It cast a shadow of his capsule on the steps that led up from the landing platform. The shadow moved as the source of light swung around behind him.

He instinctively reached down in search of his weapon, but of course it had been many years since he had carried one. He made a conscious effort to control his breathing and then squeezed himself from the cockpit toward the exit hatch.

The gates were already closed behind the Percival's land transport as it swung into the compound and came to a halt behind the two capsules. Mason stepped down into the shadows and watched as Dovac, clearly visible at the controls, powered down the motors and spoke into the console. After a few moments, the intense light from the floods on top of the transport faded from white to orange to yellow to black and Mason felt the darkness around him once again. The compound had no source of artificial light so he stepped back into his own capsule and opened its cargo bay, allowing the lamps within to chase and nip at some of the shadows.

He walked to the hatch at the side of the land transport and slid it open using the external latch. The air inside was hot and humid and smelt of sweat and ammonia, making his eyes prick. He stepped up into the passenger compartment and looked around at the Percival namesakes, still in their seats. They returned his stare, unsure of what to do next. Boots and then legs appeared at the steps leading down from the transport's observation platform. They descended slowly, carefully finding each step, one after the other, and Mason was face to face with Dovac-of-Percival.

Mason took in the bags under his eyes and the paleness of his skin. He looked tired.

'Mason-of-Trevelian, I am comforted to find you safe,' said Dovac. There was no hint of sarcasm to his voice, only exhaustion.

After a moment, Mason extended his arm.

'A long journey well-made is ended,' he said.

Dovac reached out, the two men's hands finding their place on each other's forearms.

'It seems we find ourselves united in conflict once again,' said Dovac, his voice dry and brittle, 'and we must re-assume those roles we thought confined to the past.'

Mason nodded. 'It would seem so Commander.'

Dovac released his grip on Mason's forearm and dropped his hand back to his side.

'And it is time for me to start seeing the bigger picture, Mason.'

Mason tightened his lips and gave an almost imperceptible nod. The moment passed and Dovac continued.

'My master and his son, and those we have managed to save, are in need of rest. I've been directed by the Matriarch to proceed to the tunnel entrance. If you could give direction to the Percival namesakes whilst I attend to my Family?'

'Of course.'

CHAPTER SEVENTEEN

'Thank you,' said Jess turning to the girl, 'thank you for saving him.'

She looked back through the window of the medical suite at the mass of fine white fibres almost covering her father's pale and unconscious nakedness.

'I didn't say so at the time. Thank you.'

They watched as mechanical callipers moved to and fro across the sleeper's chest, arranging strands of the fine web and adding to them as they sank through his skin leaving his body cocooned in a thin white sheen.

'Will he survive?' asked the girl.

'Yes. Given a little time and thanks to you.'

'Then I'm glad I was able to help.'

The girl felt her Mistress's hand touch hers and without looking at her, she held it. They stood together in silence for a moment.

'Mistress, we should go.'

Jess nodded.

The girl was still holding the note they had found in the chamber where they had slept. Its precise and neat hand-written letters had instructed them to come to the de-

Monte syndicate room when they woke, but her Mistress had needed to come here first.

The girl opened the door and followed her Mistress into the corridor. As far as she could determine the de-Monte estate was not a Chateau but a maze of tunnels and chambers running through the earth buried within the rock, isolated from the outside. The tunnels had smooth white walls, their sides curved but their floors flat, their darkness punctuated with lanterns set into the walls at regular intervals.

They came to a divide in the tunnel and the girl waited as her Mistress took the note from her and studied it.

'It's this way,' she said.

A few metres further on they came to a door which slid back as they approached. The girl blinked as her eyes adjusted to the bright natural light flooding from the empty room into the passageway. Directly in front of them was a large window which framed a blue sky. For the first time since they had arrived, the girl was able to feel a connection to the rest of the world, she was no longer isolated from it and that feeling drew her to the window. Her eyes widened and she held her breath. It was beautiful.

The girl had imagined that the thick defensive wall she had steered their capsule through was wrapped around the de-Monte's stronghold. She could see now that this was not the case, this side of the hill needed no artificial defences. Instead, she found herself on top of a sheer cliff, and reaching out as far as she could see was a huge expanse of water. She looked across it and at the sun held in the blue sky above the horizon. She had never dreamt that so much water existed, let alone that it could be found in one place.

The window was set at a slight angle so that its top pushed out further from the room than its base. She placed her hands on the glass, and slowly allowed it to take some of her weight so that she could look almost directly down. Far below, she could see the deep blues, greens and near-black of the water. There seemed to be no end to its depth, plunging down and down into a never-ending darkness. It was like nothing she had ever imagined.

'Quite something,' said Jess.

'Yes Mistress. It's the most beautiful thing I've ever seen.'

They stood together in silence, next to each other, almost touching, gazing through the window.

'Hello Jess.' They both jumped at the voice. 'Or should that be Jess-Nichola-Trevelian, Mistress-of-Trevelian?'

'Adam!' Jess spun on her heels to face him as he approached.

'I heard you'd finally taken on some responsibility. About time too,' he said.

He flung his arms around her and squeezed. After a moment, she pushed herself away, smiling, and hooked a stray strand of hair back behind her ear.

'I thought you were…'

'What?' he shrugged, pretending that this was just some ordinary day, pretending this was a game played in childhood.

'I'd heard you'd escaped custody,' Jess's voice was soft.

Adam smiled. 'A fugitive from the law? A lot has happened since then. Long story.'

Jess reached up a hand and touched his cheek. Fine bristles had begun to grow across it, matching those on his scalp, but the sores on his temples were still visible.

'So I see,' she said, more serious now.

'And for you too. I heard about your father. I'm sorry.'

'He's in the medical suite. They're looking after him. Is Charles with you?'

'Yes, and some of our namesakes.'

Jess smiled, taking both of his hands in hers.

'It's good to see you,' she said.

'I've been an idiot Jess, an absolute idiot.'

Jess smiled, childhood regained. 'What else?' she teased.

'I mean it. This is my fault. I've let myself be used. I argued at Council that the namesakes should be freed. They agreed. But I was just being used, it was all about putting power into the hands of Seminary. Giving them control of the farms. If you control the food supply you control the city. It's my fault. I've helped make this happen.'

'You saved my cousins?'

The girl's voice made Adam look over to her, seeing her for the first time. She was still standing by the window, but her eyes were on Adam's.

'Did you say you'd saved my cousins?' she repeated.

'You're a namesake,' said Adam.

'I was Namesake-Trevelian.' The girl nodded.

'Was?' Adam looked from the girl to Jess.

'This is, she's...' said Jess, her cheeks flushing.

'I am given to the personal duty of Jess Nichola Trevelian, Mistress-of-Trevelian,' she said. 'I have yet to be given a name.' The closeness she had felt with her Mistress a few moments before left her with this statement.

'Did you say you'd brought the Percival namesakes with you?' she said.

Adam nodded. 'Those I could.'

'How many?'

'Those I could,' he repeated after a pause, his voice drawn taut with emotion.

The girl watched as Adam's eyes turned from those of a man, to a boy's. She could see his pain and it made her feel uncomfortable, cruel for asking the question.

'You saved their lives,' said Jess, touching her hand to Adam's arm.

He looked back at her and nodded: 'I guess.'

The girl frowned: 'May I ask a question?'

Adam and Jess both looked at her.

'How will the soil be nurtured with no namesakes at the holdings?'

Adam took a step back from them both and walked over to the window. He looked out across the water, his back to them, his tone quiet and almost matter-of-fact.

'The planting, care and harvesting of crops can all be done mechanically. The machines that you and your cousins operate can be made to work automatically. The Seminary will use these devices to plant and tend to the crops.'

'My question didn't relate to the care of the crops, my question was how will the soil be nurtured?'

Adam continued to look out through the window.

'I was told about a technique for conditioning the soil mechanically,' he said. 'This is what I took to Council, what convinced them to hand the estates over to Seminary.'

'But how?' asked the girl.

Adam turned to face her.

'What?' he said.

'How? How can the soil be nurtured without my cousins?'

The girl watched as Adam frowned and tilted his head to one side, regarding her.

'OK,' he said, 'when we ask you to nurture the soil, you take the decayed plant matter from previous seasons and spread it through the sterile sand. That about it?'

The girl nodded.

'Yes,' she said, 'the decaying husks and roots of the previous year are mixed with a little soil, added to the sand, kept warm and damp. It's turned and cared for, and blessed Veneta does her work.'

'All you're doing is mixing bacteria into the dirt,' he continued, 'and as the weeks go by you periodically turn the soil to spread bacteria through the beds to make it fertile. You turn the soil but it's the bacteria in the rotted husks and plants that does all the real work.'

He waited for the girl to react but she said nothing.

'Well, that doesn't need to happen anymore,' he said. 'The soil doesn't have to be made that way, there's a new way to do it.'

'How?' asked the girl.

Adam shook his head, becoming annoyed.

'How? Chemistry. The addition of something called a prompting culture. Some chemicals developed by Seminary that contain stronger bacteria which require less care and accelerate the process. Make it much faster. The culture can be added to the soil, mixed in by machines. The fertile soil is produced in a quarter of the time and there's no need for it to be done by hand.'

The girl shook her head.

'You can't mix the soil with a machine,' she said. 'How could a machine be made to honour Eisenia Veneta?'

Adam's voice exploded as his temper took hold of him.

'The soil is made by chemistry, the reactions take place as a result of bacteria spreading through the soil, not the intervention of some minor deity that no one has heard of.'

Adam's voice filled the room, but the girl did not react. Calm and considered she turned to Jess.

'Mistress, you told me that I was to speak up when something was not right, to tell you if something didn't look right. This is not right. Eisenia Veneta is not a deity, she's the earthworm who moves through the dust and sand, turning it to soil. She's the most important and precious organism. When we say we nurture the soil, what we mean is that we care for her. She would not survive if a machine turned the soil. She would be cut to pieces. The Seminarians will not succeed, they will not be able to make soil, their crops will fail, they will have no food from the farmlands.'

***

'Ah, here you are.'

Jess, Adam and the girl turned to find Rebecca standing in the shadows near the door.

'I trust that you managed to find some sleep.' She spoke to Jess but her eyes were on the girl. Observing. Interested.

Jess smiled.

'Thank you, yes. And thanks for all you're doing for father.'

Rebecca nodded and walked over to the desk, its dark rich wood drawing a semicircle around the middle of the room. She touched a panel at its side and the section in front of her rose to the height of her elbows so that she could lean upon it from her standing position. Voices approached and Charles, Mason and Dovac entered the room. Falling silent they took up positions around the desk and Jess and Adam joined them. Only the girl was set-apart, standing alone by the window. She looked at the faces around the table, stone-solemn and silent. It was Dovac who was the first to speak.

'So. It would appear that the world unravels before us once again.'

Eyes met eyes around the table.

'What do we know to be fact?' asked Rebecca.

Dovac turned to Mason and extended his right hand to indicate that the floor was his. The room was completely silent.

'That, is absolutely the right question,' said Mason. 'Here's what we know for sure, what we know to be fact.

We know that Seminary has been given charge of both the Percival and the Trevelian holdings, ostensibly to secure Amynthia's food supply in the light of the recent attacks. We also know that Demeter has been given the task of coordinating this operation. Council would have needed someone they could trust and no doubt considered her to be beyond any suspicion as her son, Ares, was killed in the blasts at Procession, and of course she was herself injured.'

Mason pursed his lips as he considered his next words.

'Now we must move from what we know to be fact, to what we might speculate to be truth.' He paused and looked in Rebecca's direction.

'I don't need to tell you, Matriarch, that Demeter has ample experience of command in the field. She was an accomplished tactician when she served under you in The Conflict. I think she has orchestrated this entire series of events. I think we're seeing the flowering of seeds planted long ago.'

He folded his arms in front of his chest before continuing.

'I left a couple of surveillance units at the Trevelian Chateau before we left. Last night I managed to view live feeds from the estate.'

'What did you see?' asked Jess.

Mason looked from Jess to Rebecca.

'Something that we cannot defeat.'

He paused and looked back at Jess. He would spare her the details of what he had witnessed on the cockpit's grainy display screen the night before. The young boy, naked save for a loin cloth and the ribbons tied loosely around his arms as decoration. His innocent body standing on the grass outside what remained of the Trevelian Chateau. The figures, gathered in two lines to form a corridor along which the boy was passively led, others throwing what Mason took to be barley seeds in his path.

The sight of Demeter smiling benevolently at the boy and onlookers, before drawing a knife from her sleeve and expertly slitting the boy's throat. His protracted ceremonial disembowelment and the macabre sharing of his organs with the faithful. Jess did not need to hear these details.

'I saw Demeter leading a blood dedication to one of the pantheon of The Twelve gods, in contravention of the first edict of the Church of the Holy Union,' he said. 'It would seem the aspect of The Twelve and the aspect of The One true God are no longer united. Our great experiment is over.'

Jess looked at Charles and Adam, who showed no reaction.

'You knew about this?' she said.

Adam looked at her and shook his head. She looked back to Mason.

'When you say blood dedication?' she asked.

Mason put his hands behind his back and looked at the floor for a moment.

'I saw Demeter recite the liturgy and carry out a sacrifice.'

Jess frowned. She spoke under her breath: 'In our home.'

'Which of the pantheon did they honour Mason?' Rebecca's tone was cool, business-like.

Mason looked the Matriarch in the eye, 'I couldn't see.'

'What was the sacrifice then?'

He paused, recalling the images, the gentle, willing movement of the boy, the knife, the blood.

'Human,' he said.

Rebecca stood erect, reaching out her hands and placing them on the desk in front of her as if to draw strength from the wood from which it was made.

'Then it's decided for us. She honours Zeus. There'll be no mercy for any of us when they come.'

An oppressive silence grew into the space in front of the table, its weight holding tongues still.

'But we're safe here,' it was Adam who eventually spoke: 'we're safe here in the Mount. They'll leave us be.'

Charles reached out his hand to his son's.

'No. We're far from safe,' he said.

Adam shook his head.

'They'll leave us be. They have our lands and we're safe here.'

'No,' said Charles, 'you don't understand the focus they'll have. It's like nothing in the world that you've known. They mean to re-establish the worship of the pantheon of gods. They mean to bring about the glorification of The Twelve and the subjugation of The One. They must crush all those who stand counter to that. They'll want nothing other than to kill. Their gods will demand this of them. The sacrifice Mason-of-Trevelian witnessed was the first step along this path. They'll hunt us down along with all in Amynthia who do not agree to join Temple.'

Adam's face was pale. Silenced.

'Sir,' Dovac spoke directly to Adam, 'your father is quite correct. The sacrifice at the Trevelian estate means we're in mortal danger. We don't know the situation at our own holdings, but the actions of the Citizen that precipitated our departure would suggest that Demeter has control there too. They will come for us.'

'But surely we're safe here. This place is built for safety,' said Adam.

All eyes turned to Rebecca Catherine Valerie de-Monte.

'I have done what I can,' she said. 'Certain intelligence became available to me a little while ago. An old comrade of mine brought us word of a faction within the Church loyal to those who fought for the pantheon during The Conflict. This is what prompted my invitation to you,

Jess. I made provision here at the Mount such that we'll be able to survive a prolonged siege. But we have no defence against aggression. If they bring battle machines to our gates we have little by way of retaliation to offer.'

Again, silence.

'Mason,' she continued, 'you've the most experience in the front line of battle. What are your thoughts?'

Mason looked down at the desk in front of him for a moment before replying.

'You're right when you say we won't be able to defend ourselves against an all-out attack. But having been on the receiving end of the pantheon's aggression, I'm not sure that such an attack will be her preferred option.'

He looked directly at Rebecca as he said this.

'Would it not serve her purposes better to have us as prisoners?' he said.

Rebecca thought for a moment and then gave an almost imperceptible nod.

'I agree,' she spoke to Mason and then to the rest of the room, 'I agree. She'll want prisoners. She'll want to make a public show of us. To demonstrate her strength.'

'Then that is our advantage,' said Mason turning to the others. 'We can use it to buy us a little time at least. My suggestion is that we do two things. The first is to get help from the city. If we use a transmission, it'll be monitored so we must do this in person. We need to get someone away in the transport capsule, someone whose voice will be respected. They can explain to Council what's going on and ask for help. I suggest that Charles does this. They will listen to you, Sir, and will act on your words.

'The second thing we need to do is get everyone else away from the Mount. I suggest that the rest of you make for a place of safety. Take some supplies and the means to be self-sufficient for a while, and find yourselves a remote bolt-hole somewhere. If Charles is successful, and can manage to get us some help, you can return when you judge it's safe. In the meantime, Rebecca, ma'am, you and I should negotiate with Demeter, we should offer our surrender in return for the others' freedom. She won't honour any such terms but it'll buy Charles and the others some time.'

Dovac cleared his throat.

'Mason, I trust your judgement of course, but there's a great risk in going to Amynthia. Demeter will have many allies in the city, it's even possible that there's been a coordinated mobilisation of the temples. The city may already be under her control. There may be a very tight and dangerous situation there, too dangerous for the Patriarch of my Family. I suggest that I make that journey as his emissary. It'll be easier for me to find my way safely through the city should there be issues, and I can deliver his words.'

'No, Dovac,' said Charles, 'the Council and what elders will listen, must hear from me in person. It would not be enough simply to send a message; there will I'm sure need to be some persuasion applied to the matter. I don't doubt your diplomatic skills, but this task calls for my personal involvement.'

'Father and I will go together,' said Adam.

'Sir,' said Dovac, 'may I suggest that I accompany you on the journey instead of the young master? Your son's leadership and experience will be invaluable to the group in their establishment of a place of safety beyond these walls.'

'I agree,' said Charles, grateful for the way in which Dovac had phrased his words. 'Adam, you and Jess have a duty of care to your staff and namesakes, that is your responsibility. You must take them to a place of safety.'

'We should act right away,' said Mason, 'we may not have much time.'

CHAPTER EIGHTEEN

Rebecca, Mason and the girl were alone in the chamber, the others having left in a silent flurry to put Mason's plan into action. The girl could feel the heat of the sun coming through the window onto her back but the coolness of the Matriarch's blue eyes on her face made her want to shiver. The eyes were studying her. The girl lifted her chin and met them full on.

Silence.

'Tell me about this one Mason, she intrigues me.'

Mason turned from the door. He paused for a moment before replying, speaking directly to Rebecca but with his eyes on the girl.

'She was gifted to the Trevelian Family at the age of six, as you know, and has served the Family with loyalty ever since. Her service has been given without reserve.'

'Mmm. But she has a fire does she not? And not a fire carried since her gifting. One that she has acquired more recently.'

The girl could see Mason's cheeks redden slightly.

'As you know ma'am, she was caught in the blast at the Trevelian holdings. Two of her cousins were cut down in front of her and her own life nearly taken.'

Rebecca nodded slowly.

'And you say that it was this experience that moved her mind?'

Mason's silence was offered as affirmation.

'I say differently,' she said. 'I say that her mind would not have reacted so to the provocations you list, despite their traumatic nature. I say that her conditioning was designed to be robust even in circumstances such as those. Tell me, Mason-of-Trevelian, what else has befallen this "little one" to make her so…,' she searched for the right word, '…assertive?'

The girl had thought that she was the subject of the conversation, but the way Rebecca had turned her face toward Mason as she said this last word made her feel as if it were he who was being interrogated, being accused of something.

Mason looked at Rebecca. He pursed his lips slightly but made no reply.

Rebecca gave him a knowing smile as her eyelids tightened, her gaze focussing back on the girl.

'And what do you say, my dear? Does this explanation strike you as correct? Have the demands placed upon you been the forge on which your character has been struck?'

The girl looked from Rebecca to Mason and back.

'I have simply applied what I know from the fields.'

'Which is?'

The girl's serpent made her look directly into the Matriarch's eyes as she replied.

'Which is, that it is not the strongest or the fittest that survive, but the most adaptable. So it is with the crops in the field, so it is for us all. We must adapt to the world if we are to thrive.'

'Interesting,' said Rebecca.

She turned back to Mason.

'She tells me that she no longer finds meaning or truth in her faith. How does your explanation account for this, Mason-of-Trevelian?'

Silence.

'I think you've taken it from her, Mason. Tell me if this is not so.'

The girl could see that he was hit by the question, as if suddenly tripped by it. A brave warrior brought down by an expert opponent on the battlefield. A split second later he had regained his balance.

'There's been darkness and much to endure in her life,' he said. 'She's seen things that no one should have to see and has shown a great bravery in meeting them head on. And all the while showing loyalty to the Family. She's no fool. She asked how such things could be allowed and yes, when she did, I explained the facts behind the creation of the Church of the Holy Union. I explained it all, and I did so because I felt, I still feel, that she is owed the truth.'

Mason had turned side on and was now leaning on the desk over the diminutive Matriarch. But somehow it was she that looked down at him.

The girl watched as Mason broke from her gaze and focussed his eyes on the floor. How strange, she thought, that he should behave so around this woman.

'You felt that you owed her the truth?' Rebecca let the words hang. '*You* felt this. What was it I wonder that led you to believe that it was your debt to pay, or your truth to tell?'

Mason continued to look at the floor, his eyes held there by Rebecca's presence.

'And when was the last time she had caldi?' Her words were sharp and came fast, accusing Mason of something the girl could not quite grasp.

'Very well,' said Rebecca, straightening her small body and walking over to the door, 'if she's owed the truth then she must have it all. Come with me my dear, there is something you need to see.'

The girl looked to Mason for any hint of what might be in store for her, but he would not look her in the eye. Instead he walked over to the window, showing her his back and broad shoulders as he stared out across the water.

***

The doorway through which they left the room was hidden behind a gold and brown tapestry long enough to nearly touch the floor. It was old and had become faded in the light flooding through the large window, and its images of animals hunting or being hunted were well hidden in its threads. Rebecca held the curtain to one side, allowing the girl to enter the passage it concealed. As she followed, she allowed the textile to swing back into position leaving, them in an abrupt darkness.

'Keep moving straight ahead,' she said to the girl as she pushed past, 'there's nothing to trip you and your eyes will soon adjust.'

The girl followed Rebecca as she shuffled along apparently unhindered by the lack of light. After a short while she could pick out the sides of the narrow tunnel through which they were walking. There was a source of light ahead of them and dim though it was, it had made its way up to meet them. The tunnel's sides were rough unfinished stone and were narrow enough for the girl to reach out her arms and touch both sides at once. The passage was on a slight downward incline but quite straight, leading directly back into the hill.

After perhaps two minutes of walking they came to a wooden door set into the solid wall that marked the end of the tunnel. Above the door was the source of the light that had spilled up the passageway: a single lamp whose shade directed its light down around the doorway. Rebecca stopped at the side of the door and turned to the girl, the light casting an odd shadow from her nose down across the side of her mouth. She interlaced her fingers across her stomach, her thumbs bouncing against one another in a way that the girl thought made her seem nervous.

'Tell me my dear, what do you remember of your early years?'

The girl frowned, not understanding the question.

'Before you were gifted? Before you joined the Family Trevelian? What do you remember of those years?'

The girl shook her head: 'Nothing ma'am, like all the namesakes I was a foundling, rescued from poverty and hopelessness and gifted to my Family when I was very young. I don't remember that time.'

Rebecca's sharp eyes watched.

'Mmm. Now that is interesting.' She spoke to herself, lifting her chin and studying the ceiling of the tunnel.

'Why do you say that?' asked the girl.

'Why?' Rebecca looked down from her thoughts and back to the girl.

'Why do you say that it's interesting?'

'It's interesting because it tells me something new.'

The girl's serpent tightened her coils.

'And what is that?'

Rebecca smiled.

'You do have a challenging tone to your questions my dear. Well, I think it tells me that your cleaning was effective and that your atypical demeanour has indeed developed as a result of deficiencies in your care.'

The girl's serpent became angry, she could feel her twisting in her belly.

'The caldi is a drug isn't it? That's what you mean,' the girl almost spat the accusation.

'You have questions I am sure.'

Keeping her eyes on the girl, Rebecca reached out her left hand and pushed at the door. It slid to the side, allowing light and sound to spill out into the tunnel, the sudden brightness pushed into the girl's face by a wall of noise that hit her head on. She blinked and it took a moment for her to realise that the sound was that of children playing.

'In you go,' said Rebecca with a nod, 'welcome home.'

The girl stared back at those blue eyes before walking through the doorway.

The room that she entered was long and thin and brightly lit, and its white walls were painted with colourful childish pictures of flowers and trees that came up to the height of her waist. She did not count them, but there were perhaps a dozen children playing in the room, from toddlers to one who was five or six years old. It was this child who first looked up at her. She had been sitting on the floor drawing something on a piece of paper weighed down in front of her. Two young boys played a chaotic game of some sort around her. She looked up from her picture at the sound of the door closing, saw Rebecca and stood.

'Hello mother.'

As soon as she spoke, a young woman got to her feet and clapped her hands. She had been kneeling in the corner holding the arms of a toddler who had been dancing and giggling. The child now clung to the woman's legs. The two boys stopped their game and the rest of the room joined them in their still-silence.

'Ma'am,' the young woman spoke to Rebecca but stared at the girl, her expression one of surprise.

Rebecca made no response other than to nod an acknowledgement. She walked past the children-statues to a door in the opposite corner of the room.

'Come my dear,' she said to the girl.

The second door opened into a corridor decorated with childish motifs similar to those in the room they had just left. There were doors running along the corridor, each held open so that the girl could see a single, neatly-made child-sized bed in each room. She followed Rebecca along the corridor as it curved gently around to the right until they reached its end.

'That was the nursery,' said Rebecca, 'I can tell you have no recollection of it, but that was where you spent the first years of your life.'

Without waiting for a response and with no regard for any emotional reaction the girl might be having, Rebecca pushed at the door in front of them.

'And this is where you began.'

The girl followed her through the door into a room with white walls, floor and ceiling. As they entered, sterile lights flickered and blinked until the space was very brightly lit. The only furniture was a metal rack in the middle of the floor holding white coats on hooks strung along its length. The rack was constructed from white tubular metal with a bench seat that ran along either side. Under the bench were a row of open shelves on which pairs of white boots were neatly positioned.

'To keep the dust and dirt at bay,' said Rebecca as she moved to the farthest end of the rack and sat down to remove her shoes, swapping them for the ones on the shelf. 'Any of them will fit you,' she said.

The girl took the hint and pulled a pair of boots from the nearest shelf. They were simple ankle-length seamless boots that did not require any fastening. She sat on the bench, removed her own shoes, and slipped them onto her feet. She did not feel anxious. Her mind was calm. She followed Rebecca's lead and pulled a white coat over her clothes.

'Let's have a look at you.' Rebecca straightened the collar of the girl's coat and fastened the top-most clasp around her neck.

'Ready?'

The girl nodded.

Rebecca walked to the far side of the room and entered a small corridor with a metal door at one end. It was a cramped space, long enough for perhaps three people to stand one behind the other. She turned her head and spoke over her shoulder to the girl.

'Come.'

The girl walked into the small corridor.

'Close up behind me now,' said Rebecca.

The girl took a step closer and Rebecca grasped a handle that was set into the door, twisting it through ninety degrees until it was vertical. A door slid closed behind them, sealing the two women into the small space. Rebecca twisted the handle through another ninety degrees and then let it go. The door in front of them slid open and the girl blinked as she felt a gentle current of warm damp air blow into her face.

The chamber in front of them had no other door. Like the tunnels and corridors through which they had walked, it had no source of natural light. As they entered, lamps in the join between the walls and ceiling blinked into life, creating a space with no shadows. In the centre of the room a dark rectangular box was positioned on a plinth. A mess of cables and thin tubes flowed down to it from a large panel on the ceiling. There was nothing else in the room.

To the girl, the rectangular box looked a little like the medi-tubes she was familiar with, except it was shorter and was clad in a rich dark wood whose surface was ornately decorated with patterns of leaves and plants. Its beauty seemed out of place in the sterile environment in which it sat.

Rebecca walked over to the box and looked down through a thick glass window set into its lid. The girl followed suit. The edges of the glass were bevelled and they split the stark light of the room into rainbows. The designs carved around its edges reminded the girl of a mirror that used to hang in the rooms of her Mistress back at the Trevelian estate. The inside of the box was dark and the girl struggled to see its contents. She could only make out what seemed to be a dark irregular mass roughly the shape of a bowl. Its internal surface was textured, not smooth, but its contents, if it contained anything, were lost to the shadows.

'So,' said Rebecca after a moment, 'Mason has told you of The Conflict and of the struggle in which some of us engaged to bring our society back from the brink.' She placed her hands on the lid of the box and turned her head to face the girl.

'He told you something of the formation of the Church of the Holy Union. Of its origin and its purpose in keeping the peace. Of its function in keeping the religious needs of our citizens satiated but muzzled. To promote and keep a peace that would first allow us to survive and then to thrive. But the Church has another purpose.'

Her blue blue eyes looked into the girl's, lost for a moment in the deep brown pools.

'What he clearly did not explain was that it was your very existence that made the construction of the Church all the more necessary.'

The girl straightened her body slightly. Attentive.

'A secure and stable food supply is the foundation on which any society must be built. Whoever controls the food, controls the state. The construction of our society, the liberty of our citizens, the building of the city of Amynthia, none of this would have been possible without you, without the namesakes to undertake this work. Your working of the land was an absolute necessity. The Church was created, in part, to help you do this.'

The girl felt Rebecca's eyes examine her, gathering data from an experiment.

'One of the lessons learned by those of us who survived The Conflict, was that faith could drive a person to do most anything. During the war the power of faith was manifest in butchery, rape and suffering. People who considered themselves to be "good" perpetrated the most hideous deeds and wiped their conscience clean on their faith. Faith is a powerful and a persuasive master, but faith, if properly controlled, can be used to help people do good things, to serve society and to benefit their fellows. And this is the other function of The Church of the Holy Union. Both servant and monarch must be suitably motivated to carry out their duties. Faith can be applied to both cases. You, that is the namesakes, were set to servitude by the careful application of faith. Your religion is your hope. Your life is one of service but...'

'...but our faith sets us free,' said the girl, finishing Rebecca's sentence by quoting the motto that she had read and recited every time she had entered the Trevelian Chapel. For a moment, she was back in her cell, the distant voices of her cousins in the refectory as she dressed, the sweet smell of the flowers outside her window in the summer months. It was all gone and in that moment she felt its loss.

The girl looked back at Rebecca.

'Why have you brought me here to tell me this?' she asked. 'Why do you have children here?'

Rebecca continued to watch, leaving enough space for the girl to make the leap on her own.

'When you said that this is where I began, you meant that like the children back there you bring the foundlings here before gifting us to the families. You brought me here when I was a child didn't you?'

'No my dear. You were no foundling. This is where you began.' She tapped the window of the casket: 'This is where you all begin.'

'But...?'

'We needed hands to repair our damaged soil. To bring it back to life after the war. We needed namesakes, so we made you. You understand, I take it, how children come to be born? Through the union of a man and a woman, yes?'

'Yes. I understand where children come from, it's something we are asked to renounce...,' her voice faded and this time it was Rebecca who finished the sentence.

'You are asked to renounce such things by your articles of faith. You see, it's a powerful tool, and when used properly quite unobtrusive.'

She turned back to the casket and continued almost as if she were giving a lecture to a student.

'A woman will typically carry many hundreds of thousands of cells capable of developing into eggs. Oh, if nature is allowed to take its course the vast majority of these will never fully develop. But if isolated and kept in the appropriate conditions, each one has the potential to be the start of a life. Here, beneath this glass, is the womb from which such cells are harvested; where they are nurtured and cared for. When the time comes, we pluck one from its home and bring it to life. Nineteen years and forty-one days ago, that life was yours.'

The girl looked down into the dark bowl beneath the glass.

'It was given to me by a brave and wonderful woman,' said Rebecca, 'she gave it freely. She was one of the very few who were suitable for the process. She knew this and she gave her life for the greater good.'

The girl placed her hand on the glass, tried to connect with the flesh beneath her own hazy reflection.

'Did she have a name?' almost a whisper.

Rebecca looked at the girl as if considering whether to answer or not.

'Her name was Evelyn.'

Here and in this moment a daughter met her mother for the first time. In a sterile metal-walled room in the centre of a mountain, in a box on a plinth under a stark unnatural light, blood and flesh together.

The girl frowned: 'The children, out there,' she nodded her head in the direction of the corridor down which they had walked, 'they're namesakes?'

'Yes my dear, they are namesakes. They're your cousins.'

'Then why did one of them call you "mother"? You're not their mother, here is their mother, our mother.'

The girl heard the door behind her slide open and she felt a breath of warm damp air flowing down from the box attached to the ceiling above the plinth. She turned to see who had opened the door and there within an arm's reach stood The Menace; the ghoul that had come to her in her dreams. The one who's foul breath had whispered in her face, who had held her motionless to her bed, was standing within touching distance. She had banished him from her nightmare by chasing away the shadows in which he hid with the light from her mouth, but here there were no shadows and yet The Menace was unafraid, staring at her with his blue blue eyes. Fear pulled the air from her lungs and turned her legs to stone. The Menace spoke.

'Rebecca, what are you doing?'

'I am appraising our daughter of the truth.'

The man looked back to the girl. He was The Menace of her nightmares; she knew this to be a certainty. But the grip-fear squeezing the breath out of her body and the life out of her heart was giving way to something else. His eyes were telling her that he was not to be feared. As he looked into her face she could breathe again. She turned to Rebecca.

'You're quite right my dear when you say that Evelyn was your mother. But the creation of a life requires a woman and a man, and this man before you is your father and he is my twin. Through him you have as much of me about you as you do of Evelyn. I am every bit as much your mother as she.'

The girl felt as if Rebecca had been nurturing this information for years. Holding it in a nest of spite, waiting to spit it into her face. Now she had, there was nothing left for her to say. She and The Menace both looked at the girl. The girl did all she knew how to, and stood her ground.

CHAPTER NINETEEN

Dovac's eyes moved across the console of dim yellow dials. The Percival transport was still attached to its umbilical service tube but the power cells were close to fully laden. They could leave as soon as they wished. He looked out through the front window of the cockpit and watched the namesakes as they attended to the Trevelian capsule sitting alongside, filling it with crates of supplies and provisions in readiness for their exile to some place of safety. He wondered where they would head.

From his position in the cabin he could not see the faces of those box-carrying ants, not that he could tell one from another in any case. He was hard pressed to recognise a Percival from a Trevelian namesake now that they had all been thrown together. Which was it that wore their hair in a plait? He could not recall for sure. He scanned the console once again, finding some comfort in the familiarity of its backlight-glow. He flicked a couple of switches and turned dials to check the various relays he already knew to be working and tapped at the needle registering the health of the power cells.

'Dovac, would you come through please.' Charles's voice came through the speaker over Dovac's head.

He straightened his cuffs and slid his body along the console toward the door that led into the passenger compartment. It was good to see his master sitting in the plush cabin. Dovac felt that some semblance of order had been restored to the world. Here was Charles Edwin George Percival, Patriarch of the Family Percival, seated in his own environment. Never mind that the Percival holdings had been lost, nor that this great man's domain was now limited to the control of this craft and this servant. The hierarchy that Dovac sought in his life was here in front of him.

'Sir.'

'Ah, there you are Dovac,' said Charles without looking up from the display on the table. 'How's our transport?'

'We can leave as soon as you wish Sir. The power cells are fully laden and will easily see us to the city and back.'

Charles did not acknowledge his servant's reply, but continued to study the display in front of him. Dovac, well used to his master's ways, stood patiently and in silence. It was a full minute before Charles spoke.

'Good,' he said, 'I want us to get underway straight away then. Come and take a look at this will you.'

Dovac walked around his master and looked down across his shoulder at the map of Amynthia.

'You were correct when you said that Demeter may already have placed a strangle-hold on the city,' said Charles. 'It's at least foreseeable and we shouldn't ignore the possibility. I want us to get to The Step as quickly and directly as possible. We can then convene Council and allow them to mobilise what forces they see fit to put an end to this abhorrence.'

Charles paused, waiting for his servant to consider the plan.

'Sir, if I may speak freely?'

Charles nodded.

'I know you said that you needed to speak to Council, but why not let me carry the plea on your behalf? Please reconsider. I'm well known at Council and I'm sure the message will be heard and taken seriously. Please Sir, there's no benefit in us both taking this risk.'

Charles leaned back in his seat, his eyes still on Dovac's.

'I agree with you Dovac. Only one of us should take the risk. But it must be me that makes the journey. I don't doubt your skills but we can't leave anything to chance, it's my presence that's needed. If only one of us is to make this journey, then it must be me. You should be the one to stay behind.'

Dovac raised his chin and drew in his breath, as if his military ghost was pulling him up to attention.

'No Sir, I shall accompany you.'

'Very well.' Charles nodded. 'Come then, what do you think of the plan?'

'Sir, if you will allow, I should like to make a comment and a suggestion?'

'Go ahead.'

'I agree that we should undertake our mission with the expectation that Demeter will be ready to move against us. But I suggest that rather than head directly for The Step and Council, we arrive in Amynthia as quietly and unobtrusively as is possible. If Demeter has her spies in the city, the arrival of our capsule will surely be noted. If so, we will never reach The Step.'

He placed his hand on the map, indicating a region on the outskirts of the city.

'We can leave the capsule somewhere here, and make our way to Council by some other means. If we can find our way to this location under the cover of the solar collectors, we have a chance of arriving undetected. In any case this is an industrial zone so if we are spotted the arrival of a vehicle will not be unusual. We can find a transport in one of the industrial units, override its automatic functions and ride it to The Step.'

Charles considered the suggestion for a moment.

'This will delay the delivery of our message to Council, Dovac, and time is not with us.'

'I agree, but if we don't arrive at all our message will never reach the ears of those who can help. If we send a coded message to The Authority before we leave, she can assemble Council in readiness. The delay in the delivery of our message will be minimal. It's my judgement that the extra time it will take is a price worth paying.'

Charles considered the point for a moment and then nodded.

'Let's get underway then. Make the transmission to The Authority.'

***

'...I have no idea Adam, but this is the best option open to us.'

Adam and Jess stood side by side within the passenger compartment of the Trevelian capsule. Jess looked at the map on the table in front of them, Adam stared out of the porthole that faced across the de-Monte compound to his own Family's transport capsule.

Jess looked at him when he did not reply.

'Adam.'

She could not tell if he was thinking about what she had just said, or was concerned about the imminent departure of his father on what was likely to be a dangerous journey. Perhaps his lack of engagement was some feature of the interrogation he had invited at the hands of The Curate? Who knew what that could do to a mind.

'Why don't you go over and see how they're doing?' she offered softly. 'Adam?'

His attention was suddenly back with her.

'No. No, I don't need to do that. My point, put simply, is that if our job is to take the namesakes and your Family's staff to a place of safety, running off to some random point of the compass hardly achieves that duty of care.'

The patronising barb in Adam's response was not lost on Jess but she decided to leave it untouched.

'It's not a random point of the compass, it's the direction that offers us the greatest likelihood of safety. The land between us and the city cannot offer any refuge, neither can that which lies between us and either of our Family's holdings. We must cross the water.'

'But we don't know what lies beyond.'

'We know that no one lies beyond.'

'Not for certain.'

'No, not for certain but as far as we know there's no one there. Not since the war. It's the best option. The one most likely to deliver us.'

She watched as he took a deep breath. How could he not want to see his father before he left, she thought? She would not have been able to be so cold if her own father were about to leave on such a journey.

'OK. We'll do that,' he said, 'we'll head out across the water in the capsule and take our chances. We'll try to find a suitable location to get holed-up in. You're right.'

Jess waited for more but that was it. Clearly the argumentative Adam who had knocked back the idea was no longer with them. She decided that since this was the case, the conversation must be at an end.

'I'll go and check how they're doing with the gear,' she said.

Jess moved over to the door and walked down the ramp into the compound. Adam could see her speaking to one of the Trevelian namesakes. There was nodding and pointing but he could not hear what passed between them.

He looked back over to the Percival capsule. The internal lamps were on but he could not see his father or Dovac. He wanted to walk over there, he wanted to speak to his father but he felt as if his feet were held to the floor.

For most of his adult life Adam had placed a distance between himself and his father. He had wanted to show him that he could stand independently, that he could choose and follow a path that was of his own design, that he could do something significant with his life and make his father proud. His thesis to free the namesakes had been part of that agenda, and when Citizen Owen had offered him his help, he thought he had succeeded. What a fool. He had seen himself as a visionary, he had believed that no one else could see what he could see, that his insight was special and wise and superior. Once he had been interrogated by The Curate, he had thought Citizen Owen saw things the same way. But the simple truth was that he had allowed himself to believe what he had wanted to believe. He had allowed himself to be manipulated. The Citizen had seen him for the fool that he was and made use of him.

Struck by this thought he wanted no more than to be held in the arms of his father as he had been as a child. To be back in those arms in those times.

He ducked his head as he moved through the hatch into the cockpit. He wanted to occupy himself, to find some distraction and there was plenty to do. He had intended to start by activating the control panel and checking the status of the power cells, but once he had squeezed behind the controls his purpose seemed to leave him. He stood in silence, his hands limp by his side. It was as if he were in a cocoon that would not let him touch or interact with anything around him. He was isolated, numb, in his own private space where nothing could reach him. Nothing could penetrate the bubble-shield around him and he could not reach out to anything outside of it.

He stood like that for a while, in the darkness of the cockpit, until becoming aware of a rhythmic 'crack, crack, crack' from the compound. It was the sound of the motors of the Percival capsule being started. He shook away his malaise and looked out of the window. He could see Dovac in the cockpit preparing to take the capsule out of the compound and was overtaken by an urge to speak with his father. The sound changed to a low-pitched rumble as the motors came to life and began to run up to speed. He needed to see his father, to stand by his side, to share the same air. He needed to be held by him right now.

He hit the intercom switch.

'Dovac.'

Adam could see Dovac look across from the Percival cockpit.

'Yes Sir.'

'Wait. I need to speak to father, Dovac. Right now.'

Adam let go of the switch and pushed himself out of the cockpit toward the door. His father was already facing him from the Percival transport's exit hatch by the time his feet hit the dirt of the compound. He could feel his heart begin to race. It finally made sense, he needed to talk.

As soon as Charles had reached the bottom step, the hatch closed behind him and the motors ramped up to full power. A dirty skirt of dust and debris flew up around the capsule's stabilisers to the height of Charles's knees.

'No. Dovac, no.' Charles tried to get alongside the cockpit window. 'Dovac, stop.'

The capsule rotated slowly within its own length until it faced the large doors sealing the compound. It hovered for a moment as the doors groaned apart. The transport lifted itself a little higher into the air, and then its tail rose slightly, edging it forward through the gap in the great wall. There was no way of stopping it: Charles and Adam watched it leave the compound through the tightening gap as the doors closed. And then, just before they sealed, through an opening no wider than the length of an arm, a great green flash of light.

The fireball hung in the air where the capsule had been a moment before. And then there was nothing.

***

Mason and Jess had been working in different parts of the compound: Jess with the namesakes around the cargo bay of the Trevelian transport, Mason half way up the steps to the hill. As soon as the Percival's transport began to power-up, the namesakes around Jess instinctively moved into the cargo hold in anticipation of the dust that would soon fill the air. Jess remained where she was, her attention drawn by Adam's appearance at the capsule's ramp.

As the Percival transport moved out through the gates, something pulled at Mason. He would not have the opportunity to look back at this moment and consider just what it was that had pricked at him. Perhaps a sound from his distant past, or a reflection of light skimming the top of the defensive wall, in any case some tension in the air made him move quickly toward Jess. He reached her at the very moment the Percival ship was vaporised. He grabbed her body, wrapping his bulk around it, pushing her to the ground beneath him. He could feel the heat on his back in the moments it took the gates to fully close.

***

Jess was buried in Mason's chest. Pinned to the earth but not crushed. He lifted himself from her with the agility of a much younger man, and turned to check that the gates had fully closed. He held out his hand and pulled her up to her feet.

'We must get inside immediately,' he turned his face toward her as he spoke, his mouth exaggerating the shape of each word.

The shrill scream made by the disintegrating vessel had left their ears dull, and to Jess it was as if she were listening to Mason's voice through metre-thick walls. But she understood his meaning as he pushed her toward the steps leading up to the inside of the hill.

'I'll get the others,' he shouted and headed toward the cargo hold. 'Run!'

By the time she had stumbled her way up the first few steps, the namesakes were right behind her. Their movement was not panicked, but they moved efficiently, as one body. Jess turned to see Mason shepherding them along in front of him. Their tide swept her up the steps to the door that led into the hillside. Seconds later they were all inside the tunnel with the door sealed behind them and the lights flickering to life.

The tunnel was cool and dim and, except for their laboured breathing, it was silent.

Mason pushed his way through the namesakes to Jess, followed by Adam.

'We're all here,' he said.

Adam looked at him, his expression said they were not "all here". Mason acknowledged his unspoken challenge with a tightening of his lips and a nod of his head.

Jess could think a little more clearly now that they were inside.

'What just happened?' she asked.

Mason was still looking at Adam as he replied.

'Dovac-of-Percival was killed.'

Adam's expression did not change. He continued to stare at Mason. The lights gave a flicker and for a moment they were all in darkness. There was a distant groan of machinery, like a great beast trapped deep within a cave, and the lights were back.

'We must move up through the tunnel, we must get everyone to safety.' Mason turned to the namesakes: 'Make your way up the tunnel.'

Without question, the namesakes began to move up into the hill with Mason and Jess following along behind the last of them.

Adam looked around for his father and found him sitting in the shadows with his back against the door to the tunnel; crumpled, empty-looking, his face beginning to redden from the effects of the blast. He walked the few steps back down the incline toward him and knelt on one knee.

'Father.'

The others had moved up and around the first corner of the tunnel; apart from the last few shadows and the echoes of movement, they were alone.

'Father, come. We must make our way into the Mount.' He reached out to take his father's hand but Charles withdrew it.

'Father, we must go.'

Charles raised his head and Adam found himself looking into an old man's eyes that were slowly filling with tears.

'Dovac is dead Adam, the future is dead, there's no more Amynthia, there's no future.'

They looked at each other, now completely alone.

'When you were born, I made myself a promise that your life would not be wasted in war, Adam. Not wasted like mine but lived to fulfilment. Doing whatever you wanted to do with it, to make of it what you chose. I've failed you. It was a dream, a bird that could never take to the skies. Nothing I've done has made a difference, nothing has changed. The beast still hunts us. War is here and I've failed you, we all have. It's over.'

Adam wrapped his arms around his father, pulling his torso away from the door as he did so. An out of focus world snapped into clarity.

'No father, you've not failed, you've built something great and worthy. You created a world where I, where we all, could thrive and prosper away from the shadow of war. And I have thrived. But now it's time I did my share.'

Their embrace moved their worlds a little closer together.

***

Further up the tunnel Jess was still feeling stunned. She and Mason walked in silence up the stone-walled corridor, a few paces behind the rest of the group. They were walking quickly but the tunnel seemed to go on and on. Clearly the trolley that had taken them to and fro within the hill had travelled at a deceptively high speed.

'Mason, what exactly happened back there?' she asked.

Mason maintained his silence for ten or so paces before he answered.

'The transport was attacked.'

Jess felt a fear grow in her chest.

'I thought perhaps it was a malfunction of some kind. Some problem with the motors or something. Are you sure?' she asked.

'I'm quite sure. It was hit by a weapon. My guess is that it was fired from a great distance. Something focussed at the entrance waiting for the first thing that came through those gates. If it had come from something close at hand, the opening would have been breached and the compound overrun. It was something aimed at the gate from a great distance. We may yet have a little time.'

They continued to walk, the gradient now slowing their progress.

'Is there such a weapon?'

'The Conflict was a golden age for the scientists and engineers,' he said. 'No project with the potential to kill was left without resource. There's no limit to the extent to which technology can be turned to deliver destruction.'

'But all weaponry was decommissioned at the end of the war. Before the foundation of the city.'

'The last ten minutes would suggest otherwise.'

They walked on without exchanging any more words, the sound of their footsteps bouncing around the tunnel. Jess's world moved a little further into the darkness as she walked along the shadowy corridor. This was the world in which her father and Mason had lived and grown. The one she had heard of but never experienced. A world of fear and violence. She had caught a glimpse of it when her Family's holdings had been attacked but had not recognised it for what it was. She had still not understood whilst sitting in her father's wrecked office with her hand on the medi-tube that held his broken body. But now she knew it for what it was. Here was the world as it had always been. Amynthia had been an experiment born out of the desperation of war. But it had failed. It had been hopeless. The need to conquer and dominate would always rise.

War was reality.

CHAPTER TWENTY

Citizen Owen smiled: 'Fuck them,' he said under his breath, and then clearly into the room, 'connect me to Demeter.'

A second or so later the image of The Living Saint of Famine floated in front of him.

'Citizen?' it said.

'Honoured Demeter. I can report that Charles Edwin George Percival and Dovac-of-Percival are dead.'

***

The transport capsule in which Demeter stood was resting in the compound of the Trevelian Chateau. The mirror-curves of its outer skin stained with the blood-red emblem depicting her office of Living Saint. She looked at the image of the Citizen as it shimmied in front of her.

'Explain,' she said.

'I picked up a transmission to the office of The Authority.' Owen's voice was bloated with pride. 'The Patriarch and his servant were preparing to make a run to

Amynthia and speak to Council. I picked them off as they left the de-Monte estate.'

'You "picked them off"?' The silence was punctuated by the crackles that hitched their way alongside the transmission.

'And at what point did I give you permission to do that?'

'Permission? Demeter, if they had reached the city and alerted Council all would've been lost. I acted to protect us. I acted to ensure our success.'

'You acted out of embarrassment at having been outwitted by a naïve youth and a weak old man. You were tasked with holding them at the Percival estate and instead they got the better of you and escaped.'

'No, Demeter. I acted to honour the gods, you are wrong and you will give me an apology.'

'You are a fool and if I decide to I will give you your life.'

She watched as the threat twisted in his belly. She knew he understood that she could make good on such a promise, she could see it in his face.

'I had anticipated such a move by the Families,' she continued, 'and seen to it that Council could not obstruct us. If a member were to raise a concern, I've arranged for others to call for debate. Council would not be able to move against us for weeks and by that time all will have gone our way.'

The Citizen was silent.

'I had a use for the Percival Patriarch. By bringing about his death you've succeeded in making our work a little harder. And you have shown our hand.'

She gave a cold and ruthless interpretation of a smile as she watched him swallow deeply, a nervous reaction he had never been able to control or disguise.

'You will confine your future actions to those that we have discussed and which I have explicitly sanctioned.'

Demeter closed the link and spoke into the panel in front of her.

'Bring me a status report on the Trevelian holdings.'

A young man appeared at the entrance to the transport. He was tall and athletically slim and his blond hair and pale eyes marked him out as a thing of beauty. He wore a black tunic and kilt, and the insignia of The Seminary that would have run down his left sleeve had been removed: replaced with the symbolic depiction of sheaves of wheat that marked the wearer to be a devotee of the goddess Demeter.

'Give your report.' She swung around in her chair to look directly at the young man as he spoke.

'The Trevelian holdings are secure,' he said. 'We found one operational automaton in the compound this morning but it's now decommissioned.'

'And why was this not identified when we arrived?'

The young man hesitated for a second before replying.

'It was dormant, Honoured Demeter. It had been powered-down and its signature was not detected until this morning.'

Demeter considered this for a moment.

'Check for surveillance units within the Chateau. It may have been used as a signal-relay. Damn. What about the farm lands?'

'Sentinels have been sent to each of the agricultural sectors and each has confirmed that the estate is quite deserted. It's as it appeared when we arrived. The Trevelian holdings are entirely ours.'

'And the namesakes?'

'Gone, Honoured Demeter.'

The man stood tall and faced directly ahead as Demeter contemplated the situation through the porthole.

'Begin the application of the prompting-culture,' she said. 'We must make sure these lands give us their bounty.'

'Yes, Honoured Demeter.' He bowed and turned to leave.

'Wait.'

She stood and interlaced her thin fingers across her belly.

'The gods obviously have plans for us. She for whom I have been named would not have allowed them to flee the estate without there being a reason.'

Her hands moved past one another so that her thin arms wrapped around her sides as she thought.

'The goddess means us to move on the de-Monte estate immediately.'

She turned to the young man.

'Despatch all of the cherubs to the de-Monte holdings. Instruct them to surround the Mount and prevent anyone from leaving it.'

'Yes, Honoured Demeter.'

'Make sure the instruction is clear. The de-Monte holding must not be attacked.'

'I will tend to the instruction myself.'

She watched him walk down the ramp and over to the entrance of the Trevelian Chateau. After a few moments, she felt the rumble of many heavy-duty motors moving through the earth.

***

For the many years since the ending of The Conflict, the cherubs had been stored away, dormant, castrated. They had sat in silence and in darkness waiting for the order. Eyes searching impenetrable blackness for enemies and threats. Circuits and relays turning in on themselves, reacting to random spikes and surges in the depths of data-bins which contained no data. If such a machine could be said to have a mind, then surely such stagnation must have been an unbearable torture. An inevitable madness must be born from such a wait.

Then, after an age, the order came and they were brought back into the light.

The four octaves that had been deployed to the Trevelian holdings had arrived just hours before Demeter and her party. Their huge flat-sided bulks had quickly established that no threat was present on the estate. They had then slept, remaining still and silent, waiting for their next instruction.

Watching and waiting. Imposing their presence on the landscape.

Three metres in height at the rear, rising to four at the front, two in length and one in width. Matt-black with little by way of discerning features except for the lenses mounted in the mouths of the four faces etched into the raised dome at the front. Each one watching as far as the horizon to the four points of the compass.

The young man with the insignia of Demeter on his sleeve gave them the order to move on the de-Monte holdings. The cherubs would at last return to the work for which they had been created.

Each octave formed into two lines of four and set off in the direction of the de-Monte estate. The machines rendezvoused with one another, joining the formation as it passed by until a great black thirty-two-backed-beast had formed. It would kick up dust from here to there and when it arrived it would spill the blood of the unfaithful. The cherubs would carry The Word on their backs and deliver it to the enemy.

And The Word was "death".

CHAPTER TWENTY-ONE

The girl's reflected image looked back at her from the mirror.

The Menace, her father, had taken her hand and led her from the chamber. He was kind; the girl could feel it through his touch. His eyes were those of The Menace that came to her in her dreams, but he held a kindness in his heart, she knew it to be the truth. He had led her away from Rebecca and the box where she had begun. Away from the steel-walled room in which she had met the essence of her mother, of Evelyn. He had walked with her along the same corridor through which she had entered that chamber, to one of the closed doors.

'Come in and make yourself comfortable,' he had said, letting go of her hand and pushing the door open.

The room was a little smaller than the cell she had occupied at the Trevelian estate and had space enough for a bed, a standing-height table and a small set of drawers. Since they were within the centre of the mountain there was no window. Instead across from the door was a large mirror that took up two thirds of the wall. And this is where the girl found her own scarred face waiting for her.

The room was brightly lit and the usually faint scar running down the side of her face was red and clearly visible. She had forgotten that it was there. It stung as she looked at it. She watched her reflected finger trace its length from her eye to the corner of her mouth. It felt rough and uneven in comparison to the unblemished young skin on the rest of her face. She saw it as the visible part of all the changes she had been through. As if the events of the past months had opened up her body and changed something inside of her and, when her flesh had rolled back into place, it had been unable to fasten itself up properly because something had been added, taking up more room and leaving this scar.

She took off the white coat, opened her tunic and dropped it from her shoulders, her mirror-eyes examining the naked body standing before them. She turned so that her reflection could see her back. There was no other scar on her body. Somehow all but her face had escaped permanent damage and everything else that had been broken and bruised was now healed.

She pulled her tunic back on and fastened it with the cord belt, leaving the white coat where it had fallen.

'I've embarrassed you,' she said, seeing that the man, her father, had directed his eyes to the floor, 'I'm sorry.'

He lifted his eyes and looked into her face.

'No, there's no need to apologise. It's just that, well..., I'm not used to seeing a naked adult body and it seems, wrong, inappropriate somehow to see yours.'

The girl looked at those eyes, she looked straight into them. How was it, she thought, that she had seen those eyes in her nightmares? How was it she remembered him, and why did she fear him in her dreams when he seemed so kind?

'I'm sorry that Rebecca saw fit to show you your beginnings,' he said.

'I'm not. I'm glad she did it.'

'Well, I'm sorry that she did it in such a way, that must have been hard.'

The two looked at each other for a moment.

'Is it true? That you're my father, is it true?'

'Well, yes, it is I suppose. Insomuch as it was my seed that was combined with Evelyn's to make you.'

Another long pause sat between them.

'What's your name? I would like to know the name of my father.'

'I'm Laban.' His blue blue eyes and thin lips smiled.

The girl nodded to herself and repeated the name under her breath. She could see no hint of herself in this man. Like his sister, his eyes were blue, not brown, his features angular and his nose thin and pronounced.

'And my mother. That was my mother in the chest?'

Laban nodded.

She watched as he moved over to the set of drawers and pulled open the lowest. He knelt on the floor as he rolled back some clothes in search of something, and then crossed back to the table with a small box. It was made of a finely finished wood and had a shiny metal lid into which was set a large blue jewel. It caught the light, held it for a moment and then bounced it around the room. The design suggested an elegant bird strutting and displaying its feathers. Laban opened the box and handed her a picture.

'Evelyn was a brave girl,' he said.

She looked at the picture. It was of a young woman, perhaps a year or two younger than herself. Her face was only partly visible, one third covered by a shadow cast from the hood of her tunic. She had pale skin and brown eyes. She was looking up and to the right at something in the distance. To the girl the face seemed to tell of an inner strength; full of kindness and hope.

'You look a lot like her,' said Laban.

She took another look at the face in the picture, and then handed it back to Laban. He placed it carefully into the box, leaving it open on the table, unable to take his eyes from the image.

'You're not as I remember you,' she said.

He looked up from the picture, puzzled.

'In my dreams. I've dreamt of you, but you're not as you are now.'

'I had heard that you dreamed but…it's not possible that you have any memory of me.'

'I have dreamed of you, more than once, but you were not at all like this.'

'Then why do you think it's me you dream of? If your dream doesn't look like me then it's not me you're dreaming of is it?' There was a kindness, a softness in his voice.

'But that's it exactly, you look as you do now. It's your face that's in my dreams. It's your manner that's different.'

'My face is in your dream?' He shook his head: 'Not possible; you can have no memory of me, your cleansing would see to that.'

'It is your face I see, your eyes, they're the eyes that I see in my dream. You hold me in my bed or in my chair, you ask me questions, your breath is in my face. In my dreams, you are The Menace, you take the life of innocent children. In my dreams…'

'Stop. Please stop.' He was staring at her. His face incredulous. Tears were in his eyes and his voice was tight with pain

'Please. Stop.'

He sat down on the unmade bed and covered his eyes with his hands.

The girl watched as his tears came. He was fragile, she thought. She wanted to offer him some comfort. Somehow his pain was hers.

'But you're different,' she said, 'not like The Menace in my dreams, you're kind.'

He took in a deep breath through his nose in an attempt to stop the tears.

'No, I'm just as you see me in your dreams. I'm sorry for what I've done, for what I've done to you and to the others.'

He pulled his hands from his face and placed them on either side of his body, pushing them down into the mattress. He stretched his legs out in front of his body and stared at the ceiling. Air left his lungs and blew out his cheeks before leaving his mouth through almost closed lips. Moments passed.

'As a baby, and as a little girl, you and me and the others lived as a family,' he said. 'There were six in your cohort.'

He was lost for a moment, sharing a smile with the past.

'I remember each of you, the time we spent together was precious and wonderful.' He smiled to himself again as he remembered.

'When you were five your favourite game was to invent a treasure hunt for me and the others. You would make up a clue and draw it on a piece of paper. It would lead us to the next clue and so on each piece of paper taking us to the next until finally we would discover the treasure that you had left for us. A toy or a picture that you'd drawn. You were so creative. You were very special, not one of the others ever played that game with me.'

And then the sadness of those years seemed to wrap around him. The girl watched as they cast their shadows across his face.

'But that makes it all the worse,' he said. 'When the time came for your gifting, I had to...like with all of you. It's my function.'

The girl touched the man's hand and sat next to him on the mattress.

'Tell me, Laban,' she said.

'Others know me as The Curate, the cleaner of souls.'

He paused, waiting for the darkness to recede before he continued his explanation.

'At the age of six, you, that is all namesakes, are gifted to a Family. Either to the Trevelians or to the Percivals. But before you can be gifted we must be sure that you'll be… compatible with your new life. So we test you, to check that your conditioning, the way you've been brought up, has taken hold properly.'

He looked down at the floor as he continued to speak.

'It's the function of the cleaner of souls, it's my function, to administer the various tests, to see that you'll be compliant in the community of cousins that you'll join. To make sure that you'll settle in to your new life. To make sure that you'll be happy there. You're placed in a chair in a special room and I… I… ask you questions.'

The girl remembered the dream in which she had been in a room. She remembered the darkness, the sense of being watched, The Menace close and she unable to move from the chair on which she sat. She remembered the questions and the spot of blood on a girl's forehead, the empty body slumping in the chair. Her serpent awoke.

A little steel was in her voice as she asked, 'And what if you don't like the answers that you're given?'

He continued to look at the floor but the girl could feel the man's face fold up in response to the question.

'If the answers indicate that the girl will settle with her Family, then the namesake is "cleaned". She's given a potion that calms her as the memories of her early life are washed away. The process is painless and leaves the namesake ready to serve her new Family.'

He paused, knowing that he still owed the girl, his daughter, an answer.

'If the responses are not suitable, if they indicate that the namesake would not react appropriately when gifted, if she would not be happy, not be able to adjust to her new life with her cousins, not be able to settle in, then the second option is taken.'

His hands were damp with shame as he spoke.

'She's euthanized,' he said. 'It's my task to finish her.'

The serpent in the girl's belly flexed and tightened. She stood up and backed away from the bed towards the wall, looking down at him.

'So, you create us for servitude and if we can't serve we're killed. Look at me!'

Laban did not move. The serpent filled her body with anger.

'Look at me!'

His eyes stared at the floor in front of his feet.

'Lie upon lie upon lie. You tell us we're foundlings, spared a life of poverty, saved from a life without hope by the grace of the Living Saints. You tell us the gods love and protect us, that The Church is ours and we belong to it. None of that is true. The Living Saints are not real, neither is the Church. There are no gods or God. You tell us to rejoice that we're to be held in the arms of the company of our cousins. But we're not foundlings. We're not saved, we're bred and reared for a purpose and if we're not compliant then we're slaughtered. And by the person who should cherish us above all else. Our own father gives us away or kills us.'

The anger-serpent flexed again but this time the girl controlled her, not she the girl. Her voice was quiet now, but stone-solid.

'You would give me away or you would see me dead. No cause can justify this.'

Laban stood, his eyes still on the floor as he moved toward the door. He did not speak.

'Tell me,' she said, making him pause with his back to her, 'when I was here, when I was your little girl, did I have a name?' Her voice was strong and the question punched Laban between the shoulder blades.

'No,' his voice was small. He shook his head and left the room.

***

The tapestries hanging on the walls of the de-Monte conference room showed dogs and men chasing, cornering and killing wild animals. The room was full of the hunted.

'... but even if we could, we have no means of escape. Anything that goes out through that gateway will be destroyed,' said Adam. 'If we try to get the capsule out we'll be finished.'

'So you suggest that our only option is to hold out here and make a stand?' said Mason.

'Yes, exactly. We must prepare ourselves for a battle. When they arrive we must be ready, we must take the fight to them.'

Charles touched his son's arm.

'I don't think you quite understand what's heading our way,' he said. 'She'll send cherubs, and in numbers. You've no idea of the destructive capabilities of an octave of cherubs. They're machines of war, they'll act together, tactically. We'll not be able to fight them. There's little we can do.'

Adam became more animated and the pitch of his voice rose.

'We could fashion something from the power cells in the remaining capsule, rig a bomb. We could set it off as they entered the compound and...' He stopped speaking as his father slapped his hand on the table in front of him.

'No. We have nothing that can stand in front of the cherubs, do you understand? Nothing.'

The room was silent, Adam and Charles stared at each other. It was the first and only time Adam had seen his father moved to physical anger.

Another moment passed, it was Mason who broke across it.

'Charles is right. If Demeter has made us a present of cherubs, and she will have, we can't take a fight to them. The best we can do is buy a little time for at least some of our party by negotiating with her.'

Adam looked around the room at the silent, frightened faces. The only one he could not see was Rebecca's. She had her back to the room and was looking through the great window at the lake, apparently oblivious to the discussion.

'But what point is there in buying time?' he said. 'We can't get away and we can't trust Demeter to honour any terms she agrees. We must find a way to fight. We must not let them...' His voiced trailed, silenced by the memory that had walked into the room.

Laban looked directly at Adam as the door slid closed behind him. The last time they had met it had been as prisoner and cleaner of souls. He gave Adam a small bow before speaking.

'We can cross the water,' he said. 'We don't need to leave through the main gate in the capsule: we have a ship, a sailing craft in the dry dock below.'

Rebecca turned from the window, as if suddenly aware of the problem and its solution.

'Yes. We can leave undetected and use it to cross the water,' she said, 'but it hasn't been used for many years. It may not be serviceable.'

'It's in working order,' said Laban. 'I've always attended to it and kept it maintained. Its care has been my sanity.'

'Will it take us all?' asked Mason.

Laban crossed to the window and stood next to his sister.

'No, not all of us, but enough to make it worthwhile.' He looked first at Mason and then Charles as he said this. 'Those that go will be far from comfortable, and there'll be little room for supplies. There won't be room for a medi-tube.' He paused and then turned to Mason: 'How is Nicholas?'

The muscles in Mason's jaw clenched. 'His removal from the medi-tube was successful; as of an hour ago he was still unconscious. Jess is with him.'

'If he isn't strong enough to travel without a medi-tube, there's little point in him making the journey.' All those present knew the truth of Rebecca's words.

'I'll go to Jess and…gauge the situation.' Mason turned back to Laban before he left the room. 'How do I get to the ship?'

'Follow the central stairs down as far they go. We can board within the dry dock, flood it and leave directly from there.'

Mason nodded.

'Jess and I will meet you there.' He turned his broad shoulders away and left.

CHAPTER TWENTY-TWO

The girl was sitting alone in the room. Her father had left and the box that contained the image of her mother was still open on the table in front of her.

She took the picture and looked back at the mirror, comparing the two images, one reflected from the past and one from the present. It was true, she did look like the woman in the picture. All the namesakes shared her brown hair and eyes, her thin face and pale skin.

She looked at the features frozen into the picture. She thought the woman, her mother, looked kind.

She felt a coolness from the tears on her cheek that soothed the sting in her scar. She kissed the picture and held it tight to her chest.

***

Demeter was sitting alone in the transport capsule in the Trevelian compound. She stared at the display in front of her, watching the dots which marked the location of the cherubs as they sped their way toward the de-Monte holdings.

***

The girl felt the kinship she shared with her cousins. She had always felt it, since the time she had been gifted to the Family Trevelian. She had thought that it was the faith binding her community together that made her feel this way. Perhaps this had been the case. But now she knew that something else, a deeper truth united them and held them in its arms: they shared a mother and a father, they were not cousins but sisters. It was not faith that bonded them one to another but their blood. She felt closer to them than ever before.

***

Demeter felt the cool seclusion of her power as it grew with each metre travelled by the deadly guardians of The Word.

The fetid decades that had passed since The Conflict were finally at an end. From the start, from the very day that she had taken the name Demeter, the name of her own beloved goddess, she had seen the fissures in the plan. She had outwardly embraced the Church of the Holy Union but held true to her own certainty that only the pantheon of gods could provide balance to the world. For all the fine words and the knitting together of the polytheist and the monotheist traditions she had known that The Church would not be able to sustain itself. Gods would always welcome new members to their bosom, but a single God would always insist on standing alone, not above other gods, but alone. The Union could not last. It was temporary. Until the arrogant One God was defeated there would never be lasting peace, only the pantheon could bring balance to the world.

She knew that her faith would set the world alight before it could set it free, but she knew that this price was worth the payment. As she stared at the relay that showed the progress of the cherubs, she wept. Her wait would soon be over.

***

The girl and her serpent turned from the mirror, the picture of Evelyn tucked into their tunic. They left the room and made their way back up the corridor toward the room in which the children had been playing. Her sisters would be safe. All of them.

She and her serpent would see to it.

CHAPTER TWENTY-THREE

Mason pushed open the door to the medical suite. The antechamber was empty and the lights dim. He closed the door and approached the window separating him from the treatment room. He could see that Nicholas was awake, lying back on the bed, pale and weak. Jess held Nicholas's left hand, cupping it between her palms. Her lips were moving and she smiled as she spoke. Mason watched for a few moments not wanting to interrupt them.

He couldn't imagine a world without Nicholas and as he stared through his half-reflection in the glass he recalled the first time they had met. It had been in the blood and dirt of The Conflict. Mason and his platoon were cornered in what had once been a school. They had taken shelter as best they could in the rubble and dust. Low on ammunition and outnumbered they knew that their end would come in the next exchange of fire. And then, the captain of the men who had them surrounded walked into their camp unarmed. Mason had never seen anything so brave as this man's actions. That captain had been Nicholas. He had offered Mason and his men his hand. That act of mercy had propagated through the rubble and tunnels of the battlefield faster than any call to arms. It was to mark the end of the fighting. In the years that he had served Nicholas since the war, Mason had often asked himself if it were the man, or the faith the man had in his gods, that had prompted such brave and insightful action. He had never found an answer. Wherever it had come from, it had been Nicholas's strength that brought an end to The Conflict. There would have been no peace without Nicholas. How could there be peace without him now?

He tapped on the glass and Jess looked across at him, she smiled and beckoned for him to enter.

As the door slid open Mason was struck by the sterile, antiseptic taste of the air within the treatment room. He paused in the doorway.

'Hi,' said Jess. 'Come in and say hi.'

Mason returned the smile but he could see that Jess saw through it.

'I need to speak with Nicholas. Might I speak with him privately for a moment?'

Mason watched the colour leave Jess's face. She turned to her father as if to ask a question but he spoke first.

'Is that Mason?' his voice barely a whisper.

She nodded.

'Let me speak to him.'

Jess kissed his hand and carefully lowered it back to the treatment table.

'I'll be just outside,' she said, and then to Mason: 'Don't tire him out.'

Mason nodded. He could not remember ever feeling so much pain as he felt now. Jess was lit by the hope of her father's recovery and now he must take that away from her. He waited for the door to close, telling himself that it would protect her from the world for a few minutes more.

Coward.

He took the seat that Jess had been using and kissed his friend and brother on the forehead. Nicholas looked into his eyes and Mason knew that he already understood.

'You've come to say goodbye,' said Nicholas.

Mason nodded: 'A lot has happened and we're in a tight spot.'

'Is there any hope?'

'There's a chance of getting the rest to safety,' said Mason.

'…but not me.' Nicholas replied.

'No. Not you. You won't be able to make the journey. There's no room for a medi-tube and you won't survive without one.'

Nicholas turned his face from Mason and looked up at the ceiling.

'You can get Jess to safety? Keep her safe?'

Mason swallowed before replying. 'We're going to cross the lake. Try to find a place to take refuge.'

Mason watched as Nicholas's eyes filled with tears. He knew that his friend was not crying for himself.

'Look after her, Mason. Promise me.'

Mason squeezed Nicholas's forearm: 'I will.'

'Let me speak to her,' said Nicholas.

Mason nodded and got up from the treatment table.

'Mason,' whispered Nicholas. 'May your journey be well-made my friend.'

'You too,' said Mason.

The door slid open and Mason found himself looking directly into Jess's eyes.

'What's going on?' she said.

Mason dropped his gaze to the floor and shook his head.

'I'm sorry,' he said.

Jess pushed past him, and Mason walked into the antechamber. The door slid closed behind him and he turned to look back through the window. He couldn't hear what passed between them but he knew what was being said.

***

'I remember the day you were born.'

Nicholas spoke as if the two of them were reminiscing in some cosy nook. His voice, quiet, rasping a little with dryness, but still with a strength running through it. He held Jess's hand as he spoke; wanting to keep it safe, to protect it for as long as he could.

'After The Great Conflict the years were bleak,' he said, 'the taste of the fighting was still in our mouths. All the killing we had done and seen...'

He closed his eyes for a moment, pausing to gather the strength to continue. He felt himself fade from his daughter's world into a soft and comforting shadow. But he needed to say goodbye and knew his words could only be spoken in her light: without it there could be no sound. He fought the urge to fall back into the gentle silence of the darkness, and willed himself into her light.

'Fighting leaves something in your stomach,' he said. 'It's almost as if you can't bear even to move in case you wake it up and it reminds you of all the terrible things you've done... Afterwards there was work to do, we all, those of us who had survived, had to build... to build the city and the society that would live within it. All of it had to be created... a new city, a new state, a new religion... one we could all share. Build it again from scratch. But even with this work to occupy me I could feel nothing but despair. Nothing but the relentless darkness that I learnt in the war...that lived in me. Until you came. My world changed when I held you for the first time. Your mother was exhausted, you and I were alone. You gave me hope. Your tiny perfect body, wrapped and bound by your mother's maid.'

He smiled, the strength of such a joyful memory sustaining him.

'Holding you that day was the first time in my life that I felt truly afraid. War is loud and you risk your life in it, but I had never been afraid in any of those years. But you were different. Your life was so precious, one that I truly needed, a life I couldn't discard or gamble with. Suddenly it all made sense to me. That fear made me understand. The reason that rebuilding our world had to work. I realised that I was building it for you, Jess. That day, you gave me everything.'

'I love you Popos,' she said, her tears starting to well.

Speaking for so long had been a great effort for Nicholas and he closed his eyes and was silent for a full minute.

'I'm so sorry, Jess. It's time.'

Jess bit down hard on her lip and closed her eyes. She made no sound but allowed the tears to come.

'It seems that the reinvention of our world is not as robust as we had hoped.' His pale lips barely tightened into a smile as he reached for her hand. His breathing was shallow and he struggled for air as he spoke.

'There's work to be done, the duty to those in the care of the Family Trevelian, you'll have to do that work now, Jess. My time has been; your time is now. You must give me the final witnessing.'

These last words were little more than a whisper. He continued to squeeze her hand but closed his eyes, exhausted.

Jess felt a great pit open inside her stomach. It reached out its tendrils and pulled her in as he fell silent. She remembered the moment she learnt he had been wounded. How everything else in the world had become a blur as she went to him through the wreckage of the Trevelian Chateau. How she had felt relief flooding into her body when he had not been dead, when he had spoken to her. She could not go on without him, how could she? Why must everything change? Why should life have to change? She wanted to go back to how it was, to give up this new world and hide herself away, out of sight in a place that asked nothing of her. A place where she could be quiet and still and unconnected from her own pain and the pain of others. How could she continue without him?

Nicholas opened his eyes and turned his head toward her.

'Jess,' a whisper, 'don't cry.' He smiled. 'It is only by its impermanence that a life shows its beauty.'

He squeezed her fingers a little more tightly and she wiped the tears from her cheek with the back of her hand.

'I won't leave you here Popos. I can't. I'll find a way to bring you with us.'

'No, Jess, my time has come.'

'I won't leave you here, I can't.'

'You'll give me the final witnessing. You'll do your duty.'

His eyes closed. He was exhausted and the incurious world of sleep had taken him. Jess, the daughter, the little girl, sobbed and her body fell across that of her father.

***

On the other side of the window Mason was not watching. Instead he was looking at the ceiling and listening to a dull 'thud thud thud'. Moments later the whole hillside shook and then silence. Mason recognised it as a declaration of intent by an aggressor. He crossed into the medical suite and placed his hand on Jess's shoulder.

'Jess, it's time,' he said.

Jess's body shook with her sobs and then stopped as quickly as the thudding. She stood, wiped her forearm across her face to clear away the tears, and walked over to the panel to which her father's arm was connected.

'No,' she said, 'we'll bring him with us.' She threw the statement at Mason.

'It's no use Jess, he's too weak and where we're going there'll be no facilities. Your father knows that. You must let him go.'

'We can take a medi-tube then. It'll keep him safe.' Her voice was taut and desperate.

'There isn't room for a 'tube, our craft will be full to capacity and won't take its weight. Your father understands this.'

She walked over to a counter at the side of the room and picked up the azrapone sitting on its surface. She looked at the device as she held it; the clean silver strip of metal felt cool and she closed her fingers tightly around it. The dull blue jewel in its centre made it look a little like a crown. Her mind was locked tight by the emotions that filled her. She could not think, she could only feel.

She walked back to her father's pale and sleeping body and placed the azrapone across his forehead. The jewel began to glow, extending its embrace to the life it felt within its arms. The flickering of the light stepped in and out of a steady rhythm as it found and then held the mind of its patient. After a few moments, its slow glow-and-dull lullaby indicated that it had entrained its captive and wrapped him in a deep sleep.

'Jess,' said Mason.

Jess turned from her father and bent down to look in the cupboard under the counter from which she had taken the azrapone. She rummaged frantically, pulling items out and scattering them on the floor around her before finding a small field medi-kit.

'Jess,' Mason repeated. 'Jess. Stop.'

He crossed over to her and placed his hands onto the tops of her arms as she stood clutching the black and red striped case to her chest. He looked into her face. Her eyes were wide and dilated and her skin paler than usual, her breathing shallow and quick.

'We'll bring him with us under the azrapone,' she said, twisting her body away from his. 'I'll care for him with the medi-kit. His body is strong enough to travel sedated and I'll care for him.'

'No Jess, he's too weak to be moved from here. You must let him go. Give him the final witnessing. It's the right time, the right thing to do. The right thing for both of you.'

'No. Bring him.'
'Jess.'
'Bring him.'

***

Two cherubs sat within the breached compound of the de-Monte hill, flanked by the rubble-strewn gap through which they had punched their point of entry. Each faced the hillside, waiting in cold silence for any movement to show itself. They had been instructed to detain anyone who attempted to leave the compound, but these were creatures of war and this was counter to their algorithm. They must deliver The Word. They had determined to kill anything that moved from the de-Monte estate.

Outside the broken wall, thirty sets of eyes watched in all directions. Once the compound had been breached, the remaining cherubs had fanned out in either direction along the wall; from above their equidistant blocks would have looked like black gemstones on a necklace.

Cherubs could not travel across water, but they had been quick to calculate that such a route from the hillside existed. Two of the machines had positioned themselves at either end of the wall, looking down and across the water, ready to fire a salvo at any craft that tried to cross it.

CHAPTER TWENTY-FOUR

Demeter pondered the blank display in front of her. She smiled at her own reflection as she waited for the communicator to flash. She knew it was only a matter of time before it would and sure enough after a few minutes its red to green to red eye began to flash. She stood and pressed the button below the light and an image of Rebecca Catherine Valerie de-Monte floated before her. The two women were eye to eye.

'This is an outrage,' said Rebecca's image.

Demeter gave a single nod in agreement but offered no words of apology.

'Do you not seek to justify your abhorrent actions? Your attack on my estate?'

Demeter tucked her hands into the sleeves of her robe before replying.

'When your heart was dedicated to The Pantheon it was my honour to serve as your Field-Commander,' she said. 'But the day you betrayed our gods for the fiction of the Holy Union was the last day I had to justify my actions to you. What I do, I do for the glory of our gods. Your experiment is at an end.'

Rebecca's image narrowed its eyes. For a moment, Demeter could taste the anger flowing from her former commander, and then it was gone. The diplomat had returned to the screen, Rebecca's voice assertive but measured.

'Clearly you have some need for us as you have not seen fit simply to murder us.'

'Rebecca, I am mindful that you and I have history. I would honour that past and offer you a chance to accept the pantheon back into your heart. Recant your support of the abomination of the Church of the Holy Union, and do so publicly.' Demeter gave a smile that exposed her blackened teeth, a genuine smile of joy rooted in a malignant intent. 'Do so and I may grant those under your "wing" a quick death.'

A second image appeared next to that of Rebecca. Demeter nodded at it.

'Curate, I am honoured,' she said.

Laban returned the nod as the lens of the communicator moved so that only his image could be seen.

'Honoured Demeter, would not my capitulation serve your needs better than that of my sister?'

Demeter lowered her chin and raised an eyebrow. A gesture for Laban to continue.

'Is the representative of The One true God within The Church not a greater prize?' he said.

'Perhaps.'

'I am prepared to make myself a present to you, now, if you let the others live,' he said.

Demeter threw back her head and laughed.

'Huh. You seek to make a bargain with me, Curate.' She lent in toward the image. 'Know this. Not even the gift of both your heads would be of sufficient value to warrant me sparing the lives of those you shelter. There's nothing you have of such value to me.'

She stood from her chair and was about to close the comms link when Laban's next words stopped her dead.

'Not even Charles,' he said.

Demeter turned to the thin-faced image.

'Charles is dead,' she said.

Demeter watched as the image looked to its side, sharing a glance of surprise with its sister.

'Charles isn't dead,' said Laban. 'He's here. You think he's dead?'

Demeter made no response but sat back into her seat. She studied Laban's face. Was he telling the truth?

'Charles is here with us still,' he said. 'Your attack killed his servant, not him. He's here with us, I assure you.'

Demeter relaxed a little into her chair and considered for a moment before replying.

'The public humiliation of the commander of the monotheist horde would indeed be worth something.' She paused and lent forward: 'If he really is alive we may have something to talk about after all.'

'He's alive,' said Laban's image.

'I want to see him.'

'I'll bring him.' Laban's image rose and for a moment Demeter could only see his chest. The lens then focussed back to Rebecca's face.

'Negotiation then,' said Rebecca.

Demeter gave a nod. 'Negotiation. Where shall we begin?'

***

The girl had found the nursery subdued, the children had gathered around the young nursery maid and were in a corner of the room. They had felt the hillside shake and not known what else to do but to cling to one another.

'Is this everyone?' she asked.

The maid nodded, her arms full of the children gathered around her as she knelt in the corner of the room.

'Come with me,' said the girl.

The young woman did not move. The girl knew that they must not delay, that time was leaving them behind, but she could see the fear and confusion in the young woman's eyes. She walked toward her, slowly and calmly, and knelt among the children.

'We must all leave here; it's not safe. Look at my face: you and I are kin. You can trust me.'

The two women looked at each other. There it was, thought the girl, the connection that she and her cousins had always shared. No, not cousins, sisters. This was her sister.

'Will you trust me?' she asked.

Her sister nodded. 'They'll need clothes and…'

'There's no time, we must leave now. Right now.'

She picked up one of the younger children. The toddler squirmed and tried to wriggle back to the floor, but the girl held her warmness tight to her body nonetheless.

'We'll head to the compound. The others are preparing to leave, to get to somewhere safe. They don't know about you. We have to get to them before they leave.'

The young nursemaid picked up the smallest child and took the hand a young girl whose eyes were filled with tears.

'Hold hands everyone,' said the nursemaid.

The children dutifully found partners in what must have been a well-rehearsed drill. They lined up two abreast in front of the door. The girl led the way in what she thought was the direction of the entrance tunnel, followed by a train of little sisters and brothers, ending finally with the maid.

In less than twenty metres the curving tunnel ended in a mess of rubble and dust. The girl stopped and looked back to her sister.

'Take her,' she said, handing over the now still bundle. 'Wait here.'

She approached the wall of rubble and examined it. The tunnel was completely blocked. She scrambled up the slope to the ceiling, slipping as stones came loose under her feet.

'It's blocked. There's no way through this way.' She picked her way back down through the debris.

'There's no way through,' she said again.

The toddler reached out her arms to her and the girl picked her up and held her close, rocking her as she considered their options for a moment.

'Is there a room that we can send a message from?'

The nursery maid was quick to understand.

'Yes, this way.'

She led them through the corridors to a small room that was in darkness except for the greys and reds of light coming from an illuminated screen. The girl recognised the thin tinny voice coming from the display to be that of the de-Monte Matriarch. Hearing her voice made the serpent twist in her belly. She looked across at the maid, who ushered the line of children to the side of the corridor and bade them to wait in silence. They entered the room, still carrying the two smallest children. Without being asked, the nursemaid took the child from the girl's arms to allow her to approach the screen.

She could hear the conversation between Rebecca and another woman whose voice she did not recognise. Their voices were calm and controlled, they spoke of surrender and terms of safe passage, their tone cool and business-like. The image on the screen did not match the voices, it showed two black masses standing in the compound next to the smoking remains of a transport capsule. There was clearly no point in trying to find another route to the compound.

The girl looked at the controls on the panel in front of her. They were similar to those that operated the cameras around the front and rear of the Trevelian transport. Perhaps they served the same purpose. She moved the palm-sized black wheel, clicking it from one position to the next. The voices continued but the image changed to show the corridor through which they had just come, and then it showed the children lined up outside the room in which she was standing. At the next position of the wheel the screen showed the shadowy movement of ants across a leaf. The girl looked more closely at the image. It showed people, far below the vantage point, climbing into a vessel of some kind.

'Do you recognise this place?'

The nursery maid leaned in to look at the screen more closely.

'No,' she said, and then, 'it looks like it's deep inside the hill. Down at its base there's a large cavern; I've never been but The Curate talks of it.'

'Do you think you could find the way there?'

'Certainly. I know the exact way.'

She turned back to the screen and spun the wheel through its remaining positions. Each click revealed a different image, either of some room or space within the hill or from a vantage point looking out. The view of the ants crawling across the leaf was the only one that showed any signs of life.

'Then let's go,' said the girl.

***

Mason followed Jess down the tight spirals of the stairs coiled within the hill. He carried the unconscious Nicholas, his body wrapped in a white shroud from neck to foot, holding him across his own chest, one arm under his shoulders and the other under his knees. It was hard work.

The stone steps narrowed to points where they met the central pillar, and he had to take care not to miss his footing, holding his weight on his right leg, and stepping down with his left each time. His arms and shoulders were feeling numb.

At last the steps finished and they arrived at a small dark stone-floored hall. Jess was waiting for him in the shadows, and Mason adjusted the weight of Nicholas's body in his arms as she checked that the azrapone was working.

'Do you need to put him down for a moment?'

Mason shook his head: 'No, I'm fine.'

She turned and opened the door in front of them. It was made of thick dark timbers, rough and old, with black metal bands running across and from top to bottom. It opened easily, and on the other side they found themselves on a small landing from which another set of stone steps descended. These had no casing or handrail, but clung to rough walls and led directly down into the cavern below.

'Jess.' Adam's voice ricocheted up to them from the shadows of the cave.

Mason shuffled the weight in his arms as Adam appeared, coming up the steps in front of them. He watched as Adam took in the shrouded figure in his arms. Mason's lips tightened.

'You've brought your father?' asked Adam.

Jess offered no more than a nod. Adam paused for a moment, looking into her face.

'Here, Mason, let me take him.'

Mason allowed Adam to take Nicholas and lead Jess down the steps. He took a moment to look around, allowing his muscles to recover. The space had been cut into the heart of the hill and was huge, its rough jagged sides disappeared into shadows above his head and the damp slate-grey rocks of its walls reflected a ring of lights set into the floor below. The lights spiralled out and traced their way up the side of the steps to where he was standing. Far below, he could see the vessel to which they would trust their lives. It sat in a trench running the length of the cavern, terminating at the outer wall of the cave.

By the time he reached the cavern floor, Jess had already climbed up the ladder which crossed the trench to the boat, leaving Adam holding Nicholas at its foot.

'You shouldn't have brought him,' said Adam.

'I know.'

Mason looked towards the top of the ladder. The boat was taller than the trench, its side rising above him, and the ladder was at a steep angle. The hull was rounded and curved, the shape of an elongated egg cut in half down its length and lying on its side; it curved from a fair point at the prow to a broad flat stern.

A second later figures appeared over the side of the ship. Hands reached down and Adam pushed himself up the ladder, lifting Nicholas's body as high as he could. Fingers grasped the shroud and the fragile load was pulled up into the boat.

Mason followed Adam up the ladder, rolling himself up and over the side. The deck was crowded. There were the three members of the Trevelian Family staff and the namesakes from both Families, but he could not see the girl among them. He followed the namesakes as they carried Nicholas into the cabin at the stern of the ship, and watched from the doorway as they laid his limp body on the small bed that fitted along the back of the tiny structure. Jess knelt at his side and put her hand on the azrapone, as if to help it soothe the man in its charge.

Adam grabbed Mason's arm and drew him away from the cabin.

'You shouldn't have brought him, Mason.'

Mason could feel the youthful heat in his voice.

'I know,' he said calmly. 'I know.'

Bringing Nicholas had been the wrong decision. He had known that it was hopeless back in the medical suite. He should have been allowed to die.

'I had no choice,' he said, his voice still and quiet. 'I couldn't bear to see her pain.'

Adam's face reddened. After a moment, he nodded, turned and entered the cabin. Kneeling beside Jess, he put an arm around her.

Mason moved over to the control panel. It sat on top of a pedestal directly in front of the cabin. A back support ran up the cabin's outer wall to allow the pilot to remain standing if the vessel were thrown about. He slid his body into place and looked at the controls.

The design of the craft was unconventional: except for the cabin, there was no other accommodation on deck nor, it seemed, was there any way to go below. Instead a thick horizontal beam ran two-thirds the length of the vessel with forward-facing bench seats, each large enough for two adults, sunk into the deck along either side. They were fitted with padded backs and restraining straps, and were set into the deck so that each occupant's head would be almost level with the boat's side. He studied the controls for a moment and realised that the seats on the deck were positioned so that a skin could fold up and over the passengers; he realised he was standing in a life raft.

'Can you operate it?' Mason turned to see Charles standing beside him. 'I'm afraid I never was much of a sailor.'

Mason nodded.

'Yes Sir, but it'll be a crush. I'd say it was designed for a dozen or so and we're twice that number.'

Charles nodded and said, 'It's old, but from what I can see, Laban was telling the truth when he said he'd looked after it. Anyway, there's no other option.' There was a steel in the old man's eyes as he spoke. 'It'll cope.'

Suddenly their attention was drawn by the sound of voices and crying. Mason and Charles looked at each other for a moment.

'Children,' said Charles.

They crossed to the side of the boat and searched the shadows up by the entrance to the cavern. There was a group of young children and two adults. Mason felt his heart quicken; he could tell by the way the adult in front held herself, by the way she was moving, that it was the girl. She was safe.

Both men were silent for a moment.

'Unwritten namesakes,' said Mason. 'I didn't even think of it. The de-Monte's have cohorts in preparation.'

***

The girl led the way down the steps and toward the women who were coming to help them. She waited at the foot of the ladder as the children were carried up into the craft and was the last to leave the cavern floor. He was waiting for her at the top of the ladder and held out his hand. She climbed over the side of the boat without taking it.

'Mason-of-Trevelian,' she said.

She looked directly into his eyes as she spoke his name, not a greeting but an accusation. Charles's voice broke in from behind Mason's bulk.

'Some of these children are male,' he said. 'There are boys here.'

Mason did not turn or respond. She held his attention in her gaze. He swallowed.

'She showed you?' he asked.

The girl paused for a moment before answering. 'She did.'

'She showed you the casket?'

'She showed me my beginning, where it began for all of us.'

'Then you saw her.'

'I saw her, yes. I saw Evelyn. I saw my mother, the mother of my sisters.'

Her serpent, coiled tightly in readiness to strike, looked into Mason's eyes. They were damp. She could find no enemy in them. The anger left the serpent's blood and she slithered back into the girl's womb. The girl stepped toward him and reached her hand to his face.

'You knew her?' her voice was soft.

Mason nodded.

'I knew Evelyn.' He turned and started to walk away.

The girl was rooted to the deck for a moment, the scar on her face stinging. She had felt the visceral pain of loss and bereavement in Mason's voice.

'Wait,' she said.

Mason stopped for a moment but did not turn around.

'How? How did you know her?'

She watched as Mason's body seemed to sag under a weight, his broad shoulders and back taking on a greater load than they could bear.

'I just knew her,' he said.

The silence was interrupted by the sound of someone climbing over the side of the boat. The girl turned to find Laban behind her.

'Where's Charles? I must speak with Charles.'

Laban stopped when he found himself eye-to-eye with the girl, his daughter.

'I must talk with Charles.' He spoke almost apologetically.

The girl took a step back, her anger sparked by the sudden sight of him.

'Curate, what's happened?' It was Mason who spoke.

'I need to speak with Charles.'

Charles had been crouching outside the door to the cabin, holding the hands of one of the two boys who had been brought onto the boat. He walked over to Laban but said nothing.

'Demeter, Demeter will negotiate.' Laban spoke to Charles. 'She'll discuss sanctuary for some. But Charles, you are the price.'

Charles nodded. 'I'll pay it,' he said quietly.

'There's something else,' said Laban

***

Laban led Charles and Mason toward the cabin, but seeing Jess and Adam there he continued to the rear of the craft so that they would not be overheard.

'Your capitulation and your life is what Demeter seeks.' Laban looked at Charles as he spoke. 'Your position, former position, as leader of the monotheist armies back during the war, means that your public rejection of the aspect of The One true God will strengthen her cause. Help her finish the Church of the Holy Union. Help her re-establish the pantheon.'

Charles nodded. 'I know,' he said, 'I understand that.'

'She will promise anything if you agree.'

'As I say. I'll pay the price. It's a debt long overdue.'

Laban shook his head.

'Charles. She won't keep her word. No matter what she says, she won't rest until every last Percival and Trevelian is dead. Her gods won't allow her to do anything else. She'll hunt them down. She won't hold back. Once you've made a public declaration she won't hold back, no matter what she promises.' Laban took a breath. 'I need to ask you to do something, Charles.'

Charles was silent. Still. There was a steel in his eyes. The stirrings of a long-dormant command.

'I need you to help me arrange things so that Demeter will not discover their escape,' said Laban.

Charles nodded. He understood.

'I need you and Rebecca to keep the negotiations going as long as possible. Give the rest a chance to get away unnoticed. Don't concede anything, keep her talking, don't offer yourself up. Give them time to escape and give me time to make sure Demeter will never discover their escape.'

Charles nodded again. 'I understand,' he said.

Laban looked back to Mason. 'You can handle the craft?'

Mason nodded.

'Then I'll go and arrange things,' he said. 'I'll wait until I hear the launch and then do it.'

***

The girl had remained on the deck by the craft's ladder. She had not followed Mason and the others, but had watched the discussion from a distance. Laban approached her. She stood to one side to let him reach the side of the boat but he stopped in front of her.

'I am sorry,' he said, looking her in the eye for the first time since he had shown her the picture of Evelyn, her mother.

The girl said nothing.

'I'm going to try to make amends,' he said.

She gave a small nod and Laban smiled back. 'I am sorry, truly,' he said, as he went for the ladder.

***

Charles walked to the open door of the cabin.

'Adam, come out here please'.

'I'll go and speak with Jess,' said Mason, allowing Adam to leave the cabin before he entered it.

Charles looked at his son.

'Father?'

'Adam. I will stay behind to help Rebecca and The Curate. I want you to go on ahead. Find a safe place for everyone.'

Adam frowned. 'What do you mean?'

'Just what I say. I'm staying here and you're going on. Rebecca and I will keep Demeter talking while you get the others to safety.'

'No. I'm not going to leave you here,' Adam's voice gathered pace, 'either you come with us or I'll stay with you.'

'Adam,' Charles interrupted, 'I've never asked you to do my bidding, but I do so now. It's not about what you or I may want. It's about what's right. It's about duty. This is your duty. You'll take our namesakes and the others to safety. Do you understand?'

Adam stared at his father for long seconds. Charles reached out and touched Adam's shoulder, stroking it with his thumb. He let go and led Adam to the side of the boat. They each leant their arms on the rail. Side by side they looked down into the shadows of the cavern.

'Adam.' Charles did not speak for a few seconds as he considered his words. 'I know things have not always been easy between us. That I've often been distant. My life has been… focussed on things that have taken me away from you.'

'I know that father. I know that.' Adam spoke quickly, nervously. 'You're a Patriarch you've had to…'

'Please, Adam. Please let me say something to you.'

He turned and gave a kindly smile. Even though Adam was taller he had subconsciously folded his body onto the rail so that his face was where that of his little-boy self's would have been. Charles looked down into his son's eyes.

'I want to say something about your work. Adam, you're campaign to ban the use of the namesakes...'

'I can see now that this was wrong.' Adam's words spilled out of his mouth and Charles interrupted him.

'Adam, please. That's not what I want to say.'

Charles looked down into the shadows and Adam, doing likewise, seemed to find some peace.

'What I wanted to say, was that I'm very proud of what you're trying to do. I've always, I hope, made it clear that I didn't mind what you did with your life, provided you thought about what you wanted to do, and that you tried your best at it. This position you take with the namesakes, well, it's logical to me, I can understand your discomfort with how we make use of them.'

Charles raised his eyebrows as he continued.

'Oh, of course I have a different view, I've no issues with using them, they have a good life, we treat them well, and we need them. But, well, I, that is, my generation, created the world which we have around us, but it's your generation, you, who must create the next one. If you say that things must change, then they must, and maybe the time has come to make these changes. But what I want to say, is that I'm very proud of what you're doing. That's what I wanted to say, what I want you to hear, to know.'

Charles and Adam continued to look down into the shadows for a moment.

'Do your duty son.'

Adam turned and pulled his father close, the boy's eyes damp with the tears of a man.

Charles pulled himself away and placed his hands on his son's shoulders.

'You're a good man, Adam,' he said, 'and I'm very proud of you. "The future belongs to those who would change today".' He looked at his son one last time. 'God bless you.' He smiled, turned and walked across the deck to the ladder and was gone.

***

Mason was kneeling next to Jess in the cabin, his hand gently stroking her back. They knelt together in silence looking at Nicholas as he lay on the bench, held in a deep sleep. Mason had tried to explain how the others would stay behind to allow them to escape but he knew she had not taken much of it in. She had nodded and said the odd word, but her eyes had been on her father the whole time. There was room for little else in her heart.

'We need to get going.' Adam was standing in the doorway and Mason looked up at him. 'Father is staying to help with the negotiations. We'll come back for them when it's over but we must get away for now. We ready to go?'

Mason stood and nodded. 'Yes, pretty much.' He did not challenge Adam's statement. Whether Charles had been deliberately vague with his son, or Adam had simply not understood, made no difference. There would be no coming back.

Adam nodded. 'Let's get underway then.'

Mason left them in the cabin and walked across the deck to the control panel. After a moment, something made him look up from the levers. The girl was at his side, looking at him, her last question still filling the space between them. "How, how did you know her?". He would tell her. When they were away and safe he would tell her about his Evelyn and the bond he had with her, the bond he shared with all namesakes.

'Get everyone into their seats and strapped in,' he said.

She nodded and turned away from him without saying a word.

He looked back to the controls. Yes, it had been a long time but he could operate the craft. The first step would be to seal the water-tight canopy over their heads, and then to flood the cavern. He was about to initiate the launch when three dull thuds, each a second apart, made him stop. Even from within the cavern, the sound was unmistakable to him: three rounds of munitions. He held his breath for a second and then the craft shook violently. The lights in the cavern went out and they were wrapped in an intense darkness. A second later and the lights were back; rocks and debris crashed around the craft, smashing into the floor around them. Demeter must have grown tired of the negotiations already.

'We're launching now. Hold on.' He hit the launch button in the centre of the control panel as he shouted. There was a grinding of gears, the boat began to shudder and then there was nothing. He hit the button again. Nothing.

'Damn!' Mason slid himself from behind the controls. The girl had turned and was coming toward him.

'What's happening?' she asked.

'The loss of power has damaged the mechanism. Disconnected us from the launching system.'

There it was again, the dull thud thud thud of a salvo of weapons.

Mason and the girl looked at each other in the silent moments between the sound and a second rainstorm of stone.

'Here,' he grabbed the girl's wrist and put his hand on the small of her back, pushing and pulling her to the control panel like a tiny doll.

'This is a sail craft,' he said. 'Once it's out on the water a sail will open and it'll be drawn along by the wind. This lever rotates a mast to catch the wind, and this one moves a tail that sits in the water and determines your direction. It takes a great deal of skill and practice to control such a vessel. I can give you neither, you'll have to trust to luck.'

She looked up from the controls.

'You won't be here?' she asked.

'There's a control panel up where we entered the cavern. I need to get up there. For the craft to leave, the trench in which it sits must be flooded. I'm hoping that if I can do that from up there you'll be able to launch the craft from here.'

'You'll stay behind?'

'I'll stay behind to flood the dock. You'll pilot the boat across the lake and...' He paused, looked into her eyes, and smiled at her: 'and survive.'

The girl and Mason. Eye to eye. Equals.

'Once you're away I'll go and help the others buy you as much time as possible,' he said. 'We'll find a way to follow you when we can.'

The girl could feel a lie in this last statement, but chose not to unpick it.

'Think you can handle things?' he asked.

The girl looked back to the controls for a moment.

'Yes, I do.'

Mason pointed to the panel.

'When I've reached the entrance to the cavern, I'll give you a signal. Push this.' He indicated a shiny metallic cylinder sticking up from the controls. 'Push it right down into the panel. As soon as I've flooded the chamber with water, pull back hard on this lever: it'll release your moorings and launch you into the lake. Assuming it works. Understand?'

The girl gave a nod, 'I understand.'

Mason looked at her for a moment. He leaned in close and pulled her toward him.

'You look just like her,' he said softly, and then, placing his hands over her ears, he tilted her head forward and kissed its crown. 'I'm so sorry.'

As he turned to leave, the girl caught him by the arm.

'Mason.' She looked into his strong kind face, unsure as to what exactly she wanted to say. 'May your journey be well-made.'

His eyes smiled back at her. He walked over to the ladder and before he disappeared he looked back and said, 'She would have been very proud of you, your mother. I am.'

CHAPTER TWENTY-FIVE

From where she was standing at the stern of the craft, the girl could see Mason as he reached the top of the steps. After a minute, he turned and waved his hands high above his head in her direction. She waved back, crossed to the control panel, and placed her hand on the silver cylinder that Mason had indicated. Its top filled her palm and felt cold. She took a breath and leant on it, making it sink slowly into the panel under her weight. It clicked into place and remained flush with the surface when she removed her hand. The boat shook slightly and a transparent skin rotated up and over them from the underside of the vessel, sealing them in with a hiss as it descended and met the other side of the boat.

She could sense the tension in the group rise as soon as the canopy had enclosed the boat. Until that point there had been a nervous energy running through them, but now that the life raft was sealed, the space took on a claustrophobic feel; it seemed to push down on them so that they could not make a sound. Adults and children were silent, crushed together in the tiny enclosed space meant for only half their number. She looked along the deck from her position at the controls.

'Make sure everyone is securely strapped in or has a hold of someone who is.' Her voice, enclosed within the crystal canopy, carried down the length of the boat with no effort. There was activity throughout as children were held tight and seat restraints fastened.

The girl looked around to see if Mason was still at the top of the cavern's steps but the curve of the canopy distorted the view and she could only make out the greys and browns of the slate walls.

The craft began to rattle and vibrate. She guessed that he must have activated whatever it was that allowed the area to flood. Through the crystal canopy the girl could see the wall of the trench in which they were sitting begin to rise. It reached up one side of their craft and floated down the other, sealing them in. The trench had become a tunnel with their craft at one end and the external wall of the cavern at the other, the only light coming from the line of small lamps that marked out the edge of their deck.

And then a deafening noise hit them. The wall some twenty metres in front of them must have opened, and a great flood of water raced toward them. She guessed that the cavern must be lower than the lake surface and the force of the water was now flooding the tube which held them.

'Brace yourselves,' she shouted.

The water was split apart by the point formed at the front of the craft. She could feel the moorings strain as its arms held them tight against the force of the water reaching them. It rushed by, racing up each side of the canopy until it met above their heads. She could feel the currents weaken. Was the tunnel full of water now? Should she wait? Would it be dangerous to go now? How could she know?

She closed her eyes and took a slow deep breath. She could feel her heart beating. She breathed out and her heart slowed, breathed in and it sped up a little, out and it slowed a little. It was just as it always had been. One day it would stop beating and her life would be over. One day. But not today.

She opened her eyes and pulled back hard on the lever. For a moment, they floated free within the tunnel, clanking against its sides. Then a deep mechanical rumble ran through them, it quickly reached a high-pitched whir which filled their bodies, and then they were moving. The girl was thrown back against the padding behind her with a force strong enough to push the breath from her lungs. They shot along the length of the tunnel in a heartbeat and raced toward the opening in the wall.

And then they were out under the lake, sealed into their tiny craft. Inside the belly of the fish their bodies jostled and fell against one another as it carried them under the water. The vessel rocked about its horizontal access, throwing bodies left and right. One of the children began to cry and then another: the spark ran up the boat and soon all the children were screaming in terror with those holding them unable to offer any effective comfort.

She had no control of the craft, it was speeding under the water and there was no way of steering it or even of seeing where they were going. The lights set into the edge of the deck turned the canopy into a mirror, and all the girl could see was a strange inverted image of reflected bodies. If there were some obstacle in their way, the first they would know of it would be the impact. There was nothing to be done. The girl felt her serpent tighten her coils, chasing away fear. She kept her nerve.

They continued to accelerate and she was unable to get her hands to the controls. She reached out to the panel and tried to pull herself upright against her own increasing weight. If she had understood Mason correctly, there would be nothing for her to do until they broke the surface, but she wanted to be ready when that moment came.

And now she could feel the craft slow down, and as it did, fingers of light reached down into the water and took away some of its blackness. She realised that it was in the craft's nature to float: it was its forward motion that had held it under the water. Yes, as the craft slowed it was moving toward the surface of its own accord. The darkness continued to recede and she could see sky above their heads, distorted and curved by the water and the lens of the canopy. Little by little their progress slowed and they floated up. A few moments later they broke the surface of the lake and the bright light forced her to close her eyes.

The air inside the crowded craft was stale, it was damp and thick and unpleasant: the canopy that had protected them from the water was now preventing them from breathing fresh air. Someone was coughing. Anxious eyes began to turn in her direction. She looked at the controls: the top of the column she had used to trigger the boat's canopy to close over them was glowing. She pushed it further into the panel and it clicked and eased its way back out to its prone position. There was a hiss of air as the canopy slowly lifted itself up and over their heads, rotating back into the hull, stopping with a thud and allowing fresh damp air to touch them.

They had made it.

***

'We must turn back!'

The girl looked around: it was Adam who was shouting. He had come out of the cabin and was staggering over to the side of the craft. She followed his gaze: they were about half a mile from a sheer wall of rock, the top of which was a ball of flames. Adam looked at the girl and extended his arm toward the cliff; it took a moment for her to realise that it was the de-Monte hill which was burning.

'We must go back,' he shouted. 'Father and the others! We must go back. The cherubs are attacking them.'

The girl looked at the flames. Mason was back there, in danger. She looked at the occupants of the boat.

'No, we won't go back, we'll take our people to safety,' her voice was calm.

'Get out of the way.' Adam barged the girl to one side and grabbed for the controls. She tried to push him off with her shoulder.

'No, we must get everyone to safety, there's nothing we can achieve by returning.' She clung tightly to the column.

'Just get out of my way,' he said.

She tightened her grip. Adam grabbed at her fingers and tried to prize them open.

'Don't tell me what to do, you're just a damned namesake,' he said.

A deafening roar drowned out his words. He released his grip and span on his heel to face the shore. A huge fireball was rising into the air above the hill and as they watched, the rock face itself started to move. A great hulking mass, many times the size of their tiny craft, came loose and belly flopped into the lake. There was silence and then a wall of water rose up from the depths and raced toward them.

'Hold on,' the girl shouted her warning down the boat.

The wave was directly behind them and as it reached them it lifted the rear of the boat. It pulled them up to its top and tipped them nose-down as if they were balancing on the peak of a great hill. Once again the girl could do nothing but hold on and trust to luck. They picked up speed as the craft approached the vertical. Anything not securely strapped in place tumbled down the deck and into the water. The girl's body was now supported by the side of the control column which was sticking out of the deck like a horizontal beam. She was suddenly aware of Adam's body falling towards hers. Their heads connected and the girl's vision was obscured with flashes and bright colours. As she fought to hold on to her senses, she felt the crushing weight of Adam's body across her back. She struggled for breath for a few seconds, her vision clearing, and felt the boat accelerate down the face of the wave. Water flooded over the deck and spray filled the air so that all she could see were her own hands clutching at the controls. The wave roared and they picked up yet more speed. They became part of a mass of water rushing out into the lake and away from the flaming cliff behind them.

She felt the boat belly-flop back to flatter water and level out. Adam's unconscious body rolled down onto the deck and the girl grabbed at his arm to stop him sliding as the boat rolled from side to side.

And then it was over. As quickly as the wave had hit them it was gone, having folded itself back into the lake, its anger spent, leaving their craft to float on calm water.

Adam's body was belly-down in the wood of the deck. The girl knelt so that her face was next to his. His eyes were closed but she could see that he was breathing.

'Are you hurt?' she asked, her voice soft. 'Can you hear me?' She waited for a response and looked around the deck. The others were in their seats: it looked like everyone was still on board. She turned back to Adam.

'Are you hurt? Adam?'

'Is he OK?' it was Jess's voice, soft and close, that spoke.

'I can feel his breath but can't wake him,' said the girl.

Jess knelt beside her and put her hand to Adam's neck.

'He's just unconscious. That's a nasty bump he's taken to his head.'

The girl touched her own forehead.

'You too? I guess you're made of tougher stuff.' Jess smiled at the girl. 'Help me move him into the cabin.'

They each took an arm and dragged Adam's limp body unceremoniously along the deck to a spot on the cabin's floor.

The girl looked across at Nicholas.

'How's the Patriarch?'

'The azrapone has him,' said Jess.

There was silence as the two of them looked at the once great man. Father to one and master to the other.

'I must attend to the craft,' said the girl.

Jess looked up from her father.

'You know what to do?'

'Yes. Mason showed me a little of how to steer the craft.'

Mason. Rock to them both. Gone in the fireball.

'We must get everyone to safety,' said the girl.

She crossed back to the control console. A red light in its centre winked on and off to a slow rhythm. She pulled back on the lever below it and the central beam that ran between the benches on the deck rose from a pivot at the front of the craft. Its sides opened to form a horizontal beam and a sail unfurled beneath it.

To the namesakes sitting under its shadow it was as if the Saints had reached out and were pulling them along, filling the wings of a great water-bound bird with wind that steered them away from danger.

***

High above the great lake two cherubs had scanned the water.

It is possible that the existence of the life raft was not even registered before the live feeds were lost in the fireball which consumed them and the hillside. The wake left by the torpedo would have been visible on the surface, but they may not have detected it. Even if they had relayed its image to those who watched on screens from a safe distance, it may not have been recognised for what it was.

Salvation.

CHAPTER TWENTY-SIX

Jess leant on the rail which ran across the back of the boat and stared at the orange glow lighting up the horizon behind them. The hill and the shore were too far away to make out any details, but she knew what the flames meant: that she was alone now, without Mason.

It had been two hours since the wave launched them across the lake and now the sun had set, the distant fire was the only light in the sky. She had waited in the cramped cabin, sitting on the floor with her hand on her father's chest, until Adam had come to. He had said nothing other than that he was OK, before getting to his feet and stumbling slowly out onto the deck. She had let him go. She had sat with her father for a while and then, craving fresh air, she had left his white sleeping body alone in the cabin.

She stretched her neck, turned her back to the glow and looked in their direction of travel. It was pitch black and she could make nothing out beyond the bow of the boat. The light from the fire on the far shore was too dim to light their way, and the lamps that shone onto the deck from its sides made the blackness beyond the craft darker still. She looked at the prone and sleeping bodies strewn across the deck and realised how tired she felt. She took a breath and walked over to the girl.

'Can you see where we're going?'

The girl, her hand on one of the controls, did not move her head, but continued to scan the blackness in front of them.

'Only shadows Mistress, I can't see what's there until we meet it.'

They stood in silence for a few minutes, trying to pick out potential obstacles from the gloom.

After a while the girl spoke: 'They're gone aren't they? Mason and the others. Dead?'

'I think so, yes,' said Jess. 'I think that's what they planned.'

'To make it look like we were all killed back there,' said the girl.

'Yes.' Jess put her hands on the console and felt the smoothness of its wood under her fingers. 'To give us a chance to survive.'

She knew this was her responsibility, her duty to see to it that they survived. Hers and Adam's. But she had no idea how they would do this. All she could think of was her Popos lying back there in the cabin. Kept alive but cold as death. How could she think straight when he was like that? And without Mason to help her? And then Mason's voice filled her head: "Take a moment, you can't think, this is normal, let your brain catch up with you, we'll sort this." And then it was her father's voice she could hear, more than just a memory: "Show me, show yourself that you can find a way."

'They're not dead.' Adam's silhouette spoke out of the shadows as it approached them from the front of the boat. 'They're not dead. They're not and we have to go back for them.'

The lights from the deck shone up into Adam's face, making upside-down shadows above his features.

'They'll have kept themselves safe. They'll have been bargaining until the attack. They'll be holed-up deep inside the hill somewhere.'

He looked at Jess and then the girl.

'We have to go back!' he said.

There was a sudden jolt as the bow dug into something solid. Jess grabbed for the control panel in an attempt to remain upright. The stern of the craft began to swing around. There was a loud scraping noise from the hull as it grounded and the boat slowly tilted to one side. And then nothing. Only stillness and silence.

'Popos!'

Jess used her hands to steady herself against the side of the craft as she headed off toward the cabin, struggling to keep her balance on the slanted deck.

The girl looked at Adam, watched him as he watched Jess disappear into the shadows. Anger untapped, words not shouted. She gave the boy a moment before speaking.

'I think something under the craft has snagged,' she said. 'There's a tail that steers us and I think…'

'It's a rudder,' said Adam, his eyes suddenly on her, his voice calm, he was a man again.

The girl let go of the controls and allowed herself to slide to the edge of the deck.

'I think I can see land,' she said.

'I can't see a thing,' his arm brushing against her shoulder.

She turned and spoke to her sisters: 'Give me your sashes, all of you.'

The Trevelian and the Percival namesakes unfastened the cords from their waists. One of the women collected them up. The girl began to knot the cords end to end, and her sisters, seeing what was required, followed suit, creating a single length of cord. The girl formed a loop out of one end and threw it over her shoulders, threading it under her arms.

'No. I'll go,' said Adam.

The girl shook her head. 'You have the strength to pull me back. I'll go.' She looked Adam directly in the eye and handed him the end of the cord. 'Keep me safe,' she said.

He nodded.

She climbed over the side and let her body hang from her fingers. Her feet were in the water but she could not feel the bottom of the lake. She took a deep breath, relaxed her legs and let go. The cold water pushed the air from her lungs as her groin and chest went under. Her feet found soft mud that sucked at them before supporting her weight. Her chin was just above the water.

'I'm down,' she shouted into the darkness above her. 'I'm going to head away from the boat, give me as much slack as you have.'

The cord began to flow over the side of the boat into an untidy coil that floated on the water beside her. She turned and walked directly away from the hull in the direction of what she hoped was the shore. As she moved, she could feel stones the size of fists sticking up out of the mud into the soles of her feet. The water was becoming shallow and after a few more steps it was only as high as her knees.

The cord became taut.

'Can you give me any more?' she called back into the darkness.

'That's all there is,' came Adam's voice.

She turned back to face the shore. She was certain she could see it just a few metres away. She slipped herself from the cord and headed for it. She could feel the stones under her feet increase in number and get smaller, smoother. Ten steps later and she was standing on dry pebbles.

'I've made it. I'm on the land.'

She looked about her. It was difficult to make out any features but the pebbles that had led her to the shore seemed to continue back for some distance. She could see a long thin shadow lying on the ground a few metres in front of her. The pebbles made a brittle crunching sound under her feet as she walked up to it. It was a branch. Old and knurled, lying on the pebbles. She bent down and touched it; smooth and worn.

She picked it up and turned back to the water. Her eyes were adjusted to the darkness now and it was easy to spot the stranded boat. She could even see the silhouettes of those looking out in her direction.

'We can make it to shore,' she shouted, her voice the only sound, 'we can use the cord as a guide. Wait there, I'm coming back.'

She stepped carefully, using the branch to steady herself and allowing her feet to find their way through the water back to the side of the boat. The last few steps were the hardest as the water was deeper, the mud less stable. Adam was looking down at her; he reached down his hands to pull her back on board but she shook her head.

'It's only a short distance to the shore, we're right on top of it. Its deeper here but the water's only knee deep for most of the way. I'll go as far as the cord will let me, send the others along it, they can get to the land from there.

***

The girl stood alone on the hill. Dawn was breaking but the orange glow of the fire on the far shore was still visible. She turned from the horizon and looked back down the gentle slope of grass she had climbed. It had felt lush and verdant under her feet. Full of life.

The sun was not high enough for its light to reach into the little valley they had found, but she could see the still-shadows of her sisters lying next to one another under a small copse of trees. They had been exhausted and slept where they found themselves, a huddle of bodies too tired to think of shelter.

She looked back to the horizon from the top of the slope. Her muscles were stiff and her clothes still wet. She thought about removing them, but something stopped her. She didn't want to be naked in front of the others. It would not have bothered her before, but now it did for some reason. She sat on the grass, drew her knees into her chest and hugged them, feeling the warmth from her body through the damp linen.

'Hello.'

The word made her jump and look around. She stood.

'Mistress.'

'I couldn't sleep,' said Jess with a smile.

'Nor me,' said the girl, and then, 'How is the Patriarch?'

Jess shook her head. Her eyes were red and her lids a little swollen.

'The same,' she said. 'It's hopeless though. I don't know what I can do for him now.'

Jess wrapped her arms around her slender waist and looked past the girl to the water. 'I don't see how I can look after him out here. Mason was right.'

The girl reached out her hand and touched it to Jess's arm.

They sat on the grass and the girl pulled her legs back into her chest. They sat together and stared out across the water for an age, watching the fire-glow on the horizon as it flexed and danced, dim for minutes and then a sudden flash or change in colour. Heart-beats later, a dull thud, barely audible, would announce each explosion.

'You did well getting us here,' said Jess after a few minutes.

They looked at each other for a moment and then Jess turned back to the water. 'It's not what I expected,' she said. 'This place I mean. It's not what I expected.'

The girl watched as Jess pushed a stray curl of hair back behind her ear.

'In what way, Mistress?'

'I thought it would be barren. I thought everywhere had been poisoned during The Conflict. That the only fertile soil was the soil we made for Amynthia.'

"We," thought the girl.

After a long silence, Jess looked at her and smiled.

'The soil *you* made,' she said, as if having read her mind.

The girl smiled back. 'Nature has found a way,' she said.

They sat. They watched. The sun moved.

Eventually the girl broke the silence, her voice gentle and quiet: 'Did you know your mother?'

She could feel Jess's eyes on her face but she did not turn to look at her in the long moments it took Jess to reply.

'She died when I was young,' said Jess.

There was a stillness around them.

'I was six.'

The girl turned to her Mistress. 'That's the age I was gifted to your Family,' she spoke the words quietly. 'What was she like, your mother?'

She watched as Jess's eyes glazed for a moment, seeing things from a private past.

'She was kind. She smelled of flowers.'

The girl gave a slow nod.

'I met my mother for the first time back there.' The girl tilted her head to the glowing shore. 'She took me to see her. The de-Monte Matriarch took me.'

The girl pulled the picture of her mother from the folds of her clothing. It was damp, but the image was undamaged: the partially covered face protruding from the shadows of a hood. The girl could feel the scar on her face sting as she looked at the image. Mason had said that she looked like her. She took in the details of the face held in the picture. The face of her mother. It was true, they were alike.

'I don't understand,' said Jess, 'you're an orphan, all the namesakes are orphans. How can you have met your mother?'

The girl stared at the picture for a few moments more before looking into Jess's eyes.

'You don't know do you? Where I came from? Where we all come from?' She continued to look at her Mistress, not accusing, not angry. 'The way you make us, the namesakes. How can you not know?'

Jess's eyes were wide. 'You're foundlings, orphans, rescued from the streets.' Her head shook a little as she spoke. 'The Church finds you and the de-Monte's lift you from poverty and give you a home. Some are gifted to the Families, but all go on to serve the city in some way. As we all must.'

The girl searched Jess's eyes. She could see that Jess believed what she was saying.

'No,' she said, 'we're not orphans. We're made. The de-Montes make us just for you.' She handed the picture to Jess. 'This is our mother. Her name was Evelyn.'

Jess looked at the picture and then back to the girl: 'What do you mean?'

'They held part of her in a room back there. We were created from her. Created to serve you. We're told to be grateful, that we've been saved, that we are blessed by the Church of the Holy Union and held in the embrace of a Family. But none of that's true. We're created for one thing, to work the land. We're not people, we're just tools.'

Jess stared at the girl, her mouth open.

'No. How can you say that?' she said. 'Of course you're people, we don't think of you like that. You know *I* don't. You can't believe that I do.'

'Jess, Nichola, Trevelian,' said the girl emphasising each word. 'Where is my name? Where are the names of my sisters?'

Jess shook her head. 'But you're Namesake-Trevelian. You don't need a name because you're part of a community. Just because you have no name doesn't mean we think…we don't stop you having names. Being a namesake means you are free from needing one, free from rank, liberated from the burdens of rank. It sets you free. Being a namesake, being part of that community means your faith sets you free.'

'Faith does not set us free,' said the girl, her voice strong but still carrying no anger, 'it controls us, it controls both of us, monarch and servant. Only truth can set a person free, and there is no truth in the faith we're given.' The girl looked at Jess for a few seconds. 'Faith controls us, only the truth sets us free.'

The girl took back the picture and turned her head to the water. Jess said nothing.

'She's dead now, my mother. Killed back there.'

The girl thought of the room, of the taste of the warm damp air that blew from the box on the ceiling. Of her mother's essence held in a box in that cold and clinical space. A mother she would never know.

'Mason said he knew her. Knew my mother.' The girl was perfectly still for moments, and then she added, 'We should've been told the truth.'

Jess was silent for a long time.

'I'm sorry,' she said, 'I'm truly sorry.'

'Everyone seems to be saying that.' The girl's voice was calm, there was still no trace of anger: 'you, Mason,

Laban. You're all sorry. But what good is that? We're people. We're people and we should have names.'

The girl closed her eyes and tasted the fresh clean air. It did not smell like the air at the Trevelian estate. It did not hold the scent of the plants she had been familiar with in that life. It smelt heavier somehow, there was a freshness to it she had never experienced. She looked out across the water.

'It mustn't happen again.' Her voice was harder now, assertive, and she turned to Jess. 'My mother's gone, but they mustn't be allowed to do it again.'

Jess was shaking her head. She did not understand.

'Make more namesakes. They must not be allowed to do it again.'

'They won't need to,' said Jess. 'The namesakes, you were needed to work the land. To turn the sand into soil. They don't need you for that anymore. They can create the soil mechanically. They'll raise the crops without the need for namesakes.'

'No. They won't. It won't work I told you that. Their machines won't work. It's the earthworm, it's Eisenia Veneta, she makes the soil, and my sisters cared for her. Look around you. How do you think the soil has become fertile here? Blessed Veneta has been the one to bring it to life. I told you, it won't work. Their machines will kill her. Their crops will fail and they'll need us again.'

The girl paused and then, her voice distant, quiet again, 'They'll come for us. They'll have to. They'll want one of us to take our mother's place.'

'No, you're safe here,' said Jess, 'you and your cousins won't ever have to go back.'

'Sisters,' said the girl, turning to look Jess in the eye. 'Sisters. We're sisters, not cousins.'

***

'I have to go back!'

Adam's voice cut through the air between the girl and Jess. He was marching up the slope toward them both, but he was speaking to Jess.

'But there's nothing to go back for.' Jess stood and put her hand on his arm but he snapped it away from her.

'Don't tell me that. You don't know that. Father is still alive back there. We must go back and, and…'

'And what? And what Adam?' They were standing still now, looking at each other. The girl on the outside, forgotten.

'And help. And get him to safety. All of them. They created a diversion for us so that we could get away. Now we've got the others to safety, we'll go back and get them. We'll take the boat back in the dark. Now that the weight's out of it we'll be able to push it off the sandbank. We'll hide it on the shore, find them, and bring them back here.'

'Think about what you're saying.' The emotion in Jess's voice was rising along with its pitch; she spoke quickly: 'You saw the explosion. It was the whole hillside. There's nothing left. They're not hiding there, they destroyed everything including themselves so that there'd be no evidence of us escaping. If we go back, we'll be spotted. They'll still be dead and we'll be spotted. Their sacrifice will have been for nothing.'

Adam's face was red, his body leaning forward, ready to fight.

'We won't be spotted,' he spat. 'They're waiting for us and we have to go back and get them.'

They stared at each other, neither breaking eye contact. Jess took a breath, she reached her arm up to Adam's shoulder.

'Adam. He's gone,' she spoke softly, gently. 'They're all gone. All of them. You have to let go.'

Adam's eyes were wide and his face still flushed.

'How can you say that to me. "Let go", how can you say that to me! After we've dragged the carcass of your precious father with us through all that!' He grabbed her hand and threw it from his shoulder, turned and almost ran back down the hill.

The girl watched as Jess staggered back, her hand on her mouth, sank to her knees and sobbed.

***

She moved to her Mistress, folded and weeping on the ground. She knelt and wrapped her arms around the shaking shoulders, as once her Mistress had done for her. Holding, rocking, comforting.

'Shh.'

'He's right, about everything, right. He's right,' said Jess.

The girl felt tears on her shoulder and rocked Jess in her arms.

'Popos. Popos.' Jess's sobs shook her body.

'Shh.' The girl gently rubbed Jess's back and whispered, 'It's not the strongest or the fittest that survive.'

Jess's sobs turned to tears and then, after a few minutes, to silence. She looked at the girl and wiped her eyes.

'I've heard the namesakes, your sisters, say that before. What does it mean?'

The girl took her arm from Jess and looked down for a moment before replying.

'It's part of our Rule, or it was. Something we'd say to one another to give comfort. "It is not the strongest nor the fittest that survive but the most adaptable." We learnt it from the fields, when selecting and nurturing crops.' She turned back to the lake and was silent for a few moments. 'It means… it means that everything changes,' her voice was soft, 'and that we must adapt when it does.'

Jess pushed a loose strand of hair back behind her ear and took a breath.

'That's what you do, don't you?' she said. 'You adapt.'

The girl nodded.

'And so must you, Jess,' she said.

She stood and held out her hands. Jess took them and got to her feet. They looked into each other's eyes, the girl drew her close and they held each other.

After a while Jess pushed herself away.

'My father had a saying, "It is only by its impermanence that a life shows its beauty". It's from a poem.' Jess reached out, lifted the girl's hand to her lips and then held it to her cheek. 'I think it's time; would you help me, please.'

The girl understood: 'Of course.'

***

The figure of a man who would have the world bend to his view walked along the shoreline. The crunch of its footsteps on the pebbled beach went unnoticed. They left no impression, made no difference. Fully lit by the dawn but unobserved, alone, it waded out to the boat, its steps exaggerated as it pushed through the water; water that closed in behind it, no trace of the figure left in its currents.

Now that the boat was empty it almost floated freely, scraping and rubbing against the sandbank which had been its berth in the night-black. The figure pushed and pulled until the craft pointed back out into the lake and then jumped on board. Slowly it lost itself in the fret of mist drifting off the shore.

***

The girl and Jess held hands as they walked down the grass-covered hillside, back to the trees where the others were waking up. As they approached the shrouded cold-as-death figure sleeping under a tree, the girl gave Jess's hand a squeeze before letting it go.

Jess looked down at her father, his shoulders and head growing from the white sheet that wrapped around him, the blue light of the azrapone flowing between brightness and dark, holding him to her world, keeping him alive.

She knelt by his side and touched his cheek with the back of her hand. His skin was pale and cold. Stubble had begun to show on his cheek. She moved her hand across it, feeling it, and then arranged the plaits of his beard, untangling them from one another and laying them neatly down from his chin onto his chest.

'I knew it was hopeless,' she said, 'his body is too weak.'

The girl knelt next to her and put her arm around her shoulder.

'If it's time, shall we do it together?'

'Thank you,' said Jess. 'It is time, but I'll do it.'

Jess leaned forward and placed two fingers on the blue jewel at the centre of the azrapone. Its light, a tether holding a life to this world, steadied and then faded as she applied a gentle force. Nicholas Alexander Michael Trevelian, Patriarch of the Family Trevelian, her father, Popos, was gone.

'Such as you are, so we soon shall be,' said Jess, her voice brittle. 'The souls of the dead go to be weighed…,' her words trailed.

Behind them, namesakes of the Family Trevelian and the Family Percival stood together. They began to sing, one at first but then each of them joining in turn. Their song had no words or melody, it was a single chord, each woman finding a note that fitted and yet was her own.

Concord.

The girl squeezed Jess's shoulder, pulling her close.

'A long journey well-made is ended,' she said.

'A long journey well-made is ended,' repeated Jess under her breath.

There, under the trees of a new garden, the final witnessing was made. A celebration was given of the life of Nicholas Alexander Michael Trevelian, Patriarch of the Family Trevelian.

EPILOGUE

The girl who had no name is gone now. She no longer lives.

"A long journey well-made is ended."

She did not go to heaven. Instead she found a heaven here, in this garden that was waiting for her. Waiting here for all of them. Lush and verdant and fertile and waiting; ready to provide.

The others still sing to the saints and to the gods. They have been told the truth but they still sing their praise. Their music is different now, more beautiful. They find harmony in their singing. Their voices hold one another and float up into the sky. It is strange that the most tangible thing to come from all the bloodshed is such beautiful music.

When I think of the fighting, the destruction, it makes me angry; it makes the scar on my face burn. There's a serpent in my belly and when I feel this way she tightens her coils and lends me her strength. I think of Mason, I think of my mother, Evelyn, of what they did to her.

Yes, the girl with no name is gone. The girl from the cloisters who was imprisoned by faith and viewed the world through the window of her cell no longer exists. Though her heart continues to beat, she is gone.

I am a woman now and I have chosen my own name.

THANKS

A heart-felt 'thank you' from me to you for reading my novel The Namesake. I hope you enjoyed it. Please seek me out on social media and let me know what you thought of it, I'd love to know. My twitter feed, @AdamEBradbury is a good place to start.

Self-publishing is, as they say, a tough gig. The greatest hurdle is having no marketing machine to get the word out. If you fancy doing me a favour please consider posting an honest review on Amazon, or someplace like goodreads.com. Maybe you could give me a mention in your social-media universe.

ABOUT THE AUTHOR

Adam was born in the UK and grew up on a smallholding in Kent. He moved to the rain-soaked north at eighteen and has been a 'plastic northerner' ever since. He worked as a physicist for nearly three decades before figuring out that objective truth was not all it was cracked-up to be. Now he has a shed and loves the sound the rain makes on its roof. He is an advocate of creative writing and believes it is a means of finding and securing world peace.

He wants you to write.

PROFESSOR EDWIN FULLER

I am extremely grateful to the estate of Professor Edwin Fuller (1893-1975) for giving me permission to use some of his work in The Namesake (see sections preceding chapters three and nine). His painstaking research provided much of the texture and colour for the back-drop to my story.

Fuller was an interesting character who seems to have received only ridicule for his ideas when he was alive. But his theory that stories and story-telling are, and always have been, a fundamental trait of the human species makes sense to me. His idea that the stories we tell form a bridge with our ancestors at one end, our descendants at the other and us in the middle resonates with me.

What follows is a verbatim reproduction of the lecture he gave when he retired in the late 1960's. I don't remember quite how I came across it, but it gave me the starting point for writing the story you've just read. The article is reproduced here in full and is a little verbose, I guess that being the style of the man and of the time. He does raise a very interesting question though…I shall leave the final word to the good Professor with my thanks.

British Journal of Linguistic Anthropology:BJLA141969

A public lecture by emeritus Professor Edwin Fuller PhD FRS on the occasion of his retirement.

1-October-1969

Manchester Royal Exchange

The following is a transcript of a public lecture. It is given verbatim and includes some comments from those present in the audience. Such comments are indicated within the text.

Good evening and thank you, Professor Bell, for such a warm introduction and undeservedly generous outline of my career.

[clapping heard]

I was extremely happy to receive the invitation to address you all tonight. One's life in the Ivory Tower of academia has been interesting and absorbing, but one does feel somewhat cut-off from the real world, and it was with a sense of excitement and gratitude that I accepted this opportunity to share a little of my work with a wider lay-audience.

[clears throat]

What I should like to do this evening is pose a question to you. We academics are good at asking interesting questions, usually rather better than we are at answering them.

[laughter]

Before I get to that question, the one I wish you to take out into the evening and home with you, I shall ask some other smaller questions, rhetorical mostly, and explain to you a little of my work. I hope you find the journey towards the main question enjoyable and through that journey understand the significance of the question I wish to leave you with.

Let me start, not at the beginning, but in many years from now. Millennia into the future, let us say one hundred and fifty thousand years from this day.

I shall state as a given, that in this far distant future, humans still occupy the Earth much as we do today. For those of you who are not used to the tricks played by academics, when I say 'state as given', it means you cannot say that I am wrong. It is a trick to allow me to make some other, greater point. So we can, for the sake of my argument, discount any mass extinction or migration to our moon.

[some laughter]

I simply ask you to accept that in one hundred and fifty thousand years, 'we' - humans - go about our business much as we do today. This allows me to ask my first 'little' question of you, and it is this: what do you think the archaeologists of that far future world would make of us? You Madam, there in front of me for example. What would they think of you?

[pause and some laughter]

Let us say that she, this archaeologist, for she could of course be female, has been lucky and that tonight on your way home from here you drown in the mud in Morecambe Bay.

[laughter]

Not too lucky for you of course Madam, but lucky for her as you've left behind a fossilised footprint and the gold ring I can see you sporting on your left hand.

Now, let us imagine you in one thousand years from tonight. Your body will still be there, or some of it will. In ten thousand years, there may be a tooth or a bone or two, but in one hundred and fifty thousand years, in the time of our archaeologist friend, there will be nothing save for that gold ring and that fossilised footprint.

Now what will she deduce, this archaeologist? Something of your size perhaps, something of the technology available to you to work the gold, and by examining the nature of the gold, she will be able to deduce that you were part of a culture that traded widely, since there is no gold in Morecambe Bay, as far as I know. May I ask if you know where the gold of your ring was sourced?

[inaudible reply]

I see, well I had hoped you were going to say that it was Welsh gold or something, and then I could have neatly allowed my archaeologist friend to conclude that either you had travelled from Wales or traded with people who did. Unfortunately, you telling me it was from 'a jewellers' does not help me but I think you can all see the argument.

THE NAMESAKE

[laughter]

So, this perfectly competent archaeologist is unable to land on anything much that really defines us. At this great distance of years, one hundred and fifty millennia, there is so little left, so few physical artefacts, that she can say nothing of whether you owned a television, or that you listen to Elvis Presley's voice on a record, or that we have cars and roads and can fly in great metal machines. None of this, no physical evidence of these things will persist over such an enormous length of time. The trains and aeroplanes and automobiles will have long since rusted into dust. Only a few fossils, some precious stones and metals, very few physical artefacts will complete their journey into that far distant future.

[pause]

But something of you and of I may persist and find its way into that time. Any ideas as to what that might be?

[pause and silence]

It is our stories. The tales we tell one another. For example, The Bible you have at home is not itself two thousand years old, and yet its words are from that time. Or perhaps from an even earlier one. In the same way, might not something of our lives make it to the future if contained within stories that are told and retold?

[pause]

Now let me ask you another question, and this one is not rhetorical, please shout out an answer if you know it. How long have humans existed? How long has our species, *Homo sapiens*, been around?

[pause and inaudible voice from audience]

Very good, top marks. In fact, it's a little longer even than that. Current thinking has *Homo sapiens*, humans, who if dressed in our clothes would not look at all out of place sitting next to you tonight, current thinking has us around as far back as two hundred thousand years.

[pause]

Now we have established, or at least I have argued, that over that length of time, little in the way of physical artefacts will exist from those ancestors of ours. And indeed, we find the odd fossil but little else. It's not until much more recently, say just ten thousand years ago, that we start to see any number of, shall we say 'more interesting' items which allow us to piece together something of the lives and social structures of our ancestors.

But what if there were another way, another lens we could use to look back through those many centuries, back tens or a hundred thousand years? Well ladies and gentlemen, I have already hinted that there is. It is their stories that come to us, and it has been my life's work to establish this.

My discipline is a branch of what is called linguistic anthropology; a series of tools, if you will, that allow languages to shed some light on our development as a species. Specifically in my case, I study stories. Myths and legends and what they might tell us about our distant ancestors. These stories are told and retold through the generations, changing and being modified, but my work has been to trace the passage taken by these stories, back through the generations. Finding their common origins and mapping their divergent routes right up to the present day, by which I mean just a few thousand years ago.

My research has been an attempt to draw out something of the nature of our ancient ancestors, something of their culture and society; by tracing back the myths and legends we are familiar with today, right back to the mouths of our very distant ancestors, I have been able to learn a little of them.

The Garden of Eden, a great flood, the virgin birth, protecting and avenging angels. You may think, probably you do, that these are truths given to us in scripture. I cannot comment on their value as 'truth', but I do say these narratives pre-date The New and The Old Testaments of the Abrahamic religions and according to my research they do so by many thousands of years.

My work has traced these myths back through millennia into a world long-disappeared. This in itself is an amazing thing, or at least I find it to be so. But what is more astounding, breath-taking even, is that these stories, the original versions I have reconstructed from studying their passage through myriad cultures spread across the Earth, contain hints, contain what I might call 'soft artefacts' from an ancient and highly advanced civilisation.

Now, by ancient I mean perhaps seventy or so thousand years in our past, and by advanced, I mean technologically advanced, maybe more advanced even than our own society is today.

Now let me tell you something else. It has been established, by others working in the discipline of archaeology, that *Homo sapiens* underwent near extinction around seventy thousand years ago. About the same time these myths and legends first appear according to my research. The received wisdom is that this was due to some natural disaster. I say differently. My work says differently. My research tells me that our distant ancestors were highly advanced and that their near extinction, *our* near extinction, was a direct result of their own actions.

I am convinced that many tens of thousands of years ago, a highly advanced civilisation existed and that it brought itself to ruin. I am utterly convinced of this.

[silence]

My work, my life's work, has led me to this conclusion. Now that I begin to look back at my career, I can say that my greatest failing has been my inability to convince others of the validity of my conclusions. I have been unable to elicit anything more than ridicule for my opinions.

[pause]

But think of our archaeologist of the future. There she is looking at your ring and a plaster-cast of your footprint. She will, I suggest, assume that our society is less technologically advanced than her own. She will think our society primitive, that our days were lived without technology, without planes, television and long-playing records. She will find no artefacts to suggest otherwise, she will have an image of us sitting contentedly about our campfires, banging rocks together for entertainment.

[laughter]

A few months ago, Neil Armstrong set foot on the moon. This momentous achievement occurred around three thousand years after our mastery of bronze-age tools and technology. Think of it. Just three thousand years from bronze-age to space-age. Let me ask you this: how far-fetched is it really, to suggest that in the two hundred thousand years of human history predating our lifetimes, that a highly advanced society has arisen and fallen?

And this is my question, the one I wish to leave you with. Given all the above, do you really believe that we are the first technologically advanced humans to live on Earth?

[pause]

A great deal can happen in two hundred thousand years.

Thank you for your attention, and good evening.

[applause]

CPSIA information can be obtained
at www.ICGtesting.com
Printed in the USA
LVHW081813080821
694840LV00019B/1117

9 781973 970323